Tribal Spirits

FORGED FUTURES

KATHERINE MCINTYRE

Forged Futures
ISBN # 978-1-83943-807-3
©Copyright Katherine McIntyre 2019
Cover Art by Erin Dameron-Hill ©Copyright May 2019
Interior text design by Claire Siemaszkiewicz
Totally Bound Publishing

FORGED
FUTURES

Dedication

To those struggling with loss —
this story is for you.

Chapter One

The house never felt as empty as it did in mid-winter.

Lana thought the loneliness would've gripped her by the throat in the early summer nights after Greg died, but those didn't compare to the brittle ache that descended with the new year.

Even though she was standing right beside her microwave, the beep made her jump. She pulled the now-steaming mug of coffee out and took a sip. Since it was nine at night, she needed this to keep from being comatose after the double whammy of a shift on the ambulance followed by three sessions with her massage clients. She might have both bare feet planted on her hardwood floors, but her mountain lion hadn't stopped pacing from the moment she'd returned home.

Her skin prickled. *Something's off.*

She cast a quick glance around her kitchen. The shadows sloped with the dim overhead light splaying across chrome appliances and rustic hickory countertops. Nothing slunk through her kitchen. The heat from the mug of coffee soaked into her palms — the closest she'd come to feeling something all day.

Almost eight months had passed, and still she walked into the house waiting for his deep voice to answer her back. Greg's worn spot on the couch remained empty, almost as empty as the hollow chamber where her heart had once beaten. She headed over toward her living room, winding around a stack of paperbacks that teetered precariously. Her coffee sloshed over the rim, the hot liquid stinging where it splashed her hand. Lana glanced at the windows, waiting for something to pop up, for eyes to be staring back at her.

Great Spirits, I'm going insane. Lana took a seat on the weathered corduroy couch and placed her mug on the scratched and dented coffee table. She needed a roommate, or at least a cat. Maybe a dozen — her local SPCA would be a danger zone for her. She should cave and take Ally up on her offer to move in.

Skritch, skritch, skritch.

Lana sat straight, her mountain lion perking to alertness. That wasn't a squirrel in the bushes. Her heart raced, as it had the night of the bombings. She could still feel the burn of the colloidal silver ropes against her skin. And all she would ever see again on her floorboards was the crimson splatter as her husband slumped to the ground, dead.

Lana's nails turned into claws on instinct, and a low growl built in the back of her throat. The scent wasn't a woodland critter prancing through and didn't belong to her pack.

She crept in the direction of the sound coming from the backyard. Her bare feet jolted with a shock of cold as she stepped onto the cool tile of her screened-in porch. Her heart pounded loudly, becoming almost all she could hear while she crept forward. Any moment, the door would fling open. Any moment, whoever stalked outside would attack.

Night-time breezes swept in through the screen, the chill of winter causing goosebumps to prickle up her arms almost as much as the distant hush that descended. Her throat dried, but she took another step. Even with Marcy and Rick living next door, if someone murdered her here, they wouldn't hear a sound. Who knew if she'd even be found for days? Her eyes throbbed with the familiar pulse of phantom tears—she'd cried so much in the first month that they no longer came.

Her nose twitched from the unfamiliar scent. Where was it coming from? Lana took another tentative step, a heartbeat away from shifting. Her mountain lion paced inside her, begging to break free. Her cheeks iced, but she continued forward, her core temperature rising with the need to shift even as her outside froze. Ever since they had taken down the Coalition of Human Rights in September, quiet had reigned through Ricketts Glen. Too much quiet.

If she hadn't been paying attention, she would've missed the sound—the soft *whump* of padded feet on grass.

Her teeth transitioned to fangs and she stepped closer to the door. *Focus.* Her skin prickled, the fur begging to emerge. She strode up to the handle and rested her palm on the icy knob.

Two sets of eyes glowed on the other side, feet away.

Her gaze landed on the two approaching grizzly bears, and she leaped back, as if the flimsy screen might protect her. With the poised control of their limbs and the menace in their eyes, Lana didn't question for a second that the hulking shifters wanted her dead.

By the time she dived through the door and back inside the house, the bears had begun to charge. Their growls slashed through the air, and her heart leaped into her throat. Lana had made many, many split-second decisions to the point they'd become reflex. She raced through the house, her bare feet burning against the hardwood with the force with which she slammed on the planks. Mesh ripping resounded through her place, and a second later, the heavy pounding of the bears' approach reverberated all the way to her.

She needed to reach her front door. If she got there, she could shift, and in her mountain lion form she stood a chance of outrunning them.

Lana's breath caught in her throat as she crossed the distance from the living room to her front door, running closer and closer. The weight of the bear shifters echoed through the house, their footfalls like tolling bells. She didn't dare look back at the intruders who raced for her, their snarls making their intent clear. They were closing on her, like a noose sliding around her neck and pulling tight.

Her home wasn't safe. Again.

An icy sweat broke out on her palms as she lunged for the handle, scrambling to grab the knob. She fumbled with it, trying to turn it and failing.

The bears crashed through her house, getting closer by the second.

Lana yanked the door open and vaulted out. She shut it behind her, the door slamming so hard she almost took the doorknob off. With all the trouble the Landsliders had caused in the region, she didn't question that they were involved. Roars quaked behind her, muted by the door, and she rushed down her front steps. They'd bash their way through within moments — she needed to take advantage of the seconds while she had them.

The shift overtook her liquid-fast, already brimming on the surface. Her creamy fur pricked across her skin and her nails changed into sharp claws. Lana's surroundings altered with the shift, the crystalline night growing even sharper in her mountain lion eyes, and within seconds she settled her weight onto four paws.

Lana lunged forward, slicing her way through the wilted grass at top speed.

At least, until an unknown wolf stepped between her and the road.

Lana skidded to a halt, churning grass and mud with the force. The inkstain wolf shifter bared her teeth, the golden eyes glowing like lanterns. Quaking came from the house behind her as the bears slammed at the door, straining the timbers. Once they broke through, she was dead. No way could she fight all three at once.

The wolf in front of her growled, the sound reverberating between them in the stark air. Cold filtered through her veins. She needed to escape.

A bang echoed through the air, and her front door burst open. The first of the bears barreled through.

Her world shrank to the wolf before her and the bears behind. She would die. Just like Greg.

Lana lunged to the right, trying to find a way past the wolf who paced in front of her. The moment she moved, the wolf leaped, snapping for her leg.

The ground shook as the bears raced across her front lawn, closing the distance too fast. Dread rushed her in one dizzying sweep, even colder than that winter night. These shifters would kill her, and she'd never know why.

A single roar sliced through the night, loud enough to fracture the sky.

A massive Siberian tiger crashed onto her front lawn, one she recognized from the attack on the Coalition. Lucas, a member of the East Coast Tribe, had arrived.

Those were odds she could work with. Lana whipped around to face the wolf, baring her fangs. Lucas crashed on past her, moving with a grace that defied his size as he charged for the bears. The wolf lunged for her at once, the gray fangs shining in the sparse moonlight. Her paws crushed the withered grass beneath her as she whipped around.

Once the wolf snapped with those lethal jaws, she didn't step back or try to dodge. Lana slammed right in, using the flat of her skull like a battering ram. The collision echoed through the air with a *thump*. The wolf emitted a low, pained sound as she sank onto her paws. As if the Silver Springs pack hadn't spent time sparring with their Red Rock wolf brethren.

Growls lit the air from the two bears, but Lucas raced circles around them, moving with a familiar feline swiftness. The tiger leaped in to scratch one along the muzzle and whipped around to slam into the other before either could react. The way he fought was pure poetry.

This time, she took the offensive. Lana didn't give the shifter a chance to rebound, charging forward with her head down, ready to ram in again. The wolf reared on its haunches. The moment she dove in, the black wolf sprang, sailing overhead.

Lana pivoted around, right when the shifter landed. They both lunged at the same time. The hot breath of the wolf puffed against her fur, and Lana launched in for the kill. The jaws snapped in her face, the fangs scraping against her head, but she'd ducked.

She clamped down on the wolf's throat and tugged. Crimson blood spurted across her cheeks, the heat staining her fur as she refused to let go. Her heart hammered, her adrenaline surged and, like this, the hunt, the chase and the kill commanded her.

The wolf let out a moan before she collapsed to the ground. Lana tried to steady herself. The specks of blood on her face might as well have been acid. A pool of crimson grew around the body, and a violent urge to heave rolled through her. Her mountain lion might've taken the reins in a fight or flight situation, but she should be saving lives, not taking them.

All she could see was Greg's body lying on the floor as they'd done the same to him.

She stepped back one pace, then another, numbness descending. The ground shook when one of the bears dropped, flesh rent as if it had been tossed through a wood chipper. Lucas tackled the other bear, the two locked in their fight, a tangle of limbs and claws.

The moment the bear landed on his back with a crunch, the shifter was sentenced. Lucas tore into him with a similar ferocity, the sort of formidable expected from one of the Tribe. The governing force of the shifters wasn't one to be underestimated — on top of their enhanced skills, they possessed elemental magic and a compulsion they used to force their kind to comply.

Lana prowled, trying to ignore the ache in her heart and the sickness that dizzied her mind like the flu. Blood soaked into her fur, and even her pawprints left smudges on the grass as she stalked forward.

The bear let out one last gasp before Lucas' claws sliced right across his throat. Blood spurted in droplets onto the grass, leaked in pools beneath the massive body and stained the pristine coat of the East Coast

Tribe member who for some reason had showed up here at the perfect time. Not like she wasn't grateful — she'd have been dead otherwise.

Lana began to shift, needing some space from what she'd done in this form. Her fur changed to smooth skin and her legs lengthened until she stood back on two feet. Lana's long hair tickled, growing until it brushed her back. She touched the wet spots on her skin, trying to rub away the blood even as she approached.

Lucas prowled over from where he'd left the two bear corpses on her lawn. He'd begun to shift as well, the beautiful orange fur and the white stripes disappearing when he returned to his human form. By the time he stood in front of her, he towered at well over six feet of pure muscle, his tawny, desert-sand skin marred by the blackened flecks of blood across the surface. The Tribe tattoos traveled all the way up his arms and legs, bands of complex linework she couldn't help but stare at.

His dark eyes crinkled with his smile as he came to a stop. "I'm guessing this isn't how you expected to spend your night?"

The sardonic tone drew her out of her shock and she responded on autopilot. "How else do you think I stay in shape? This is my nightly ritual to get to sleep — you might want to try it. Works better than whiskey." She wanted to groan when the words left her lips. She was two steps from vomiting on the lawn, yet here she stood sounding like a homicidal maniac.

A laugh burst from his throat, a rich rumble. The sound calmed her like nothing else and a breath escaped her — the first deep inhalation she'd taken since she got home.

"What are you doing back in the area?" Lana asked, her stomach sinking with the realization. If the Tribe members had returned, so had trouble.

He skimmed a hand through his jet-black hair before glancing at the bloodstains spattered across his chest, his legs and his arms. Lana followed the trail on reflex, but when his eyes met hers, her cheeks flushed. Like she didn't have enough to feel bad about, she might as well add gawking at the hulk of a Tribe member on her lawn.

He lifted his eyebrow and shook out his hands, sending a couple of droplets flying. "Why don't we discuss this inside? If you've got a shower I can co-opt, I'd be in your debt."

Lana nodded before heading toward the door. His dark gaze burned into her, and she should feel unsettled with this big guy she barely knew entering her house. However, her front door hung off the hinges, and she'd been feeling neurotic at every creak and groan for months now. Lucas Diaz was one of the good guys—she'd known within five minutes of meeting him—and he'd saved her from ending up as a body on her lawn.

They stepped to the doorway, and Lana trailed her fingers along the wooden edge as she looked to Lucas. "Just tell me one thing," she said, unable to ignore the gravity settling inside her. "You're here for that reason, aren't you?"

Lucas nodded, the shadows deepening the scar in his cheek, the sharp curve of his nose and the grim line of his lips. "The Landsliders have returned. I'm here to find out why, then I'm going to stop them."

Chapter Two

Lucas had been in worse places than a stranger's shower, washing the blood off his skin, but right now he'd give his left nut to be back at Dusty Pines Motel by his lonesome. The sheer amount of time he and the other Tribe members had spent there over the past year had made it feel somewhat home-y, even if the felted cat décor and paisley curtains were backwoods horror movie chic.

It didn't help that the woman he'd happened to save was Lana Bennett.

He'd be lying if he claimed he hadn't noticed her on his prior visits. With those heartbreaker green eyes, smooth olive skin and sensuous lips, she was impossible to miss. Besides, her wry sarcasm spoke to him even as she wielded truth like a pistol.

Except she was off-limits. He'd have to be the worst sort of bastard to hit on a widow, and from what he'd heard around town, she and her late husband had even grown up together. That loss didn't fade. Hell, bottles of men's shampoo and conditioner still sat half-used on the shower rail.

He scrubbed his hair even harder, the water turning pink as more droplets of blood circled the drain. Those shifters had been stalking her house, and he needed to get to the bottom of why. Little had they known that he'd been trailing them for the past day.

The heat scoured his skin, and he heaved a reluctant sigh. Once he left the shower, the Landsliders' return would become real. Mackey had remained just as elusive as his right-hand shaman, Joe Ganzorig. However, the last Landslider he'd caught up with had spilled that the shaman had returned to Ricketts Glen. Lucas stepped out of the shower, clouds of steam gusting with him.

Ganzorig was number two on his shit list, second only to Mackey Kendricks after the trouble he'd been causing. Lucas would never be able to erase the sights of the house upstate they'd entered months ago, plagued by the coppery scent of blood, one that sent him back to memories best left buried.

The shaman had led the Landsliders through the house and murdered cubs.

Unforgiveable.

He snagged one of the gray towels hanging up and wrapped it around his waist before stalking out of the bathroom. The sound of clinking came from the first floor, so he headed down the steps and followed the noise.

Lana stood in her kitchen with her back to him as she scrubbed at a mug in the sink — the same one, over and over again. She'd pulled on a pair of leggings and a long, gauzy tank top in the interim.

"Hey," he said, announcing himself after a minute had passed and she hadn't turned around.

She almost leaped to the ceiling. "I…I'm sorry," she said, tugging at the bottom of her ponytail. "Realized I didn't have many mugs clean. I don't get company too often, so dishes sort of stack by the wayside. Next they'll be mobilizing into an army."

"You don't need to on my account," he said, waving a hand. Her gaze traveled to the towel wrapped around his waist, and he tried his damnedest to ignore the surge of heat that spiked inside.

"Ugh, I'm shit at hosting," she said, running her palm down her face. "Let me see if I've got something upstairs that'll fit you. If you're thirsty, I've got a pot of coffee that needs warming up, or tap water." Before he could respond, she bolted for the steps, which creaked as she raced up them.

Lucas wandered farther into the kitchen, over to the dishtowel where an array of still-dripping mugs and dishes rested. The one she'd been fixated on sat in the sink, worn green and blue ceramic. Either she was coming down from the excitement outside, or maybe the mug had been her husband's. His chest twisted at the thought, at his own bone-aching loss that still crept in on holidays and birthdays.

He snagged a different one from where they were drying on the towel and poured himself some cold coffee, bringing the mug over to the microwave and putting it in. He leaned against the counter, the buzz of the microwave a comfort in the quiet of the house. A rose and orange scent lingered in the air. He assumed it was Lana's, since she seemed to be the only one living here. A beep sounded behind him, but before he could grab his mug, Lana reappeared with a stack of clothing.

"Here, you're welcome to try these," she said, thrusting out the stack. "I'm hoping they fit. Greg wasn't as big as you." Lana ducked her head at the comment and scratched the nape of her neck. "Not saying you're some behemoth – just might be a size differential."

Spirits above, she's adorable. Everything about her brimmed on the surface and after he'd met so many cagey, hidden people in his travels, this woman shone like a gem.

"I'm sure it'll be fine," he reassured, taking the pile of clothes from her. She wasn't wrong – her late husband had been a lot skinnier, but the pair of sweats and stretchy white tee had some give. He tugged the shirt over his head and slipped the sweats on next. Lana took to staring holes into the hardwood floor. "It's safe to look up," he responded, folding the towel before he handed it over. "I'm decent." He couldn't help the amused grin that rose to his lips.

"Right. So now that you're all settled, let's have a chat about why the hell Landsliders are prowling around my house." Lana looked up, concern gleaming in her green eyes. *Shit.*

"I was hoping you'd be able to tell me," he admitted, reaching past her to grab the mug of coffee from the microwave. Her eyebrows furrowed, but she didn't say anything as she led the way to her living room where a full mug sat on her table in front of her corduroy couch. By some miracle her drink hadn't been disturbed, even though muddy prints tracked across her floor and chairs had been toppled in the mad dash the bears must've made through her house.

Lana sat on the couch and picked up her cup of coffee. Her nose wrinkled after the first sip. "Man, it went cold." Lucas stood with his mug, not sure if he should snag the spot on the couch or the armchair next to it.

She glanced to him and patted the seat beside her. "I only bite on Tuesdays. You're safe."

He shook his head and took the spot, unable to help the grin that rose to his face. This close to her, he noticed the sprinkle of dark freckles across her cheeks. "So, I've been tracking those guys all day. They've been prowling around the area, and I thought they were interested in striking against the Silver Springs pack again. However, all three of them zeroed in on your place. Don't suppose Ganzorig has been camping out in your backyard?"

Lana shivered. "God, I hope not. Thanks for the nightmare fodder. I'm already concerned there are about half a dozen ghosts and creepy-crawlies camping out in the corners of this house. Having the Landsliders tromping around my place isn't going to help me sleep at night."

"You're here by yourself?" he asked, the words coming out unbidden. He wanted to smack himself after. Of course she was.

Lana's expression softened, and he regretted his slip at once. "I need to get a roommate or something. I'm not cut out for this living-alone thing. Too vivid an imagination."

"Sorry," he apologized, running a hand through his hair. "I didn't mean to bring up anything." Guilt pulsed in his chest and awkwardness spread through the room like a stain.

Lana lifted an eyebrow. "Oh, stop," she said, meeting his gaze with a pointed look of her own. "I'm not going to break just because my husband is mentioned. Besides, sometimes it feels good to hurt a little, to get the pain out there in the open. My own friends and family are tiptoeing around the subject with me — I'm not going to start with acquaintances too."

Lucas opened his mouth and shut it again. She wasn't what he'd expected at all — Lana's sharp humor enchanted him, her directness in the face of a grief that would leave most people fragile and three steps from shattering. "Well, I'm right at the Dusty Pines Motel if you run into any trouble again. I'll bring up tonight's incident to your alpha, and we'll see how he wants to proceed."

Lana pursed her lips, and her gaze darted to the surface of her coffee. "Or you could crash in my spare bedroom while you're in the area. I mean, I can't compete with those sweet, sweet motel amenities, and I don't have nearly as many needlepoint cat pictures as Dusty Pines, but I've got a steady supply of coffee. Also, did I mention I hate living alone?"

A laugh escaped him. "You're telling me you're not afraid to have one of the East Coast Tribe staying at your place? We're not exactly well liked."

That was an understatement. Humans avoided them on principle, and even most shifters backed away once they caught sight of the tattoos. Not like he blamed them — Tribe compulsion abilities tended to freak folks out.

Lana shrugged. "So, you're telling me I should be upset about having the biggest, baddest tiger in the region keeping my place safe? Seems like a common-sense move to me."

"I can't argue with that," he responded, sinking back into the couch. "I'll be able to better figure out why the Landsliders might be coming for you if I stay here."

Her rose and citrus scent wafted his way, stronger with how close she sat, and he couldn't help the way his pulse sped up. The logic was sound, but in no way could he admit his real hesitation in staying at her place. He'd been drawn to her from the moment they'd met, and staying there wouldn't help smother that attraction.

"Awesome," she said, a grin reaching her lips while her shoulders relaxed. He hadn't realized she'd been bracing herself this entire time. She possessed the sort of smile that reached her warm eyes, like sitting by a hearth fire. "Seriously, you're doing me a huge favor. Thus far, all I've discovered in my widowed life is that I suck at living alone. Even before Greg and I got married, I lived with Ally. This coming home to an empty house thing is the pits."

Lucas shook his head, spreading his arms out on the back of the couch. "Try constantly revolving motels. If we're working jobs together, we have roommates, but most of the time I'm back to a random place by my lonesome."

Her eyebrows knitted together as she pulled her knees up to the couch and rested her chin on them. "Man, the changing places combined with shifters getting freaked out by your status as Tribe has got to be lonely."

Lucas dipped down to grab his mug, as if he could hide from the way his chest squeezed tight. One single sentence and she'd summed up his existence for the past decade. When he'd been younger, they'd worked in pairs more, but the older he'd gotten, the more time he'd spent alone. Most days he didn't mind. Navi, Jess and Akio were his family away from home and he saw them often enough.

However, some nights, when he lay on his bed staring at the rotting ceiling tiles of another shit motel, the loneliness corroded what remained of his vacant heart. He'd given away too many pieces over the years — small chips and fractures — until little was left.

"Damn, you don't mess around in the shallow pool, do you?" he responded, unable to voice how she'd reached right in and clutched his heart in her slender hands. Not like he minded. He'd skated the surface with so many people that someone who dove right to the real stuff was like the first dunk into a lake in midsummer.

Lana dipped her head, an impish grin on her lips. "It's a problem of mine. Feel free to tell me to knock it off — I don't always realize I'm digging too deep."

"Dig away, *carina*," he said, trying to ignore the way his chest melted like butter. "I don't mind." Even in the middle of winter in her cold house, being around her was like basking near a radiator, and his tiger wholeheartedly approved. "Not to switch subjects from my maudlin existence, but if the Landsliders are after you, your house, whatever, I'm going to need your help."

"These are the same assholes who murdered my husband," Lana murmured, her voice growing dark with a cavernous fury. "I'll do whatever's necessary to stop them."

"Good," he responded. Lucas tipped back the rest of his coffee in a single gulp, the warm liquid rushing through him. "I'll come by tomorrow with my stuff. Thanks for offering a place to stay." He glanced her way right when she looked at him with those big green eyes. Lucas forced himself to stand, otherwise he might have lingered there the rest of the night.

"Thanks for coming to my rescue earlier," she responded, clutching tight to her knees as her chin burrowed into them. "I was seconds away from the same fate as my husband."

His fingers twitched at the sight of her curled up on the couch, emanating a vulnerability that tangled with the fibers of his heart. She could fight—he'd seen her take care of the wolf out there—yet she remained so wide open with her grief, with her fear, with everything. He wanted to wrap his arms around her.

"Any time, *carina*," he responded. "I'm a sucker for a dramatic entrance." He tipped his fingers in her direction before he headed for the door. Each step across the hardwood pounded another reminder into him of why staying there classed as a bad idea. Her gaze bore down on him, and he couldn't ignore the flush of attraction or even the sheer comfort he'd felt being around her for the short time he had.

If he stayed at her place for any extended period, he was beyond screwed.

Chapter Three

Lana had trouble sleeping on a normal night. After the Landsliders had attacked her in her own home, she didn't stand a chance of catching a wink.

She poured herself a fresh cup of coffee, steam wafting from the surface. Lana could've tried to sleep longer — her first massage client wasn't until later — but shut-eye wouldn't happen. The trill of the songbirds and the gold of the sunbeams that poured in through her windows got her moving even when she felt stretched like tallow on the inside.

A knock sounded on her door, followed by a creak as it swung right open. The door almost toppled forward onto the floor.

Her alpha's eyebrows furrowed while he stood in the middle of the doorway, his hand still lifted.

Lana had to restrain her laugh at the pure bemusement on his features. "Come on in, Dax," she called out. "The door got broken last night when two bears decided they wanted to play battering ram."

Dax shook his head when he entered, his thumbs hooked through his belt loops as he sauntered inside. The man had always been cocksure arrogance even as a kid, though Dax paled in comparison to his brother, her former best friend and the guy responsible for her husband's murder. Lana swallowed the tightness in her throat as she grabbed her cup of coffee and approached.

"I had to see this for myself," a familiar voice came from the front door. Ally's blonde hair gleamed like honey when she poked her head in, and her eyes crinkled in amusement. A broad smile ripped across her face, Ally's own brand of armor that she donned at all times. Her best friend slunk through behind Dax with a sanguine grace that hadn't gotten ruined by the limp in her leg where the silver had scorched her back in the bombing.

Lana's heart warmed, and she crossed the space between them to tip her head onto Ally's shoulder. Ally stroked her hair, and relief rushed through her at once. If her pack hadn't been so close, she would never have survived after Greg's death—touch starvation alone would've sentenced her.

"Lucas told me the Landsliders were stalking your place?" Dax asked, his thick eyebrows knitted together in concern. "If you're in danger, there's no way we're leaving you here alone."

She tipped two fingers in salute. "Got that figured out, boss. I offered my spare bedroom to the big growly tiger."

Ally snorted and tugged on Lana's hair. "Of course you did. Who cares that the Tribe members are stupidly strong and use compulsion against our kind? I'm guessing you've already made a gut call on him and he's a fluffy teddy bear inside."

Lana pursed her lips as she straightened and folded her arms across her chest. "Maybe he is. Regardless, if the Landsliders are after me for whatever stupid reason they've got jotted down on their world domination memo, he's the best person to keep me safe."

Dax lifted his hands. "Not arguing there. I'm just the bearer of bad news."

Lana frowned, and Ally let out a sigh. The knowing look in her best friend's eyes as she delivered a look to Dax made her stomach flip.

"Rip the Band-Aid off, D," Ally said, placing her hands on her hips. "None of us likes this anyway."

"We're going to have to work with Drew on this one," Dax admitted, his gaze skating the ground. "He's got the locations of the Landsliders' last known spots. If any are active, we'll excise them from the area, and if they aren't, we'll collect whatever scraps we can on Mackey and Ganzorig."

The air left the room.

Drew might not have been there the night of the bombing, but he'd worked alongside the Landsliders and had splintered the Silver Springs pack to hurt her people. And the attackers that night hadn't just set bombs to torch their houses — they'd walked right up to Greg and slit his throat with silver. The friend she'd once trusted with her life had been the very one to sentence her husband, and like wounds from a silver weapon, that didn't just heal.

"You want me to work with the guy responsible for Greg's death?" Lana asked, her voice faint.

Dax shook his head as he heaved a sigh. "I know. My brother's a piece of shit. You get to make the call on this one, Lana. Drew's a necessary part of the operation, but I understand if you need to sit this out. We can find a guard for you while Lucas is on the job. No way will we leave you unprotected."

Her skin itched. She didn't fall into the camp fighter category, not like half of her pack, and she wasn't keen on prowling through Landslider locations with the intent to make an attack, maybe even kill. Even more so, she'd rather mainline Drano than work with Drew.

Except, the empty hours had started to suffocate her. When she wasn't at one of her jobs, the silence had begun sawing at her sanity until threads remained. Every creak of the pipes and every groan of the house settling crawled under her skin like a nightmare. The nearest night out on the town involved bars at least an hour away, and only a few in her pack were willing to single it up with her. Not like she wanted to go out anyway. If some guy hit on her—Spirits forbid—she wouldn't know what would be worse, missing Greg even more or the guilt that would follow if she felt anything.

Lana tugged on the end of her ponytail. "I'll do it," she said, lifting her chin, as if that might convince them that she meant what she said.

Ally's manicured eyebrows rose so high they almost lifted off her face. "If you're going, then I am too," she said, half to Lana and half to Dax.

Their alpha shrugged. "No two pack members I'd trust more. I'd join you guys, but I need to hold down the fort here."

Ally strode past them, heading for Lana's kitchen. Within seconds, she dove in the fridge and pulled out a can of strawberry kiwi seltzer Lana kept stocked for her—she only drank them sometimes, but Ally was a seltzer fiend. Dax followed her, making a beeline for the mostly-full coffeemaker.

"No one's blaming you, D," Ally said, cracking the tab open with a hiss. "The second Sierra started to show, you've been getting growlier and growlier. I'm assuming any sort of distance or road trip away from your pregnant mate would make your head explode."

Lana snorted before she nabbed a mug for Dax. "You and Sierra make the snarliest pair in the known universe. I'm fairly certain your child is going to leap from the womb growling."

Dax grinned as he snagged the cup from her and filled it with coffee. Her heart twisted. If someone had told her that the perennial bachelor from her younger years would be settled and expecting, she'd have called them a liar.

She and Greg had always been the ones everyone pegged as having kids first. Lana clutched her mug a little tighter, trying to ignore the dizzying sweep of envy. Not only was Dax having kids first, but he'd found his mate, someone who brought out his best self. Greg might've been her forever friend, but she'd never had the key-in-lock connection people described with the mating bond.

"If the kid's anything like Sierra, everyone's in trouble," Dax muttered, tipping back his cup. "She's like a Molotov cocktail wielded responsibly."

Ally leaned against the hickory countertop, her strawberry kiwi seltzer in hand. "So, who are we waiting for?" she asked Dax. Ally had earned her spot as the Silver Springs beta with determination and cleverness alone. She'd manipulated her way around any other contenders until she was the last one left. "I'm assuming there's a reason you haven't filled us in on the details yet."

"I wanted to clear it with Lana first," Dax said, scratching his nape. "They're close behind."

Lana's heart squeezed tight. Meaning Drew was close behind. He hadn't entered her house in ages, even before Greg had died. The day half of their pack had sabotaged the fight for alpha and run Dax out, she'd been pissed with him even though Greg had teetered on the other side. She lifted her mug of coffee in salute. "Here's me, prepared."

She was too transparent to keep the bitterness out of her voice, and Ally passed her a sympathetic glance. If anyone should be nervous or upset, it should be Ally. After all, Drew was her ex.

A knock sounded on her door, and her stomach flipped. Dax got up, but Lana lifted a hand.

"I've got this," she said, trying to summon her determination even though nausea rocked through her. Too many memories haunted her on a normal day, and this would bring them all to the surface.

Lana grabbed the handle of her door, not even needing to twist the knob before it swung open. She needed to get that repaired.

When she looked at her entryway, her shoulders sagged with relief.

Lucas stood before her, the earthy scent of him, all sage and rosewood, calming her nerves a touch. He cracked a grin that gleamed in his dark eyes, those fierce features betraying the softness that she suspected existed beneath. His hand curled into the top of the doorframe as he shifted the large rucksack he'd slung over one shoulder. Even with the sheer size of him, the deep scars marking his arms and along his temple, she didn't find him intimidating in the slightest.

"Hey there," he said, his voice a low rumble. "Hope you don't mind, I brought my stuff with me."

She let go of the knob and gestured him inside. "I made the offer, didn't I?"

As soon as the relief of Lucas' arrival descended, it got snatched away. The moment he stepped inside, Drew appeared in her doorway.

"Hey, Sunshine."

He ducked his head, unable to look her in the eyes while he drilled holes into the pavement with his stare. The old nickname on his lips, the one he and Greg had always called her—she couldn't take that right now. The man had once been pure cockiness, always with the carefree smiles like his brother, but even though he kept an arrogant look on his face, she could feel the hesitation. Grief rolled over him in such a fierce wave that she took a step back. Lana swallowed bile.

"Come on in, Drew," she said, clenching her jaw so tightly her molars ground together. She took a couple more steps back. Even though she'd told Dax she could handle this, an icy chill swept through her. All she could see was Greg's body lying on her kitchen floor. The tang of blood flooded her nostrils.

A hand rested on her shoulder, and the warm, heavy weight drew her to focus. Lucas stood in front of her, concern creasing his forehead even as he lifted the strap of his rucksack.

"You mind showing me where I can put this?" he asked.

Spirits above, she could kiss him for the escape he offered. Based on the way those dark eyes shone, he knew what maneuver he'd pulled. "Yeah," she said, the word coming out like someone else had spoken it. "Follow me."

Lana wasn't even aware of her legs moving, but all of a sudden she was heading up the stairs, away from Drew in her house. Sure, she'd seen him since the bombing, but witnessing from a distance was one thing. It was another having the reminder of Greg's death in her face, in this house. She shivered, the cold sweeping through her until nothing else existed, an Arctic terrain she couldn't escape from.

Her footsteps creaked as she headed to her second floor, Lucas following close behind. The bedroom she'd shared with Greg for years lay at the end of the hallway. Ally usually nabbed the guest bedroom when she crashed out at their place, or it got claimed by any of the pack who needed a room for the night. Now, someone else would be there for the time being.

She stopped in front of the guest bedroom entrance, trying to ignore the glare of her own room, as if Greg still sat on the bed watching her. Lana swallowed hard. Lucas stepped behind her, looming with his sheer height as his shadow stretched into the room.

"So, you'll be staying here, right next to my room," she said, pointing inside. "If any creepy-crawlies try to sneak up on me, it's the perfect position to intercept."

He slipped past her with surprising ease, his cat-like agility on full display while he placed his rucksack on the floor. Lucas sat on the bed and smoothed the sheet beside him. "We don't have to head back yet if you're not ready," he murmured. "I'm not judging, just offering an out."

Warmth suffused her from the inside out, as if she'd been wrapped in a blanket. In all her brief encounters with Lucas, he'd been the source of the comfort, from his whiskey-and-gravel voice to the firelight glow in every single smile. Some might view him as menacing, with the deep scars, Tribe tattoos and the gruff face, but all the trappings couldn't hide a softness that set her at ease.

Lana took a seat beside him. Her shoulders slumped, and the breath she'd been holding escaped. Her fingers curled into the down comforter beneath her. "I should be able to handle this."

Lucas lifted an eyebrow. "Seriously? You handle this however you need to. Drew and the Landsliders caused a lot of harm to your packs, in your case irreparable. No one but you gets to choose how you grieve, who to forgive or how long it takes for you to feel like your feet are on solid ground again." His voice heated when he spoke, those dark eyes flashing with something that looked a lot like experience.

"Who'd you lose?" she asked, the words slipping out before she could help herself.

Storm clouds reigned in his expression. Lana licked her lips, which had dried in the wake of his ferocity. Beyond the anger, the searing, searing anger, she could reach out and pluck the chord of loss in him that resonated with the depth of her own. *Not like everyone's comfortable having their past paraded out on front street.*

Lucas let out a sigh as he offered a smile that didn't reach his eyes. "Has anyone told you that your levels of perception are staggering? Because, *damn*, woman."

She grinned in response, a real one. His answer gave her enough of a cue — that wasn't a subject he was ready to broach. "If I could turn this off, I would. The flip side is I can't hide my own shit worth anything. Every time I steel myself for something, all I can see are the bloodstains on the floor in this house. Kinda fucks up any attempts at normal social interaction."

"Ghosts tend to linger," Lucas responded, pushing off from the bed. He stood, looming over her as he extended a hand. "So, we'll make a deal. If things get too intense down there, ask me if I need something — coffee, food, where to find the bathroom — I'll go with it, and you can take a breather."

"Where have you been all my life?" Lana asked, accepting his hand. Her heart thumped in double time and warmth flushed through her. She couldn't put into words how his kindness gave her the strength to stand and face her fears. Even as she stood, she found her grip on him lingering. She didn't want to let go.

Lucas pulled away first, clapping a hand on her shoulder. He gave her a gentle nudge forward. "You've got this."

Lana's eyes burned. The empathy and understanding from someone she barely knew meant the world to her right then. Some folks she'd known for years she hadn't felt this kinship with, but from the moment Lucas had thundered to the rescue last night, their conversations had been as easy as a lazy day by the river.

"Thank you, seriously," she said, glancing to him. "I'm glad I'll have someone like you in this ol' empty house."

She headed for the corridor, taking the lead as they traveled down the hallway again. Unlike before, when she'd been off-kilter, having gotten those feelings out in the open had her feet on solid planks again. As they creaked down the steps, her breathing returned to normal, even when she caught sight of Drew leaning against the polished counter in her kitchen. If she were honest, the sight was a familiar one—he'd spent many a night at their place—but the ping of familiarity made her feel guilty as sin.

However, Ally's and Dax's grim-lipped expressions didn't fill her with ease when she approached.

"What's with the dour looks?" she asked, wanting to rip the scab off. Whatever bad news they'd discovered couldn't be much worse than Drew having shown up in her house. "Let me guess, Mackey Kendricks has raised a zombie army to overrun the region next after dabbling into some deep, dark necromancy."

"Lana…" Ally trailed off as she took two steps forward, reaching out as though already trying to offer comfort. "You don't need to know." She looked to Drew, her blue eyes flashing with fierceness. "She doesn't need to know this."

Lana arched an eyebrow even as her stomach bottomed out. Lucas approached, standing beside her, a big form she had the urge to sink against.

"Tell me," Lana commanded, a firmness in her voice despite the chaos inside. Dax and Drew exchanged looks, with an understanding there that she didn't like.

"It's about Greg," Drew started, meeting her gaze at last. Those blue eyes were so familiar, yet so strange at the same time, as though they belonged to someone she'd known in a different lifetime. Her stomach squeezed tight at the mention of her late husband, and fear descended like vertigo. He'd already died, though — the worst had happened. Whatever Drew told her now, she would handle.

Lana balled her hands into fists. "What about him?"

"Lana, he was one of us," Drew murmured, guilt splashed on his features. "Greg was a Landslider."

Chapter Four

Lucas gripped his mug of coffee tight as he leaned against the counter in Lana's kitchen. Every ounce of him longed to close the distance between them to wrap his arms around that woman, but he didn't want to cross any boundaries. After the news Drew had dropped, he didn't know how Lana remained standing.

Ally rested a hand on Lana's shoulder as she faced Drew. "Way to make things worse, asshole."

Drew shot her an irritated look in return. "What did you want me to do? Lie? If she's wondering why there's a massive target painted over her home and person, then ding, ding, ding, that's why."

"How long?" Lana asked, her voice coming out hollow and lost.

Drew ran a hand through his hair, his features softening when he faced Lana. "Almost as long as I was. Look, I wanted to tell you, but there were things I just couldn't."

Lana's eyebrows drew together. She clenched her fists so tightly her fingers might fracture. "Oh, so all the times you came over to hang out, it just slipped your mind?" Her voice grew glacial.

Lucas tipped back more of his coffee and exchanged a glance with Dax. This was beyond personal and not his place to intercede.

Drew shook his head. "No, you don't get it. There are things I still can't say." The caustic edge to his voice belied the depth to which those words had affected him.

Lana opened her mouth as her eyes narrowed, but then she glanced at Lucas. Shame washed over him at the clarity that descended. If he could take a Brillo pad to his skin, he still didn't think he'd be able to scour the look away as Lana made the connection. As much as the packs in this neck of the woods loathed Drew Williams, Lucas held nothing but sympathy for the man. He understood intimately what Mackey was doing to the shifters unlucky enough to join the Landsliders, and if he dwelled on those thoughts too long, he'd hurl.

With the hold Tribe members could command over shifters, Mackey was the sort of criminal that nightmares were made from. Since he'd defected, he'd violated so many minds, forcing shifters to commit atrocities that would haunt them for a lifetime.

"You mean he gave the command, and you had to follow," Lana murmured, horror blooming in her gaze. "Both of you?"

Drew nodded. "By the time we realized we'd fucked up, it wasn't like we had an easy escape route."

Ally lifted her chin, staring him down. "You're the one who chose to take the step in the first place. Don't take a bump of coke and act surprised when you get addicted."

Drew looked away, not responding, but Lana placed a hand on Ally's arm. Her comment had been sharper than necessary, deeper and more personal than most of the annoyed and disgusted stares he'd collected. The awkward silence spread like a stain, and Dax didn't do anything to step in, standing with his arms crossed over his chest as he drilled holes into the floor with his pensive stare.

"Look, we can discuss the past later, but right now we need to address the immediate concern. If Greg was a Landslider, then why did they kill him in the attack?" Lucas brought up, drawing the room's attention his way. Drew took a step away from everyone, as though he'd mired himself in memories where he stood. Lucas caught his gaze and nodded, trying to offer encouragement to continue.

"So," Drew began again, turning to face Lucas as if he talked to him alone, "we'd been working there for a while when Mackey started developing some sort of Doomsday device. Supposedly, it would fuck up shifters real bad. Thing is, Mackey gave us plenty of orders, but Greg seized on the loophole. He stole the device."

Lana bit her lip and nodded. "So, he was trying to do some good," she murmured, her gaze flickering to the ground.

"Yeah," Drew said, his tone as cool as a cave. Lucas didn't need to be a mind-reader to know that was a load of bullshit. However, Lana had dealt with enough surprises today—finding out her husband might've had bad intentions didn't need to be on the list. Drew paced a step or two before continuing. "Problem is, the device is still missing. Landsliders were supposed to get the device then kill Greg, in that order. Except, we all know how that played out."

Lucas heaved a sigh. "So, we're looking for the device before they can get to it. Ganzorig's probably heading the search team. If he created some anti-shifter weaponry, guaranteed there's shaman mojo involved."

"We should have a shaman of our own if that's the case," Dax said, placing his mug on the countertop. "I've got the number of one we can call."

"That's a good step," Lucas said, rolling into command mode. After years of working in the Tribe, leadership came as naturally as shifting to him. "We'll head out in a team tomorrow to start checking the former Landslider spots as well as anywhere Greg might've considered hiding it. I can start with a full search on the house tonight, with Lana's permission, of course."

Lana's shoulders jumped at the mention, and she glanced his way. "Sure thing," she murmured. Her tone grew distant in the wake of the napalm dropped on her. If possible, he'd do the search himself to give her a night to rest and soak all this shitty news in.

"Ally, Drew and Lana, I'll need you to reschedule clients or work shifts you might have tomorrow. This is going to be a long day, because we're on a time crunch. If they're back in the area searching, we're steps behind."

Ally fired off a salute. "You've got it, boss."

Dax cast a glance to Lana then the rest of the room. "Why don't we clear out for now, so everyone can start fresh in the morning?"

Lucas nodded, drawing the same conclusion. Lana needed a break right then from all this mess rather than having a bunch of people crowding her space.

"Right," Drew said, taking the cue, "I'll be up the street if you need me." Before anyone could say anything, he'd already made big strides for the door. Dax followed close behind, as if he wanted a word in private with his brother.

Ally clapped a hand on Lana's shoulder and squeezed. "I'm around if you want a drink. Or a hug. Or to watch shitty horror movies. Whatever the deal, call me."

"Thanks, Ally-cat," Lana murmured, leaning against her friend's shoulder for a moment. She let herself get pulled into a fierce hug. Lucas shifted his stance, feeling as if he were intruding on something private. Spirits above, he should be clearing out too, yet he'd just accepted her offer to stay here.

As Ally slunk to follow the Williams brothers out of the door, gravity descended between Lucas and Lana, as subtle as a concrete wall.

Lucas scratched the back of his head. "Ah, I can leave if you need space," he said, taking a step back then forward again.

Lana looked at him, the sadness in those green eyes like the tangled, lonely part of a forest. "I know I'm a wreck right now, but you don't have to leave. I mean, I don't blame you if you want to. Right now, I kind of want to cry my eyes out, but the tears don't come anymore. I think I exhausted myself of them in the first couple of months."

Lucas nodded. The grief consuming her prickled his skin with familiarity. "Okay," he said, slowly. "So, say I stay. What can I do to help you right now?"

Lana let out a breath and rifled a hand through her hair. A shaky smile rose to her lips. "Throwing your hat in the ring for canonization, Mother Theresa? Seriously, though, you're some sort of special, Diaz. Right now, I want to lie on my couch, be a little numb and drink my damned coffee. If you care to join me, you get to choose what we watch."

A grin quirked his lips—he couldn't help it. Everything about this woman charmed him, whether she was tired, upset, whatever. The ease he felt around her was dangerous, as was the thrill gripping him every time their gazes locked. Yet he couldn't pull himself away.

"Deal," he said, taking the lead over to her couch in the living room. He sank into one side while she took the other, and as he grabbed the remote and scrolled through the channels, they both descended into numbed silence for the blissful moments they could grab.

* * * *

Lucas had spent the rest of the night diving through room after room in the house, searching for anything Lana's husband might've left regarding this device or his time in the Landsliders. Wherever Greg had kept his secrets, they sure as hell weren't on the surface of the house, or even in the tucked-away desk drawers. Lana was keeping her distance, occupying herself with cooking chicken and rice she didn't have to share with him, but did anyway.

He lay in her guest room bed, staring at the ceiling. Even with her husband gone, this house felt like a home. It wasn't the couple of bright, splashy pictures or the different colored walls in each room. It wasn't even the stacks of papers lining the desks or the books leaning askew on the shelves. No, it was her presence.

Even a room over, he could feel her like a living heartbeat. He'd be lying if he claimed to have ever felt that immediate connection with anyone.

However, she was recently widowed, and he was transitory at best.

Lucas let out a sigh and rolled over, attempting to close his eyes and force some sleep. At least, until his skin prickled. He sat up and prowled to the windows, looking out on the front lawn for any sign of intruders.

A knock sounded at his door.

Lana entered a moment later. "Hope you're decent," she called, lifting her hands over her eyes. "I caught a scent in the breeze from the open window," she said. "Smells coyote-ish."

Lucas leaned down to yank a gray tee over his head. When he pulled the shirt the rest of the way, Lana's gaze had drifted to him. She looked away at once, but he caught the flare in her eyes.

"I'll go check out the spot," he said, heading for the door.

Lana hugged her arms tight as she wrinkled her nose. "I'm joining you."

He lifted an eyebrow while he gripped the edge of the door frame. "You don't need to. I didn't scent an army out there. It's probably a lone scout."

"Yeah, on my property," Lana said, striding past him. She'd put boots on, which clicked against the hardwood as she walked down the hallway. He followed close behind, his bare feet not making a whisper. They descended the steps fast, and he barely paused to slip into sneakers before making for her back door.

"Follow my lead," he said, stepping out into the inky darkness, the cold breeze causing his skin to pebble. As he stared out into the forest stretching behind her house, he took a deep breath of the air. A coyote must be feet away, but from what Lucas could gauge, there was only one.

Lucas took one careful step forward, then another, to head down the steps of her back porch.

Despite the murky darkness threaded through leaves and tree branches, Lucas caught movement, and the slender form of a coyote emerged. It trotted ahead a couple of paces, its eyes gleaming silver in the moonlight. The shifter was carrying something in its mouth. Lucas' fangs threatened to emerge at the foreign scent, and his tiger paced in his chest, restless to hunt or strike at this intruder.

The coyote stopped and whipped his head to the side to toss whatever he carried.

Lucas threw his hand out to push Lana with him, and he staggered back. However, the thing landed in the grass and didn't explode. The coyote bobbed his head before he trotted off to the woods. Once the shifter reached the cover of the pine trees, he launched full speed through the forest.

"Stay back," Lucas warned as he took a few steps forward. Lana stood behind him with her arms crossed even as her focus remained steady on the woods. The way she watched his back without being asked made him feel like he was among the other members of the East Coast Tribe. He crouched to where the item had been tossed in the grass.

It was a scroll. He picked the fragile thing up with his fingertips, the paper damp from being carried in the coyote's mouth. Now the Landsliders were sending their peons as a delivery service — like the mail or even an email couldn't do.

By the time he'd unrolled the paper, Lana crouched beside him. "What does it say?" she asked, her voice echoing in the cold night air.

The stark words were scrawled out on the pale note.

Return what Greg stole, or your pack will suffer. You have until the end of the week.

A growl slipped past his lips before he could help himself. They'd caused her so much suffering already, and now they'd hold the lives of her pack hostage. Lana sat so close to him that he could feel the vibrations in the air when she began to shake. It wasn't from the cold.

The scrap of paper dropped from his hands. He found himself slipping an arm around her shoulders. At first, she froze in surprise and he almost pulled away. However, a second later, she sank against him, and the tears she'd been holding back coursed down her cheeks. He kept his arm around her, unable to convey the tightness in his chest at the sight, or how something intrinsic longed to protect her.

As if maybe, in saving Lana, he could somehow atone for not saving Josefina.

Liquid imprinted on his shirt, and her shoulders shook. Lucas didn't dare say anything to interrupt as the tidal wave the woman had been holding back roared forward. Her nails curled into her thighs as she leaned beside him, still in a crouch. He focused on his breaths, keeping them steady, soothing. While he might share a deep connection to the other members of the East Coast Tribe, he hadn't experienced this much up-close interaction since the last time he'd visited his mother and father at home.

If he were honest, he craved the connection like he did a crackling fireplace after a run through the snow.

Lana pushed herself away from him before tapping his chest with her fist. She looked him square in the eye, her eyes glassy. "Great host I am. Here, come stay at my place so I can be a bawling wreck. I'd say this is a new widow thing, but I've always been a crier."

Lucas shook his head and pushed himself from the crouch, his legs protesting at the quick movement. He offered her a hand. "I grew up in a loud, close family with three sisters, so I've done my fair share of offering a shoulder to cry on."

"No wonder you're so good at this." Lana offered him a half-smile, soft in the wake of her tears as she accepted his hand up. Lucas snagged the scrap of paper — he'd be needing to show it to Dax and Sierra in the morning. Together, they walked toward the house, leaving the whisper of the wintry breeze curling around the desiccated leaves.

The moment they stepped inside, Lana locked the door behind her, the click echoing through the room, then ran her hands along her arms. She glanced at Lucas. "Let's see if counting sheep can combat my paranoid twitches at every sound I'm going to hear tonight. I was jumpy to begin with, so these assholes didn't need to amplify that."

He gave her shoulder a gentle nudge. From his brief interactions with her, he'd come to realize how well she responded to touch. "That's why you have me here, remember? I'm in the room next to yours, and it's not like any shifters can levitate to your window."

Lana shuddered. "Spirits, but what if they could?" A second later she cracked him a grin that didn't quite reach her eyes. "You're right, though. Any of those assholes try to sneak into my place and you could just command them to stop, right?"

"Yeah," he said, feeling like he was walking over bubble wrap, ready to pop at any moment. The subject always made him uncomfortable, because so few of their kind understood why the Tribe needed compulsion. It didn't help that monsters like Mackey roamed out there abusing their powers.

Lana stopped in the middle of the living room and stared at him, her gaze piercing right through. "Hey, I wouldn't have invited you into my house if I thought you were prancing from city to city using those powers for evil. I trust you, Lucas Diaz."

Her words socked him in the gut. If he hadn't been smitten by her before, he was now. "You don't know how rare that is," he murmured, ducking his head. "Come on, let's head up and catch some shut-eye while we can. We've got a full day tomorrow." He hightailed it up the steps before she could see the flush on his cheeks.

They both reached their respective rooms around the same time, and Lana paused with her hand on the knob before she turned around. "Good night," she responded with a genuine grin this time. "See you in the morning."

He waited for her to head into the room. Once she'd closed the door, he stripped out of his clothes and tossed them into his room, his nails pricking out in transition. He shifted with the ease of years of experience, his bones mutating and fur sprouting along his arms as he went from standing on two feet to all fours. Lucas prowled back and forth outside Lana's door a couple of times before he found a comfortable spot and settled. He could rest here for the night.

If any Landsliders wanted to threaten her life, they'd have to go through him first.

Chapter Five

Lana stepped through the entrance of the Beaver Tavern, the bar emanating silence since it wasn't open to the public yet. She felt a presence at her back and turned, ready to tease Greg to stop dragging his heels. When she spun around, Lucas stood behind her, casting a massive shadow. Lana swallowed hard, trying to ignore the burn. She lifted her hand to shield her eyes and squinted as if she were staring at the sun streaming in through the door past him.

Grief was stupid. She'd be floating, floating, floating, then all of a sudden it'd jump out of a bush to sock her in the face.

"Anyone here yet?" Lucas called, his voice ringing around the room.

"Be out in a second," Sierra shouted from the back. "Go find a seat."

Lucas grabbed a chair at the nearest table and pulled it out, gesturing for her to sit. This man needed to stop being so damned sweet. Warmth burned in her chest at the memory of opening her door a crack last night to spot the massive tiger curled in front of it. Seeing him out there protecting her settled the unease that had buzzed through her veins like caffeine. For the first night in far too long, she'd fallen into a deep sleep, and the rest had been glorious.

Lana sat and skimmed her fingers through her hair. Her brain turned into a hornet's nest at the thought of Greg, his secret past and her present, still without him. Guilt throbbed inside her, a living pulse, when she looked up at Lucas and smiled. She couldn't help the relief she felt at having another presence in her lonely house, but she hated herself. She should be stronger, like Ally, who could live by her lonesome and toss out snappy comebacks as if she wasn't hurting most of the time.

"Guess it's too early for a beer, right?" she said, glancing at the taps. A mere year ago, she never could've imagined herself a loner barfly, hanging out at Beaver Tavern for too many nights. But clinging to a pint here was better than the alternative of returning to an empty house.

Lucas tapped his fingers on the surface of the table. "Never too early. All the barley and wheat—it's like liquid cereal."

Lana couldn't help the impish grin that curled her lips. "That's quite the roundabout justification, Diaz."

Sierra emerged from the back, carrying a six-pack. "I could hear you guys whining from where I was." She stepped out past the bar, her rounded stomach making an appearance with her. For a while, Sierra hadn't shown at all, but now the bump was growing more apparent with every passing week, since she was five months along. Lana tried to ignore the twinge in her gut, which was faint but always there every time she saw families with young kids, or ones just beginning.

She and Greg had been heading in that direction, preparing to have cubs of their own one day. Those dreams had gotten severed the moment he'd crashed dead on the floor.

Her nails turned to claws that bit into the wooden table. Lucas' gaze glided over her, too knowing, and part of her wanted to blurt out the mess in her head on the spot. Sierra plunked the six-pack in the center of the table.

"For everyone but me, because I no longer get to enjoy nice things." Sierra glared at her stomach, and Lana couldn't help but smile. Even as she felt her own sadness, joy candy-coated her insides at the thought of the Dax Williams she'd grown up with forming a family with Red Rock's fire-and-brimstone alpha. They were going to be a fantastic team.

Lucas cracked open an IPA right as the door swung open. Ally stormed inside, irritation written on the crease in her forehead. The source followed close behind her as Drew entered.

"You don't own a stake in every breakfast joint in Pennsylvania," he called out, heat rising in his tone.

Drew still scraped Lana raw, even knowing his actions might not have been his own. She couldn't stop the bile in her throat at the memories of finding out who'd been behind the bombs, the way she'd curled into a ball and cried and cried and cried in the wake of Greg's death.

"Yeah, but that one was ours," Ally spat, stomping her way to the table and plunking into the seat. Her blonde braid slapped against her back with the force, and she didn't bother with a greeting. She reached straight for a beer and cracked the top off. Ally turned to look at Drew again. "Find a different diner."

He let out a snort as he took the seat beside her, most likely to piss her off.

Lucas heaved a sigh, looking weary before they'd even begun.

Lana nudged his foot to snag his attention as she leaned in. "They're always like this," she murmured. "Doesn't mean they can't snap to focus when it counts."

"Both of you, stop fighting," Sierra stepped in, slamming her palms onto the table between them. "Ally, the man's got to eat somewhere in this area, no matter the problems he's caused. And, Drew, if you're antagonizing her on purpose, you deserve what's coming to you. Regardless, we're here to discuss more important things."

Drew and Ally silenced at once, both of them tipping their bottles back in an attempt to avoid Sierra's ire. Lana pursed her lips to hide her amusement. Pregnant or no, the Red Rock alpha tolerated zero bullshit.

"Right." Lucas took the cue to step in. "So, I'll drive us to the first location. It's about a half-hour away and should be abandoned, but everyone needs to be on the alert and ready to fight and shift. Got that?" He focused on Ally, not that Lana could blame him. Drew, he had already run missions with, but Ally possessed a stubborn streak an ocean wide, which was probably why she worked so well with a fluid and changeable alpha like Dax.

"Sounds good," Sierra said, tapping the tabletop. "Let's head out."

Lucas stared her down, his gaze lingering on her swollen stomach. "I don't think that's a good idea." Sierra bared her teeth the second the phrase left him, but he continued on, unintimidated. "You're at half-strength due to your pregnancy and slower than ever. We can't afford to have a weak link in the chain here."

Sierra jutted her chin out. "Which is why I'll be bringing this," she said, pulling out a Glock. "I've hit the bullseye every time at practice. Even if I can't fight in the thick of things, I refuse to sit back and be useless." For someone born a regular shifter, the Red Rock alpha showed little fear.

Lucas met her gaze head-on. "If I tell you to retreat, you listen. If you don't, I'll be forced to make you comply." She nodded in response as he let out a sigh and pushed up from the table.

Lana couldn't help but like this man. He could've turned Sierra down, but instead he'd listened and offered a fair compromise. If more people were like Lucas Diaz, the world would be a far better place.

Lana strode a pace faster to the door, taking Lucas' cue. "I call shotgun."

Ally let out a groan loud enough to resound through the whole bar, and Sierra's keys jingled as she whipped them out to lock up. They'd driven over together in his Explorer, one which would feel smaller than ever once they crammed all five of them inside. She slipped into the passenger seat and the engine rumbled to life. Lucas already sat behind the wheel.

He passed her an amused glance. "I should've given us earplugs, right?"

Lana snorted. Ally hopped into the back seat, moving to the far right as she called for Sierra to sit in the middle. "They wouldn't have helped. Where are we heading first?"

Drew had barely closed the door when Lucas pumped the gas, gliding onto the highway. He tapped a beat along the steering wheel while he sped down the strip of asphalt.

"We're heading to Harvey's Lake today," he announced to the car, answering her question.

Lana's insides lurched. Harvey's Lake had made the papers as a local spot for fantastic views and picnics — she knew from experience because she and Greg had spent their last anniversary there. His suggestion. Her insides dripped with acid. At that point, he'd been working for the Landsliders, lying to her face. It could've even been an excuse to make a stop-off — she'd met him in the town, after all.

"What work were you doing there?" she asked. Her voice sounded hollow, as if someone had gutted her like a jack-o'-lantern. Part of her wanted to know — needed to know. Another wanted those secrets to stay buried with the dead.

"You know, your average sort of villainy. Drug smuggling, planning to take over the region," Drew muttered in the sardonic tone that always fit him so well. His experience with the Landsliders had changed him, though, deepening the notes with a bitterness belonging to funerals and broken homes. "Ow." The sound erupted from Drew as Sierra elbowed him in the side. Lana watched through the rearview mirror.

Lucas focused on the road ahead, speeding down the open highway, but even though his gaze remained forward, she couldn't help but shiver. Even when he wasn't looking her way, he paid attention when so few did nowadays. No one wanted to meet her eyes, but she understood — witnessing her truth hurt, like she'd smacked them in the face with rock salt.

"Didn't you go to Harvey's Lake recently?" Ally brought up, her best friend blurting things out on instinct before she thought them through. Lana winced, and at once she caught the flash of regret in Ally's blue eyes. "Shit, I'm sorry, Lan. I forgot."

An awkward silence descended through the car at the mention of Greg, one she'd begun to loathe. Everyone was so afraid of bringing him up around her even when she just wanted to talk in the open about those things. Ally might be a stampede through a Sunday picnic, but Lana appreciated her friend for slicing past the quiet, for her rambling honesty.

"Greg was a Landslider," she said out loud, as if the words might sink beneath the skin. As if the truth might somehow imprint over her memories of the man she'd spent afternoons fishing with, the one she'd made turkey, craisin and relish sandwiches for because, even if it was weird, he liked the combo. "Only stands to reason some of the things I thought were ours belonged to them too. They already robbed me of his life, so why not his memories?"

Her bitterness burst through the car like an explosion. At once, shame flushed through her. She could've died on the spot.

Lucas tapped the back of her seat. "That's why you're on the team, Bennett. We're going to make sure those fuckers don't get what they want."

Lana sucked in a breath of relief at the out. "Call me Renoir," she murmured. "My maiden name."

Even though his eyes never left the road, Lucas noticed her, and again, the man had come to her rescue. His words shattered the silence in the car like a crowbar smashing glass.

"We'll create some new memories," Ally said. "Like setting their secret lairs on fire and roasting marshmallows over the wreckage."

"I've got a pretty finite deadline for getting Mackey Kendricks and his filth out of this region," Sierra said, patting her rounded stomach.

"Honestly never thought I'd be an uncle," Drew murmured, even as he stared out of the window. A note of longing, impossible to miss, crept into his voice.

Sierra's nose wrinkled. "Trust me, we're not thrilled to have you either." The Red Rock alpha had mistaken the distance in his voice, but Lana had known Drew long enough — he'd always wanted to be a father. Sierra might not catch the flicker of a wince in those eyes, but the rear-view mirror let Lana see it.

The stretch of highway filtered to smaller, winding roads as they got closer and closer to Harvey's Lake. Out of everything she worried about encountering on site, the Landsliders were the least of them. After all, once Greg had died, the places and things they'd shared had become a minefield of memories. Too soon, the familiar sparkle of Harvey's Lake glimmered into view.

The surrounding area was a quintessential sleepy lake town, small buildings and boating docks. Trees stretched around all sides, sloping into hills that cast their shadows over the large expanse.

Within minutes, they rolled through the small dusty roads, past the main slapped-together stretch of asphalt they called their town street and reached the fringes of the lake where the glittering waters lapped the shore. Lana pulled at the sleeves of her jacket. She didn't bother with gloves — she'd shredded through too many pairs in the past, and besides, shifters ran hotter than the average human.

In the back seat, Ally murmured something to Drew, her tone agitated, and Sierra dove in to stop the argument. Their annoyance rolled across Lana's skin, but she had no desire to get involved.

Her gaze rested on Lucas' corded forearms as he clutched tight to the steering wheel, since he'd rolled his sleeves up while he drove and hung his jacket off the back of the driver's seat. The Tribal tattoos were dark black strokes against his sepia skin, the markings tethering him to an ancient spirit. Something so simple, yet so potent.

The car jerked to a halt, and he put it into Park, but before Lana could tear her gaze away, Lucas' landed on her. She tugged on the end of her ponytail before she met those dark eyes, which to some might look forbidding. Lana offered a genuine smile she felt deep in her bones. His full lips twisted with a smirk.

"All right, crew," he called out to everyone in the car, bringing their bickering to an end. "This is where Drew's going to take the lead."

Drew nodded and hopped out of the back seat first. Lana cracked the door open, a bracing wind blasting in. She pursed her lips, settling her boots on the firm ground of the gravel parking lot. This section of the lake glittered like carved crystal when the sun struck it, and even with the chilly breezes roving past them, the pale rays fought to warm them.

Lucas slipped his jacket on and walked in line with Drew, who started striding toward the lake. The two of them were murmuring, but when Lana tried to tune in, they only talked about a live music show they must've swung into while on the road. Somehow, the two had patched a friendship out of their time together.

Ally scampered after them, and Lana kept a deliberate pace while Sierra took the rear, her hand gliding toward the pistol she carried. Each step caused

Lana to remember the day last March, their wedding anniversary. It was mere months away, the first one she'd be spending without him in four years.

The thought formed a pit in her stomach, one that widened as they continued toward the wooded section. The winding path was familiar, the same one she'd walked with Greg that day, their laughter threading through the pines as they'd joked about the latest fit Greg's mother had had over her best silverware going missing. As usual, she'd forgotten she'd packed those boxes in the basement.

Ally slowed to walk side by side with her. "Hey, is this weird?" she asked in a lowered tone. "I mean, do you need a moment?"

Lana shook her head, but then nodded. "Ugh, got that backward. Yes, it's weird, but no — moving is better." The shadows fell over them, and she hated that she didn't even have to look to follow the trail Drew was leading them down. If she'd had any doubt that Greg had recycled places with her that he'd spent time in in a different life, the secret one she hadn't been privy to, the way Drew slowed as they neared the small boathouse confirmed her hunch.

Her heart pounded louder and louder until the sound drowned out the whistling birds, the gentle thrum of the lake and even the soft crunch of their footsteps. The path opened to an exposed shoreline, the mix of sand and dirt trailing into the sparkling waters of the lake. She almost stopped mid-stride when she felt the shiver of the cool lake around her feet. Except back then, Greg had been sitting there with her, their plaid blanket streaked with dirt and the bottle of wine finished between them.

Drew passed the spot where they'd sat, blissfully happy.

Where she'd been blissfully unaware.

He tromped right over to the nearby boathouse, and Lana swallowed bile. The Landsliders had been right here. His secrets had been right here, and she'd never even known they existed. Naïve had a new definition in the dictionary — her.

Lucas took the lead and stepped up to the boathouse. The interior was in far better condition than the weathered paint of the exterior, Lana recalled. He listened while they approached before facing them and offering a nod. Lucas opened the door, a devouring darkness waiting inside.

Time to discover the other life my husband led.

Chapter Six

The boathouse smelled like algae and wet wood. It also smelled like metal and wolves.

Lucas stepped in first while Drew followed close behind. They'd scouted some of the initial spots when he'd last arrived here, but then the Coalition had caused so many problems they'd just done a cursory sweep of the old Landslider meth operations. Mackey had somehow created a spiderweb network sprawling through the entire region. It wasn't like the intricacy or fervor surprised him. Mackey Kendricks had always been angrier than the rest of them, and, armed with his charisma, he was destined to cause trouble.

The boards creaked under his feet, but his eyes shifted to those of the tiger dwelling inside him, the ancient being he ended up going toe to toe with half the time. Like back in the car when the simple fucker had rammed him in his chest, begging to mount Lana after he'd caught her staring. So yeah, he didn't listen to his beast's cues most of the time. With his cat's eyesight, he was able to discern more shapes in the room, nets for skimming algae and a couple of canoes stacked against the wall.

Drew wove by him to crouch on the floor. He tugged at a ring, which opened a set of steps.

"Is this area rife with hidden compartments, or do the Landsliders hire creative contractors?" Lucas asked as he hunched beside Drew. Ally switched a flashlight on from the pack she carried, while Lana and Sierra trailed in last.

"Mackey keeps a team on retainer just for secret passageways," Drew murmured with a wry grin. Despite the hate Drew Williams had earned around this area, Lucas understood him. The man was another of Mackey's victims, and from the slips of the past he'd shared on the road, the atrocities he'd been forced to commit haunted him every night.

"Glad to know he's got his priorities straight," Lucas responded with a grin before lowering to the first step. He glanced to the rest of the crew. "Sierra, you stand watch up here. Any sight of other shifters and you nab us. Everyone else, follow me." He then set to climbing down into the darkness, trying to ignore the prickle across his skin. *Not like anyone needs to know the big bad Tribe member is afraid of the dark.* His childhood fear had gotten cemented into his brain that night. The one when he'd flipped on the light in Josefina's room.

Lucas gritted his teeth as he descended, trying to ignore the creeping feeling that something was watching him. The moment he shed some light on the pit he descended into, he'd find this place teeming with monsters worse than the ones he'd confronted as Tribe.

His feet settled onto solid ground, and he viewed the room through the eyes of his tiger, making out a far larger space than anyone would believe after seeing the miniscule boathouse up top. This stretched out like a cellar, tall stacks of shelving in every direction. He couldn't catch a single noise apart from the scraping shuffle of their footsteps as the others descended with him. Ally brought her flashlight, the beam slicing around their inky surroundings.

His nose twitched from the metallic scent of the shelves, the lingering trail of all the shifters who had tromped through here and the rich earth beneath his feet. Lucas headed in the direction of a long iron-studded workbench on the far end of the room, where papers sat stacked or scattered across the surface.

Ally dragged her flashlight to the opposite corner, while Drew hit the other side. Lana crept beside him, her presence already becoming a comfortable one.

"What do you think they'd even leave here?" Lana asked, her voice echoing through the room.

"This was one of the meeting spots for Mackey and Ganzorig, but a couple of us got dragged along for the ride to help out with the next step of his crazy complicated agenda," Drew called. He opened a filing cabinet with a creak. "The guy had contingency plans for his contingency plans, so chances are, most of this information is outdated. We were given enough to fumble in the dark."

Lucas' gaze drifted to a list pinned to the wall containing a bunch of names that had all been crossed off—like a hit list. He snagged it and folded the paper into his pocket. Lana fingered through the stacks of pages on the workbench in front of them.

"Anything of use?" he asked, leaning over her shoulder. He feigned curiosity, but her presence calmed the nerves that consumed him at being down in this dark, confined space. Not like getting closer was a good idea. Even here, in the middle of this dank basement, his libido thrummed to life at their proximity.

She glanced at him, her eyes glowing the amber of her mountain lion. "This is a ton of research on shamanic techniques. Looks like they did a lot of assembly or experimental work here. Think they'll notice if we take all their shit?"

"I don't like this," Ally grumbled from her corner while she crouched to examine another stack of shelving. "No way would Mackey just allow us to waltz in and look at anything important. This has got to be a trap."

"Agreed," Drew said as he stepped to the center of the room. "I don't like how quiet this place is. I know they abandoned it a while back, but Mackey isn't the type to leave anything to chance. I expected they would've scoured this place clean or filled the space in."

"Grab what you can, then we'll get out," Lucas called, taking command with ease.

"This stuff looks newer," Lana said, walking to the other end of the workbench. A few half-folded papers lay scattered across the surface, a bunch of handwritten notes. She picked them up but froze mid-grab. "Oh fuck."

Lana didn't need to say another word. Lucas discerned the metallic stench that had been lingering here. A bomb sat ticking on the counter—it had been buried under the pile of papers, but the neon-red numbers clicked down, closer and closer to zero.

Under a minute left.

"Run." Lucas gave the order, not needing to throw any compulsion behind the words.

Ally and Drew already bolted for the ladder up. Lana grabbed the pile of papers she'd been scanning and took off, but he outpaced her in seconds. Lucas slowed to throw a hand out. She grabbed it, and together they raced for the steps at the opposite end of the room. He cast a single glance back.

Less than a minute left.

His calves burned as he sprinted across the room, his grip tightening on hers. He slammed into the base of the ladder first, but he didn't climb. Lucas nudged Lana forward, and she set to climbing at once, even with the bundle of papers in her hands. Lucas rested his palms on the rungs beneath her, ready to bolt. His gaze rested on the neon numbers flashing down.

They must've tripped off a timer once they'd stepped inside the room. No one was supposed to leave this place alive.

Lana scrambled to the top, and he followed close behind, vaulting up the rungs at top speed. She didn't bolt out of the boathouse, waiting at the top for him instead.

"Go," he called to her, closing in on the final ones. She shook her head, her mouth pressed into a thin line. A beeping echoed through the room.

Lucas leaped past the last rung and into the room of the boathouse. This time, Lana grabbed his hand and yanked him with her, right as the weathered planks began to tremble.

The resounding boom followed a moment later.

They raced through the boathouse, and the heat traveled from below, gusts of noxious fumes from the explosion. The floorboards crumbled beneath them, creaks and groans sounding as several tumbled below.

Lana staggered out first, and he followed. More of the aged floorboards either lit with crimson flames or cracked and fell to the basement beneath. Her nails dug crescents into his palms from the force she gripped him with. He spluttered, trying to suck in clean breaths of the cold, wintry air. She heaved forward, letting out a couple of ragged coughs. Her hand remained in his for a few more moments, and they stood drawing in breaths before she pulled away.

"I mean, we should've expected bombs," Sierra said, standing out by the lake with her arms crossed. "Not like we haven't seen that MO before." The suspicion in her voice locked and loaded at Drew.

Before Drew could argue or Lucas could even speak up, Ally stepped in. "Drew and I were both having our concerns down there. It was a clear set-up." Drew's eyebrows furrowed, and he skimmed a hand through his hair rather than saying anything in response.

"Hey, not a total waste," Lana said, stepping past Lucas to the others. She handed out papers from the stack she'd nabbed from below. The list he'd found burned a hole in his pocket, something he wanted to investigate. After all, despite the immediate concern of Ganzorig and the threat to deliver what Greg had stolen, Lucas had a bigger agenda. More than all the sideshow acts the Landsliders pulled, he needed to stop Mackey. The man had been East Coast Tribe. The longer he ran free and the more atrocities he committed, the more guilt gnawed away at all of them.

"On to the next spot, boss?" Drew asked, looking to him for confirmation.

Lucas nodded. "Only this time, we'll toss a stick in or roll a ball to test for more explosives. We won't get caught off guard again."

* * * *

By the time they'd cycled through the other spots on Drew's list, the sun had already set. The locations, all withered shacks and boarded-up gas stations, were either emptied as expected or set to explode. Only this time, they took necessary precautions rather than getting caught in the blaze.

After all the time tromping through the bitter cold from place to place, sinking into Lana's couch was like heaven. She heated a container of lamb stew, which they devoured, then they both settled in on the couch to work. She sat on one end, and he had slumped into the other, but as the hours whiled away, they ended up inching in closer every time he took a look at something on the pages she was scrutinizing or when she peeked over to see the names he was searching.

"These notes are dated," Lana mentioned. She adjusted the reading glasses she'd donned when they'd set to work. "More recently than last August, when Ganzorig ditched his home. He must have somewhere else he's camping out." She sat curled on the couch inches from him, her sweater slipping off one of her shoulders to reveal the strap of the tank top beneath, and she wore rumpled plaid pajama pants. Several strands of hair slipped from her messy bun, drifting along her neck, all tan, olive skin. She couldn't have looked sexier if she tried.

Lucas nodded, setting his laptop down for a moment. "I know thinking about Greg must hurt, but if you get any ideas of other places to check, I'm listening."

Lana heaved out a shaky sigh. The weight in her gaze as it descended caused the breath to catch in his throat. "I hate this, you know? Having to question everything we did together the past couple of years. And I'm pretty sure Drew's holding stuff back from me on purpose. I'm not an idiot. But at the same point, I don't think I'm ready to know either. I mean, I knew Greg my entire life."

"Christ, apart from my family, I don't think I've had any attachments that long," Lucas murmured, closing the lid of his laptop. He leaned into the couch to face her. "The East Coast Tribe is the closest we've got to pack, and even then, we're running off on independent operations most of the time."

Lana shook her head. "You know, sometimes I wish I could escape. Don't tell Ally or Dax, but that's the drawback of growing up here. The grief is all around me, minefields just waiting to be stepped on. But I'm avoiding your question, aren't I? Finding this device is vital, so I'll try my best to figure out where it might be."

"What was being with someone that long even like?" he asked, the question leaping out before he could help himself. He winced a moment later, but Lana's lips quirked with a grin as she shook her head.

"None of that guilt," she murmured. "It does me good to talk about things. You know, the same favor's extended to you, whenever you're ready." The glance she gave him over the rims of her glasses was pointed, like she saw straight through to the scars that had never fully healed. "It's comfortable, like this old blanket," she said, lifting the one she'd tugged over her legs. "A weight you know will be there, a respite at the end of a long day."

"Sounds nice," he responded, trying to shut out the longing in his voice.

Lana tilted her head to the side. "Don't tell me the Tribe makes you take some vow of non-commitment or something. Navi managed to mate with Finn."

"Nothing is hidden from you, is it?" he responded, a grin rising to his face again. As much as dredging some of these things to the surface hurt, he could feel himself healing with every one of their talks. "Sure, we're allowed to mate, but apart from getting lucky enough to find yours, most relationships don't stand the test of long-distance or a life on the road. Not like I have room to complain, fuck."

Lana lifted an eyebrow. "You're allowed to be as pissed as you want. And I might've lost my best friend and husband, but we weren't mates. Hell, maybe if I'd waited to find mine, we would've had the soul-deep connection where nothing was hidden. Sure as hell not working for our enemy on the side."

Lucas' heart pounded faster in his chest, a hope he fought to suppress. His attraction to her was undeniable, and not just because she had the sort of stunner curves that would stop him mid-stride. Her presence, her words and her touch grounded him like nothing else. And for someone who'd been on the move from an early age, the feeling was more powerful than any he'd experienced.

"Yeah, no luck in that department for me either," he responded. "Instead I've become King of the One-Night Stand."

Her eyes glimmered as she nudged him in the arm. "Hey, at least you're getting some." She tilted her head to stare at the ceiling. "Even before Greg passed, it had been a while, and now no one will touch me with a ten-foot pole. Apparently being widowed means I also became celibate."

A deep hunger burned inside him, and his tiger thumped in his chest, a rumble that traveled up and down. His fingers buzzed with the need to skim across her smooth skin, to grip those hips, and he couldn't stop his tongue from slipping out to wet his lips, which had suddenly grown too dry.

Lana's gaze transfixed on his mouth, making him even more aware they sat inches from each other. Her lips parted, the pristine shade of roses in early morning, the same scent that lingered around her. His need for her grew painful, a tug in his chest, a kick to his libido that had him shifting in his seat. He'd been trying to tamp the lust he felt for her from the moment they'd met, but it grew into a Herculean task when he saw the same flare in her dew-green eyes.

Fuck it.

Lucas leaned in, closing the distance between them. He brushed his lips against hers, soft at first, until a sinful breath of relief came from her. She deepened the kiss, surrendering to him as though she'd been wanting this just as badly. He had kissed many women over the years, but the moment his lips met hers, he knew this would be one he remembered. She melted into him, resting her palm on his chest like a brand, her taste all bitter coffee and sweetness.

He twined his fingers through her hair, cupping the back of her neck. He slipped his tongue in, caressing her mouth as their lips met again and again. *Too much.* Heat flared through him with a demand he wanted to sink into, but he wouldn't do that. Not now. Even though his entire body protested, he pulled away from her.

"See, someone's willing to touch you," he murmured against her mouth. His cheeks flushed from the surge of warmth he felt. He snagged his laptop and stepped away from the couch before he could witness the look in her eyes, whether it be temptation or the sort of disappointment to break him. Lucas made a quick retreat up the steps, heading for the guest room.

Great Spirits, I've made a mess of this.

Chapter Seven

Lana needed a drink since yesterday.

She settled onto her usual bar stool at Beaver Tavern, the clink of pool balls echoing behind her and the scent of polished wood and dark ale rich in the air. Raven caught her gaze and winked. Lana lifted a finger, and her favorite bartender began pouring her a Scotch and soda. Lana still wore the yoga pants and tank top from when she'd been working on massage clients earlier, but she'd thrown on a flannel overtop in an attempt to look presentable. Raven sauntered over with the drink to place it in front of her.

Raven's eyes gleamed often, even months after her mating bond with the Red Rock beta had been made official. Happiness was a good look on her.

"Haven't seen you in a couple of days," Raven said. "Everything okay?"

The fact that skipping a few nights at Beaver Tavern caused concern slammed into her like a bear at full charge. The words wanted to spill from her lips like a waterfall after everything that had happened in the last few days. But Raven was working behind the bar tonight, and Lana was nursing her single drink like she did every time she didn't want to return to an empty house.

Lana forced a grin and raised the glass. "Let's say this was well earned."

Raven nodded before she darted off to pour a pint for Gene, who'd arrived at his normal spot. Lana lifted the Scotch and soda to her lips, willing the alcohol to burn away the scum coating her insides.

Lucas and Drew had left early in the morning to check out another lead, at least as far as the scrawled note said. She hadn't seen the formidable Tribe member since last night. When he'd kissed her.

And Spirits above, what a kiss. She hadn't realized how touch-starved she'd become until relief had shuddered through her when their lips had met. His mouth had been rough and hot, his movements filled with the competent control he exuded. Kissing Lucas was like standing at the top of a cliff only to dive into the icy depths below. The way they'd collided had left her with heart-pounding exhilaration she'd never experienced before.

As fast as the relief had swept in, the bone-aching, heart-searing relief that had made her feel like she was more than a vessel for all this grief — the moment Lucas had pulled away, the guilt had descended.

Worse, the warmth she felt toward Lucas hadn't diminished. Instead, heady sensations swept through her at the mere thought of him, an attraction she found her body awakening to anew. Lana shifted in her seat, staring into the pale yellow contents of her drink. She wasn't blind. The man's rugged good looks elicited a visceral response, and whether she wanted to admit it to herself or not, she'd been looking.

Lana drank deep from her glass. *Kissing another man when my husband hasn't even been buried a year.* She was the worst sort of monster. The door creaked, drawing Lana's attention as a familiar blonde entered the tavern. Ally locked eyes with her at once and strode over.

By the time Ally had settled into a seat, Raven had dropped off a pint of lager for the Silver Springs beta.

"Figured I would find you here," Ally said, circling her palms around the tall glass. "You've got a lot to process with all the news about Greg." She sank in the stool, her hair pulled back in pinned, perfect curls, and she still wore her all-black attire from work. Lana had only ever trusted Ally to cut her hair, and her best friend had become one of the top stylists in the area.

"That's just a stone in the avalanche," Lana said, her heart twisting tight in her chest. She needed to tell someone what had happened, but Ally had been friends with Greg—her husband, the one she had sworn to love for better or for worse. Yet, if she was destined to remain alone for the rest of her life after he'd passed, she might as well kill herself now, because she'd wither away.

Ally's eyebrow quirked, and foam coated her upper lip once she took a gulp. "You're giving me that look."

"What look?" she asked, tugging on the end of her ponytail.

"The one you always give when you've got something on your mind and want to talk. So, spill." Ally flicked her in the shoulder, a grin on her face.

A pit opened in Lana's stomach. After everything that had happened, she didn't think she could handle her best friend hating her. "Just tell me I'm terrible now and get it over with," Lana blurted out. Her mouth betrayed her every time.

Ally leaned back on the bar stool, a skeptical look in her eyes. "And why do you think I'd be calling you terrible? You've been beaten down ever since Greg died last year, and it hasn't been getting any better."

Lana's fingers skimmed her lips on instinct before she wrapped her hand around her drink.

Ally's gaze flashed with curiosity. The woman might be a blunt battering ram, but she paid attention. "Oh, that's one guilty look, sister. Did you hook up with someone?"

She shook her head even while she lifted the Scotch and soda to her lips. The dry bite of the liquor wasn't scraping the surface of her guilt tonight.

"Lucas kissed me last night." The words came out so low they were almost a whisper.

Ally's ocean eyes grew huge. "Go big or go home, I guess," she said, her lips twitching. "Because the guy is massive. Like, muscles on muscles."

Lana's eyebrows drew together, her throat dry. Her heart ached as if someone had dragged their claws over it and she'd barely managed to stop the bleeding. "Why aren't you mad at me?"

Ally wrinkled her nose before she chugged the rest of her pint. The glass hit the polished mahogany bar with a solid *thunk*. "Look, I'm not going to lie. It's weird. I've only ever known you with Greg. But it's stupid to think you're going to shrivel up and die just because he did, Lan. You're so much bigger than that, and you're allowed to heal. You're especially allowed to hook up with a stunning specimen of a guy while he happens to be in town."

Heat rose to her eyes, and when she blinked, a couple of tears slipped free. "Ally-cat, did I ever tell you how much I love you?" Lana leaned forward just as Ally wrapped her arms tightly around her. Even though she couldn't dispel the uneasy churn in her gut at what she'd done, at the attraction she could no longer deny, Ally's words gave her the space to breathe.

While the pack had been supportive since Greg died and Dax checked in on the regular, Ally had been her rock. Her cheeks burned in embarrassment at the emotional display, but Great Spirits, she'd been drowning.

"I mean you've told me, but I never tire of hearing it," Ally said, squeezing her hard. "Besides, I'd much rather listen to that than the grating sound of my ex's voice."

Lana pulled away, smudging the tears from her eyes with a thumb. She sucked in a shaky breath. "How've you been feeling with Drew back in town?" While she hadn't sorted out her stance on the ex-Landslider yet, her confusion had to pale in comparison to what Ally must be going through. Lana and Greg had been the stacked granite, stable couple, while Ally and Drew were drawn to each other like wildfire to dry wood. And when they collided, they turned into the sparks and twisted metal of a car crash, again and again.

"Pissed off, but hey, what can I do?" Ally shrugged, bringing the pint to her mouth a little too fast. Ally would denounce the truth until kingdom come, but Lana knew her best friend's tells. No matter what had shattered between them, the attraction remained.

Lana shrugged. "I'm having to re-evaluate all my opinions on Drew because of Greg. My husband's death was this sudden tragedy, at least that's what I thought until the Landslider secret slipped out. I can't sit here and hate Drew for what Mackey Kendricks forced him to do while excusing Greg's actions in the same breath."

Ally pursed her lips. She clearly wanted to argue but couldn't without condemning Greg. "That doesn't make Drew any less obnoxious."

Lana couldn't help her grin. "He always has been, but you fucked him anyway."

Ally's jaw dropped and she smacked Lana in the arm, even though her gaze glittered with amusement.

Their bickering was a reminder of her youth filled with Dax, Drew, Ally and Greg. Her heart hurt at all that had shattered through the years, at everything they'd lost. However, the change wasn't all bad. Raven caught her eye from across the bar and offered a genuine smile. In the process, their pack had grown to accept the Red Rocks, and those who remained clung together for dear life against the Landsliders' threats.

"Let's drink all this bullshit away," Ally said, lifting her glass. Lana grinned and they clinked their drinks.

"Deal," she said, taking another blissful sip of Scotch and soda. She might not be able to sort through the tangle in her mind now or scrub away the guilt coating her skin, but for a few precious moments, she could laugh with Ally and exist free from grief.

* * * *

By the time Lana left Beaver Tavern, her chest hurt from laughter and she was buzzing on the high of sitting and swapping old Silver Springs stories, as if the Landsliders weren't closing in on them with every passing day. As if the looming deadline at the end of the week didn't exist. Lana pulled up to her house, the porch light still on.

Lucas hadn't returned yet.

Her stomach twisted into knots. Part of her felt relieved at being able to ignore the guaranteed awkwardness to follow. However, the disappointment sauntered in, followed by a hefty helping of the ever-present guilt. Lana put her car into Park and heaved a sigh, slamming the back of her head against the seat.

She needed to brew some coffee and scan over the stack of papers again. She'd allowed herself a night's reprieve, but her husband had stolen the device before they'd murdered him. There had to be a hint of where he might've hidden it somewhere in the nooks and crannies of the house. Lana stepped out of her car, trying to ignore the prickle that raced along her neck at walking up to the front door to her empty house. Spirits above, she needed to stop being such a wuss.

As Lana settled her feet on the ground, a scent pricked her attention.

The coppery stench of blood.

Bile rose in her throat, and she staggered like she had that night. Her claws pricked out and her mountain lion rose to attention, the feline aware even when her own brain was stuck on repeat. If the Landsliders were prowling around here, she was screwed. Lucas wasn't nearby to come to the rescue again.

Lana took one step forward, then another, the ground feeling foreign, as if she was floating across the asphalt. She followed the source of the copper scent even though it came from multiple directions. With the number of times she'd returned to that night, who knew, maybe she was hallucinating.

More blood. As though she was wading through a sea of it. Lana gagged as she stepped into the wilted grasses, the stench overwhelming. Another step forward and she discovered why.

The twisted body of a squirrel lay in front of her, all shattered limbs and pulp leaking onto the ground. Though the carcass had been shredded to pieces by predator's teeth, a breath escaped her.

She'd been expecting to find Greg's body there. All over again.

Another breath snagged in her throat when she scanned with the eyes of her lion. The mutilated corpses of squirrels, deer and foxes lay draped across her lawn in a checkerboard of twisted, bloody flesh and patches of grass. She didn't question who'd created the menagerie of horrors before her.

She hadn't taken another step forward before her sneaker nudged against a body, this one a rabbit with the eyes gouged out. Lana's stomach seized. She leaned over, her palms slamming against her knees as she vomited onto the ground. Her gut pulsed in response, and she heaved up her drink from the night. The number of animals they'd killed to send a message — the winter air no longer felt remotely cold. Her body started to tremble, even as she searched around her yard for a sign of life, or any movement from whoever had dragged these bodies to display.

The roar of an engine sounded from farther down the road, and neon headlights peeked into view, aiming at her house. Lana wiped her mouth with her forearm and tried to catch a glimpse of the approaching car. The familiar sight of Lucas' SUV sent a shuddering wave of relief through her as he pulled into her driveway.

Lana staggered from the dead animals littering her yard, forcing her gaze away before she ran a hand through her hair. All her prior worries faded in the wake of the horrific display across her front lawn. The Landsliders hammered their message in clear. If she didn't deliver the device Greg stole, there was no limit to what they'd do to her packmates.

Lucas slipped out of his car, the slam of the door echoing in the brimming night air. His thick eyebrows furrowed and his nose twitched. A second later he loped in her direction.

"What happened here?" he called upon approach.

Lana swallowed, trying to find her voice. She couldn't help but meet him midway, needing to put some distance between her and the miniature massacre. "I'm assuming they wanted to make their point," she murmured, the words coming out raspy.

"*Ay mierda*," Lucas breathed as he came to a halt. He ran a hand through his dark hair even as his gaze skated across the grass. "What a waste."

"You're telling me," Lana muttered, her legs wobbling beneath her. She needed to sit, now. "Mackey's crew has a sick sense of humor."

Lucas scratched his nape and continued looking at the ground. "I'm going to need to stay here if they're trailing around your house."

Her forehead wrinkled. "I thought you already were?" Her stomach attempted to twist, but the contents had been wrung out. Her fingers and toes grew numb at this point and not from the chill.

"After last night…" Lucas licked his lips, meeting her gaze head-on. "I crossed a line. I'm sorry."

Lana's throat dried, but Ally's words pounded through her, a reminder that maybe she could try.

"Look, I'd be a liar if I said the kiss didn't fuck with my head. I felt like I cheated on Greg, even though I buried him eight months ago." Lana raised her head, refusing to look away. In the wake of all this fear, in the wake of the threats against her home, her person and her pack, she was allowed a little boldness. "However, I'd also be a liar if I said I didn't like it."

His dark eyes flared gold with the heat threatening to devour her where she stood. She was tangling with an apex predator, one of the East Coast Tribe, and yet from the second he'd entered the picture he hadn't frightened her once. Around him, Lana felt the safety she'd been robbed of the moment the Landsliders had descended upon her pack's homes with pipe bombs.

The tension between them grew molasses-thick, and it dripped through her with the way he looked her over, the hunger evident in his gaze. Lana's heart thundered as she focused on him, the one lifeline she had right now. Otherwise, she'd see the bodies surrounding them. Otherwise, the scent of blood would smother her until the breaths ceased coming.

A rustle from the bushes deep in the woods snapped them both to attention.

As fast as the spell had been cast, it shattered.

"Come on," he said, an adorable gruffness to his tone. He offered a hand. "Let's get you inside. I'll take care of this mess."

Her heart squeezed tight as she slipped her hand through his, as though touching him was the most natural thing in the world. The guilt lingered a heartbeat away, but she clung to the relief the connection granted in the wake of what the Landsliders had done. She had a long night ahead of her, because they weren't fucking around with their threats. She'd learned that the hard way.

Chapter Eight

Lucas had thought he was an early riser until he'd started staying at Lana's place. The woman rose with the first rays and had coffee brewing in accompaniment every time. After last night, though, he'd been the one in the kitchen first. He had cleared out half the yard by the time she'd emerged again to help, even though the sheer carnage had caused her arms to shake with terror by the end of their work.

The coffeemaker growled, spitting out sludge while he sat at the kitchen table, the sun's buttery beams streaming through the window. Lana's footsteps creaked above, and his heart picked up pace. The woman made him feel young and fumbling, something he hadn't been allowed even when he was. After all, as the big brother of three sisters and one of the Tribe from an early age, Lucas had been in charge his entire life. Creaks sounded down the stairs as she descended, and his throat dried.

He had expected she would kick him out and never want to see him again after he'd kissed her. Yet she had an honest streak a mile wide, and her words last night lingered like a phantom touch.

Lana stepped into the kitchen wearing cargos and a skin-tight tank top he wanted to peel off with his teeth. Even as she maneuvered to grab a cup, her gaze flickered his way. The interest was a tangible current in the air, something he'd only hoped for before.

"Sleep well?" he asked before lifting his mug to his mouth.

Lana cast him an arch look, a grin curling those petal lips. "How could I not with a tiger resting outside my door?"

His cheeks flushed at once. Whenever he'd heard her start to get up, he'd hightailed back to his room, but she must've snuck up on him at some point over the past couple of nights, a feat in and of itself. "We're going to be checking Greg's old worksites today throughout town to see if he might've nestled anything away there. You're welcome to join, but I understand if it would be too hard."

Lana's head popped up at the mention, her gaze sharpening. She set her untouched cup of coffee on the counter. "You know, there's one place I didn't think of checking. I placed Greg's old business front on sale a month or so after he passed, but I haven't cleared everything from the place yet. I figured if someone was interested in the property, I'd handle the rest of the mess then."

"That's absolutely worth checking out," Lucas said, tapping the side of the porcelain mug.

"I'll go there while you guys scour the other sites," Lana responded, tugging on the end of her ponytail.

Her nervous reflex stirred something deep inside him, a warmth both he and his tiger clamored to claim. He wanted to protect her with every neuron in his body, this bright, strong woman who bypassed the internal borders he'd erected like they didn't even exist. No one else managed to coax him out, yet all Lana needed to do was crook her finger.

"After last night, no one is going anywhere by their lonesome," Lucas argued, the words coming out in a low rumble. "I'll go with you." No one needed to tell him what a bad idea that was, since he'd been obsessing over her from the moment he'd arrived back in town. Yet he also wouldn't be able to live with himself if something happened to her. He'd failed with Josefina, but maybe he could keep Lana safe.

Her scrutinizing glance told him plenty.

Lucas lifted his hands in defense before pushing himself from his seat. "Please don't make me suffer through another round of Ally and Drew's bickering."

Lana snorted. She drank down her mug of coffee before setting it on the counter. "We'll leave that to Sierra. I think she's scary enough to get them to stop. You're not nearly as intimidating."

He placed his mug in the sink beside hers, standing an inch away from her. He might loom at six foot four, but she met his eyes regardless, staring with a brazen boldness that had him falling fast. Lana was a grenade with the pin pulled, a distraction he couldn't afford. A one-night stand with a gorgeous girl was one thing, but she'd begun peeling past his layers in their first conversation. If he fell any deeper, she wouldn't just be a fling when he left—she'd be a regret.

"Obviously I'll have to work on my growl more," he responded. This close, he wanted to reach out and touch her, skim his fingers along her smooth skin, trace the curve of her jaw, the elegant line of her collarbone.

Lana's lips twisted with a smirk while she broke away, heading for her coat rack. "That adorable blush on your cheeks doesn't help either, Diaz."

As if the mere mention had summoned it, his face flushed. Spirits above, this woman turned him upside down. He snagged his wool coat from where he'd left it draped over the arm of the couch and followed her out of the door. The icy wind grew bracing as he made the quick phone call to Sierra to babysit Drew and Ally for the day. By the time he reached his car, the situation had been dealt with. Lana leaned along the passenger's side, staring at the bleached-bone clouds in the sky.

"You know, I could drive us," she offered. "In case you didn't want to feel like a chauffeur, carting everyone around all the time."

He lifted an eyebrow and approached the driver's side. "I'm way too much of a control freak."

She offered a grin as she slipped into the passenger's seat. "I know. I just figured I'd give you the option."

Lucas revved the engine and set off down the road, the grip on the steering wheel a familiar comfort. Behind the wheel, he could cling to a semblance of order. Truth be told, he'd had choice ripped from him at an early age—the day the shamans had tattooed him—and he'd been chasing after any scrap of control ever since. Life seemed to want to teach him the opposite every chance it got.

"So, what's up with the list you found back at the Landslider hangout?" Lana asked as they sped along the highway. Occasionally, she'd point to guide him in the direction of her former husband's company. Guilt clung to him every time he thought of that, as if they

Forged Futures

were sneaking around to cheat behind his back. No matter what logic he used on the situation, he couldn't dispel the feeling. She must be going through even worse turmoil.

"It's all shifters from the area who have died so far," he said. "I've been going through the names to try to draw some correlations."

"Sounds like you've got a better lead than mine." Lana leaned against the window. "The pages of shamanic research are all about shifters — our creation, our history, the process of shifting to our animal selves and the different packs we've formed. So, in essence, useless."

One-story buildings began to crop up, the small stretch constituting a town in this backwoods area. The Landsliders could be anywhere here, crawling around the same spaces on the hunt for this device. At the end of the day, his most important task remained keeping it out of their paws.

"His place was a little away from the main sprawl," Lana said, pointing to the road. "One of the reasons I'm having such a hard time finding a buyer."

"The leftover tasks are one of the hardest things to deal with," Lucas murmured, the tap-tap-tap of his finger against the steering wheel increasing. When Josefina had died, he had taken leave from his Tribe duties to return home and don the mantle there as well. While his mother had tried to handle what she could, his father had turned into a husk for a long time. His sisters had been distraught, and so he'd stepped in.

Fingers skated across his arm, the gentle touch so electric he almost veered off the road.

"Whoever you lost, that's still eating you up, isn't it?" she asked, her voice soft, tentative.

85

Most of the time, his work as East Coast Tribe kept him too busy for contemplation. Sure, the thoughts might crawl in at night, but he pushed past them and kept moving, moving, moving. Until he'd arrived in this town and met Lana fucking Bennett, he hadn't realized how much he'd missed out on. The past couple of days he'd spent in her house had been the first time he'd felt peace in longer than he could remember.

"Yeah, it is," was all he could force out as he tried to ignore the scrape of his voice. "The grief doesn't have an expiration date."

She pointed to a building ahead, and he pulled into the empty lot. When he settled the car into Park, Lucas met her gaze. "Look, I might've taken the leap a few nights ago, but when it comes to anything between us? You're driving that car, *carina*. I am never going to tell you how to manage your grief or judge where you need to be, because I've been down that terrible fucking road, and I'm still struggling years later."

Lana's throat bobbed. She swallowed and pursed her lips. Her eyes glowed the amber of her mountain lion, so intense he lost a breath. "Thank you," was all she said before she slipped out of the car. The moment the door shut, the tension deflated and he remembered how to breathe again. Lucas skimmed his fingers through his hair before he locked up and loped after her.

Lana's keys jingled as she fumbled with the lock on the door that, based on the paint chips and weathered handle, hadn't seen use for some time.

"Aren't you trying to sell this thing?" Lucas asked, scanning over the rust.

Lana fixed him with a stubborn look, resting a hand on her hip. "And whose super-handy husband passed away? Oh wait, mine. I'm about as good with a wrench as Sierra is with taking orders."

Lucas snorted and followed her inside. The fluorescents flickered on, casting their sickly rays over a couple of desks and chairs, along with a few filing cabinets placed behind them. There were some peeling posters tacked to walls which could use a good coat of paint, and a few dented lamps clustered in the corner of the room.

"I'm shocked the Landsliders haven't broken in here yet," he muttered, striding across the linoleum to the nearest desk.

"It's still listed under the former owner's name," Lana said, her steps slowing as she waded through the place. "The business, at least. The building was ours to sell. Though, who knows if we had a tail."

Lucas crouched in front of the first desk before pulling out drawers. They were filled with documents, thin yellow invoices, random old pennies and a few fishing lures. He tugged out the papers and began to flip through as fast as possible. "We shouldn't have a tail," Lucas murmured while he scanned. "I kept a close eye when we drove over."

"Not questioning your prowess," she responded, amusement welling in her voice. "However, the Landsliders are worse than cockroaches around this area, and I can guarantee they can ID your car on sight, big, fearsome Tribe guy and all."

"Nice to know that's the reputation I've got around here." Lucas tugged out a couple of the more recent invoices, as well as the job information. Something nagged at the back of his mind when he examined them, but he needed to sit and digest the information to figure out what.

A laugh escaped Lana's lips. "Right, you would like that. Then no one will know you're a huge softie underneath all the scars and growls."

He shrugged. She wasn't wrong. Out of the Tribe members, Akio and Navi were the hardasses. He and Jess belonged to camp stability. A *skritch* came from outside.

"Stay here," he said. "I'm going to check out back."

"Those are some horror movie last words," Lana said, clutching the folder she held even tighter. "Don't finish with 'I'll be right back' or you're a goner."

He saluted before jogging for the door. His tiger perked to alertness and as he stepped outside and caught some wolfish scents on the breeze, his nails had already turned to claws. Lucas tugged off his shirt and unbuttoned his pants once he'd slipped around the side of the building. His sneakers weren't even fully off by the time he began to shift. His tiger took over, the indomitable force contesting his will, always. As much as the beast had grown into an integral part of him, it was also an ancient spirit he tangled with daily.

His bones shifted to transition, and orange and black fur sprouted across his arms as he became a Siberian tiger. All too fast, he switched to four paws, and the clearing grew even brighter, the scents more potent and sounds louder in this form.

Another *skritch* came from the back of the building, this one sounding like claws on glass. Lana was inside. If they got through the door, she'd be in trouble.

He prowled, one paw in front of the other, as he stepped closer and closer to the back. Lucas peeked around the corner of the brick building. Three wolves were ramming a back entrance, alternating between blunt force and the scraping of their claws. Lucas' arrival at the site had been noticed. Even though the other Tribe members were off chasing after Mackey Kendricks, the concentration of Landsliders in this area of late had increased with Ganzorig's arrival.

Best to stop them now.

Lucas leaped into the clearing, not giving the wolves a chance to register his presence. Before they even saw him, he bounded toward them at top speed. The gravel trembled around him, begging to be used. He had possessed the ability to manipulate the earth from the day they'd connected him to the Great Spirit, and ever since, stone and dirt responded with ease.

The easiest solution would be using compulsion — however, Navi had had issues in the past regarding the Landsliders. Mackey must've used a loophole or gotten Ganzorig to perform a spell so anyone with the Landsliders' mark carved into their skin only responded to him.

No matter — fangs and claws would do.

The wolves whipped around to face him, too late.

He descended through the middle one with the force of a battering ram. The wolf went flying. Before the others could lash out with their claws, Lucas pivoted to the right and swiped. He caught the other wolf in the flank, sinking the points of his claws into flesh. Teeth scored his back leg. Lucas didn't follow the knee-jerk reaction to yank — instead he thrust his leg farther back. The motion kept the fangs from latching hard, and he waited for the break in pressure before twisting around.

He slammed his paw into the wolf behind him, claws first. His nails sank in past the thick coat of fur until the wolf skidded backward. The other two panted, the harsh sounds giving away their approach. He towered over the three of them from size alone, but the shifters still outnumbered him. No point in gaining senseless injuries. One of the wolves lunged from behind — he could feel the shift in the air.

Lucas leaped past them and jerked his head up. The surrounding gravel that had been waiting for him, all those tiny pieces buzzing on the ground, flew into the air.

He slammed his paw to the asphalt.

All the gravel descended like a monsoon. The chunks pelted the shifters before him, bits of chipped stone slamming into their pelts. The grit billowed in clouds, blinding them. Lucas crouched, teeth bared as he waited for the dust to settle to finish this fast.

One of the wolves leaped through the roiling grit, half-blinded. Lucas rammed into the guy mid-leap, sending him flying back from force alone. Then he caught the blur of movement in front of him as the other lunged.

The muzzle snapped near his face, but Lucas slammed his head right into the nose. A yelp came from the wolf as he stepped away. The third one backed off a pace, hesitation in its stance. Before he could target that one, the wolf to his right lunged for him again. Lucas caught the snap of the limbs, but he waited until the pointed gray teeth were close to descending.

He whipped his body into a roll, slamming against the wolf.

Right as a smack sounded through the air, the other wolf gnashed its teeth at him again. Lucas sprang forward, closing his massive jaw around the shifter's exposed neck. The rip echoed as he tore into the flesh. The wolf's head lolled to the side.

The other shifter sank her claws into his flank. She dug her tips in, but Lucas ignored them — they were small enough to feel like pinpricks compared to some of the beasts he'd wrestled with. Copper coated his teeth, and he spat out the residual liquid before turning to face his attacker. She lowered on her hind legs, tensing as though she'd spring.

Bring it.

From the corner of his eye, he caught the third wolf continuing to back away, one pace at a time.

The shifter facing him launched. Lucas ducked when she sailed high — she was aiming for his throat. Before she could soar over him, he clamped his teeth down on her hind leg. He whipped his head to the side and let go. The force of the swing sent the wolf careening toward the back wall. She hit the chipped bricks with a *thump* that echoed through the clearing, then she crumpled to the ground.

The third wolf loped away, disappearing behind the neighboring pines.

Lucas heaved a sigh, spitting out more blood as he padded toward the side of the building. Already, the shift began to take hold, his fur transitioning to smooth skin and his bones adjusting until he no longer stood on four feet but two. His claws turned to smooth nails, and Lucas strode forward to gather his clothes from where he'd left them.

Footsteps pounded from the side of the building, and he froze.

Lana whipped around the corner. Her eyes widened, but he didn't miss how she scanned him up and down. The way her stare scorched made the blood go straight to his cock.

Lucas held up a hand. "I'm just grabbing my clothes," he said, bending to snag the pile he'd left on the ground. "There were three Landsliders hanging around out back. They're dealt with."

A laugh escaped her, and she shook her head. "Three Landsliders, no big deal. Only you, Diaz."

Even as he pulled on his clothes, she kept her gaze averted, a gorgeous blush spreading across her cheeks. Not like that did anything to tamp his libido. His heart still thrummed with the rush of the battle, the burst of adrenaline making him want to fight or fuck until he wore himself out.

Lana lifted the stack of files in her hand. "If the Landsliders know about this place, we're going to need to pack up everything we can. Unfortunately, I figured out another of my husband's secrets."

Chapter Nine

Lucas parked in front of Zip's Diner and the sight of the familiar place made Lana let out the breath she'd been holding

The sign for the diner dominated the space to make the bright letters clear from the roadside, and the snug spot with its faded red and white canopy felt like a slice of Americana. Since noon had already arrived, the walkers-and-canes gangs that descended at breakfast had passed on by, leaving the normal lunch rush of contractors and local business owners who made this their normal stop. Most of the Silver Springs pack had been patronizing this joint for years.

Lana gripped the folder in her lap tight, the sweat on her fingers printing on the manila surface. Her gut churned in the wake of her discovery, but she wanted to wait until they took a seat before she delved into what she'd found.

"Please tell me they've got scrapple here," Lucas said as he slid out of the car. "I'm starving."

Lana made a gagging sound. "That stuff is nasty, but yeah, you're in Pennsylvania. Scrapple is a given."

He took the lead toward the front of the diner, and Lana's throat dried as she followed. Now that she had the image seared in her brain of what he looked like sans clothes, she couldn't forget it. The Henley and jeans combo he wore clung to those defined muscles, the ones she'd seen in all their sun-kissed glory earlier. Combined with the dark tattoos that wound up his legs and arms, the scars on his face, and his corded thighs, he was the sort of gorgeous that caused a reaction. Hell, the mere memory had her pussy pulsing like she was in heat.

Lucas cracked open the chrome door and gestured for her to step inside. The warmth in his chocolate eyes was so scorching she barely noticed the shift into the heated interior of Zip's Diner. She licked her lips on instinct, a little helpless to stem the intense crash of her newfound feelings. The past eight months had turned her into a brittle tree in midwinter – isolated, covered in ice and straining under the weight she carried. For the first time since then, she'd begun to melt.

They headed for one of the back booths where they could get some privacy. The place bustled, servers dodging around the patrons as they carried out massive trays laden with club sandwiches, burgers and waffles. Conversation buzzed throughout the small space. Lana soaked in the familiar comfort, even as she dipped her brush into the sadness of the many memories she'd collected in this place, most of them by Greg's side.

Lana slipped into the cracked vinyl booth and picked up one of the plastic menus, as if she could deflect her body's reaction to the big bad Tribe member. *Spirits above, I'm in trouble.*

"So, what did you find out from the papers?" Lucas asked, skimming the menu. A waitress swung over to grab their drink orders — both more coffee, as if they hadn't drunk enough this morning — which gave Lana enough time to get her brain back on track.

Not like I want to return to what I found. The mere thought made her queasy at how little she knew about what Greg had been up to during their last year together. Lana tugged out his company's books and placed them in the center of the table. Her skin prickled and she tapped her fingers on the surface.

"Before you think I'm a total idiot, we kept his company separate from our finances. I, like an idiot, trusted him to handle shit on his own and to be transparent with me." Lana lifted her hands in defense. Shame trickled through her, thick as oil, melding with an anger that had begun burning from the moment she'd found out Greg had been a Landslider.

Lucas let out a low whistle. "Oh, *carina*, I'm sorry," he said, flipping open the books. His thick eyebrows furrowed, the serious expression causing his scar to crinkle. The smart man had pieced together in a second what had taken her minutes of scanning through the documents.

The waitress chose that moment to swing by with their coffees, and Lana gripped the porcelain mug for dear life. Whenever her mind dipped too far into thinking of all the things she hadn't known about Greg, numbness infiltrated to the point where even the scorching heat could barely permeate through to her palms.

"What can I get for you folks?" the waitress asked, tapping the end of her pen to a pad. The woman's soft smile contradicted her harsh wrinkles and wild hair.

"I'll have the bacon omelet and a side of toast and scrapple," Lucas ordered before passing over his menu.

Lana handed hers over, not needing to look. She got the same thing every time. "Biscuits and sausage gravy. I need the extra carbs today." The waitress' eyes crinkled with her grin as she nodded and headed off to place the orders.

"So yeah, I get why Drew didn't want to tell me," she muttered, running a hand through her hair. "'Hey, Lana, your husband was doing jobs for Mackey Kendricks, otherwise his business was about to go bankrupt.' Chances are, he didn't steal the device to keep Kendricks from using it. He probably wanted to pawn the thing off to get out from under his thumb. Greg leaned toward practical most of the time."

Voicing the words out loud made the truth impossible to hide from. Lana sucked in a shaky breath.

Lucas stretched his hand across the table, tilting his fingers so they brushed against hers. Lana's throat tightened at the simple act. The man read her better than anyone she'd ever known. She laced her fingers through his, gripping tightly to the tether he offered.

Her heart strained as if it might break. Everything about this had become endlessly complicated, whether it was the new, shitty things she kept finding out about her dead husband, the memories of Greg that crept around every corner or the emerging warmth that coaxed her out every time she met Lucas' gaze.

Lana forced a grin. "This whole situation is building a good case for never trusting again, but here I am anyway."

Lucas squeezed her hand tighter. "Keep that hope," he said. "Life is going to do its best to beat it out of you, so if you can retain even a flicker, you're leagues above the rest of us." His tone might have been wry, but Lana caught the helplessness there, the hint of despair. He wasn't speaking just for her.

Lana shrugged, a shudder of vulnerability coursing through her. "I like people too much to stop. It also doesn't hurt when some of them keep proving the opposite to you, that there are folks worth taking a chance on." Her gaze locked in on his, and all oxygen departed the diner.

"*Ay dios mio*, woman, you're killing me here." His voice was a rumble she felt deep in her core, and the smile was as genuine as they came. Those dark eyes gleamed with an intensity she'd forgotten about, like the fluttering of her first kiss. "I'm trying to maintain a respectable distance, I swear. Then you say shit like that and turn me into a stupid teenager."

Lana couldn't help but be charmed by him even though she should be backing away. As much as he could be a tumble in the sheets and maybe one she needed, Lana would get attached to a pair of mittens if given the chance. And Lucas Diaz, even with all the sweetness and a protective streak that touched her heart, was Tribe. He would always be on the move, and when his assignment here ended, he would leave.

Lana swallowed hard, not wanting to think of the inevitability. Not wanting to imagine returning to the aching emptiness of her house that threatened to devour her.

The waitress carrying the laden tray of food was a timely interruption. Lana dragged the steaming plate of biscuits and sausage gravy closer and speared a fork in to start off the destruction. She took a piping hot bite, the top of her mouth burning even while she chewed on the fluffy biscuits and the savory, peppery zest of the sausage gravy. Lucas dove into his food as fast, a flurry of forks and knives. He set to the omelet as if he'd never get another meal.

"Enough focusing on the shitty course my life has taken as of late," she said, jabbing a fork in his direction. "I want to know more about you, Diaz."

Lucas lifted an eyebrow, and a slight bit of shyness descended when he ducked his head. The man might be amazing at protecting others, but he obviously wasn't used to the reverse. Lana's heart squeezed tight. He might be outmatched in the protective department. She might not be barreling in to smack down Landsliders, but she wanted to guard his feelings and protect the softness that emerged from the big, gruff man with an intensity that surprised her.

He shrugged. "There's not much to know. I go where I'm sent with the Tribe, sometimes in a group, sometimes by my lonesome, and I get to see my family on holidays."

Lana fixed him with a look. "Who are your friends? What's your family like? What do you want out of life?" A grin perched on her lips as she delivered the rapid-fire questions.

A laugh escaped him and he shook his head. "No one warned me this was an interrogation. Friends aren't an option when you're on the road like I am, and the East Coast Tribe is family as much as my own. As for my family, they live in Arizona. My mother, father and my two sisters, Maria and Isabella." He leaned back in the seat and lifted his cup to his lips, taking a deep sip. His movements were languid, powerful in a way she couldn't help but trace. He focused on her. "What about you?"

Lana pursed her lips. So much for deflection. "I mean, you've seen most of what's going on in this town. My folks live locally too, and we've got a semi-functional relationship."

Lucas placed his cup of coffee onto the table with a clink. "Fine then, I'll share what I want out of life if you do." A predatory gleam had descended in his eyes, one that made her feel as though she'd caught the attention of something far more dangerous than she'd anticipated. They weren't just sharing scorching glances at this point, and this was where she sank in deep.

Lana's glance shifted to her coffee. "If you had asked me a year ago, I could've given you a clear answer. I'm a massage therapist and an EMT—I love helping people, and I want to keep doing that. But I also wanted a family, something Greg and I had always talked about. It's not like we were married ages, though—we had four years together." Lana took a quick sip to try to wet her dry throat. Not like it worked.

She shrugged. "Now I'm stumbling through day by day, trying to reconstruct a whole new life plan by my lonesome. It sucks." She dared a glance up, but once she caught his stare on her, the breath hitched in her throat. With those long lashes, his square jawline and his thick, careful eyebrows, Lucas was a breathtaking sort of gorgeous. She never doubted for a second that this surreal, powerful man belonged with the Tribe. "Your turn," she said.

Lucas leaned back in the seat, flexing his arms behind his head. The movement caused those powerful muscles to bulge, visible under the thin layer of his

Henley. "When I started with the Tribe, I had these lofty visions about saving the world, but this business wears at you. We travel from place to place and there are always conflicts that need resolving, more and more situations that need handling by the day." His gaze rested on her, and she found herself licking her lips.

"I want to keep people safe as best I can. If fortune smiles on me and I get as lucky as Navi or Akio to find my mate, well—that's all I could ask for." He glanced away, staring into his coffee cup. "Let's be honest, no other relationship would survive the long distance or traveling on the road bullshit."

Lana speared more of her sausage gravy and biscuits into her mouth. She'd waded into far heavier territory than she'd intended. Her chest burned as though she'd struck a match, and she wanted to reach out and touch him so badly. Even though the guilt lingered like it did every time her thoughts drifted to Lucas, her current anger at the new discovery granted her a brief reprieve. Deep in her heart, she wanted the same. The bond her parents shared, that Sierra and Dax had found—she wanted the connection with a fierceness that corroded her insides.

Lana pointed the end of her fork at Lucas while she chewed on her last bite. "You need to stop making me like you so much. It's not fair."

"Same could be said of you, *carina*," he rumbled. "You don't know how rare it is to meet people who bother to get to know you, or, hell, who will even talk with me once they see these." He lifted his tattoo-covered forearms. When he rested them back on the table, Lana couldn't help herself. She reached out, tracing her thumb along the black whorls lining his gorgeous copper skin.

Her heart pounded so hard she guaranteed the whole diner could hear it. The connection between them was a lit fuse, a jolt of electricity that somehow brought her out of the interminable winter she'd been living with.

The waitress swung by, snapping them both out of the moment. Lana pulled her hand away, and Lucas snagged the check.

"We're on the job, so I've got this." he said, before pulling out cash to cover the bill. Her stomach twisted with the weight of the folders by her side. They sure as hell had been on the job, since Lucas' car was loaded with her husband's secrets. She only hoped they'd be able to find the location of the device from them.

"Let's get back to sort through the documents then," Lana said, even as every ounce of her wanted to stay seated in this booth with him. For those brief moments, she wasn't a grieving widow, and she wasn't Lana Bennett, wife of Greg Bennett. She was Lana Renoir, newer, wiser than the girl she'd been. A woman unafraid to go toe to toe with a tiger.

He pushed himself from the seat first, and she slipped out after as they headed for his car. Her heart hadn't caught the memo to slow, beating so hard it pulsed in her ears. The sunshine glowed down on her, citrine afternoon beams, and she shivered when she stepped into the cold.

Lucas wound around the passenger's side to grab the door for her, and Lana was so distracted she bumped right into him. He loomed over her, all hard muscle, but she had seen the grace in his movements and the gentle ferocity in his gaze. He turned around to face her, but she didn't back away.

Instead, she leaned in closer, her mountain lion prowling with the same intention as the pulse of her heartbeat. A bravery gripped her by the throat, one she would've never expected from herself. She reached up to trace the scar on his face, her fingertips traveling down the divot to the firm line of his chin. Her mouth watered as his jaw dropped in surprise, and she took another step forward, closing the inch between them until her body pressed against his.

His eyes burned and his dark eyebrows tugged together in surprise. With the way she pressed against his furnace of a body like this, the cold didn't come close to permeating her. He settled his hands on her hips as if it was the most natural thing in the world. The crisp air sharpened his scent, all sage and rosewood, making her core pulse in response. His gaze traced hers, a wonder there that broke her heart, like no one had bothered to see him — the real him — in far too long.

That bolstered her like nothing else. Lana leaned forward on her tiptoes and pressed her lips to his. The moment they kissed, he needed no prompting. He tightened his grip around her waist, and he drew her flush to him before claiming her mouth. His kiss was possessive and demanding, with a hunger that curled her toes. She melted into the heat of his body, the solidity of his frame. His kiss grew into a slow inferno, a steady coaxing that lit her from the core out with the way his tongue stroked against hers, in how he nipped at her neck.

Lana twined her arms around him — the most she could do to keep upright. Her legs forgot how to work, trembling, useless things. If their first kiss had been memorable, this one tattooed itself on her skin. He tasted like coffee and spice, and as his hot mouth caressed hers, all she could do was kiss back, hungrily seeking everything he offered. When his teeth scraped against her skin, the shudder had her clenching her legs tight with need.

He slipped his hands beneath her jacket, his fingers on her bare skin, and it wasn't enough. She wanted those hands over every inch of her body, wanted him like the sun after weeks of rain. Her synapses sparked to life each time their lips met, the rough scrape of his causing her to shiver. Lana sank into this oblivion with him, the chilled breeze against her skin a delicious contrast to the inferno inside.

"Hey, Lucas," a familiar voice called out from the opposite side of the car.

As fast as they'd collided, they separated.

Her shoulders heaved, and her heart pounded. She gasped for breath, coming down to earth. Dax looped around from the opposite side of the car. Lucas ran a hand through his short strands of hair in an attempt to look casual, even though his lips were still parted, and he was a little breathless.

"Thought I recognized your car," Dax said, slipping his hands into his pockets as he eyed them both. "What are you guys doing here?" The underlying question made his words dig deeper. Lana had escaped the guilt for a moment, but as Dax tipped his baseball cap and met her gaze, it flushed right to the surface.

"Going over Greg's business forms," Lana volunteered, attempting to draw his attention elsewhere. "We're trying to see if we can suss out a location for the device from any business communications."

Dax nodded, tapping the brim of his cap. "Right. Well, good luck to both of you. I'm meeting with Jer to go over the Coalition case. Never-ending joyride." He flashed them both a quick grin, but his smile didn't quite reach his eyes. Lana swallowed bile.

She didn't bother responding before she hopped into the passenger's seat and closed the door behind her. Her shoulders dropped and a breath escaped her. *Fuck.* She'd just been making out with Lucas in broad daylight, smack in front of Zip's, the place she'd gone with her husband thousands of times.

Part of her needed Lucas' touch. She craved it so badly. He offered the first glimpse of hope for her in far too long. Trouble was, every time she made one step forward, guilt crawled across her skin like spiders, as if she was cheating on her husband or desecrating their past. All she knew was that the more time she spent around Lucas, the deeper the hold he had on her. *Spirits above, I'm in trouble.*

Chapter Ten

The tension in the car grew as thick as soup.

Dax's appearance hadn't done any wonders for them, throwing a bucket of cold water over their kiss, and Lucas was rolling on adrenaline he needed to burn in the aftermath. However, his phone buzzed the moment they got into the car. Ava had arrived in town and needed to be briefed, and Ally, Drew and Sierra would be meeting them at the Red Rocks' cabin.

"I could always drop you back off at the house," Lucas offered, trying to dispel some of the awkwardness. When Dax had shown up, she'd shut down like she'd been caught cheating.

Lana glanced his way. "It's probably a good idea so I can sort through the rest of these papers." She let out a shaky sigh. "I'm not trying to cold-shoulder you, side note. If you've got the insta-fix for this dose of guilt I get slammed with any time I try to move forward, I'll take it."

Lucas' forehead creased, and he gripped the steering wheel tighter. "Try a different tactic. When I lost someone, one of the worst parts was avoiding talking about her. Why don't you tell me about Greg? Not the current bullshit you're dealing with, but the guy you married." He turned his gaze to the road ahead, trying to avoid the prickle of discomfort at both the mention of her dead husband and the memories of Josefina.

Lana let out a throaty noise. "I'm still wondering what I did to deserve you coming into my life right now. Okay," she said, sitting forward in her seat. "Greg had this easy laugh, one that made you feel like you were walking into a sunlit room whenever he was around. I miss hearing it in the house — the rooms have been dark and cold ever since."

Lucas' chest tightened at the mention. He didn't know how he could compare to the powerful connection she'd had with her husband, but he also couldn't help the inexorable draw toward her. Being around Lana felt as natural as his connection to the earth, an intrinsic part of him.

She let out a shuddering sigh, staring out of the window. "He used to bring me a bundle of forsythia every anniversary. Not because they were my favorite flower, but because I could never pronounce the name growing up."

"He's a part of your past. A large part of it," Lucas said with a shrug that was a whole lot more cavalier than the maelstrom brewing inside. His skin prickled. "Whatever this is between us, we're not going to get anywhere if we hide mention of him or treat this like we're sneaking around behind his back."

"You might want to take your own advice there, Diaz," Lana responded, a wryness in her tone. "Bringing stuff out in the open can really help heal."

Lucas could feel her stare on him, the too-knowing look in her eyes. He'd darted around the mention of Josefina enough, but he wasn't ready for that level of vulnerability yet — with anyone. Shit, he'd been the big brother, the protector and the Tribe member for too long to even know how to let go.

Her house appeared at the end of the cul-de-sac, near so many others belonging to the Silver Springs pack. Lana hadn't stopped staring at him, an amused grin lingering on her face.

"It's okay, keep your secrets for now," Lana responded. "You'll tell me in your own time."

Truth be told, she was right. Even as he held those pieces tight, every ounce of him begged to let the dam burst free. She was the first person he'd ever wanted to share every ugly little thing with. Lana had become a lighthouse in the middle of an icy storm, the safe harbor he'd witnessed from afar but never believed he'd reach.

He parked in front of her house, but once he stepped out of the car, his internal alarms started clanging.

Her door was ajar.

Lana stepped a couple of paces in front of him but stopped mid-stride, her hands balling into fists.

"Looks like the Landsliders got impatient," Lucas muttered. His nails turned to claws, and a deep rage percolated inside him.

"Well, it was a matter of time," Lana murmured, a hollow resignation in her voice while she strode for the door. She had fucking suffered enough. Lucas stormed past her, ready to plunge his claws into the first beast to step in his way. A growl ripped from his throat, and his fast stride turned to a run. He raced into the house.

They'd only been gone a few hours, but apparently the Landsliders had only needed that long to tear her house apart. His stomach clenched tight as he surveyed the damage. They'd upturned her cushions while the claw marks along the carpet and the coffee table made it clear others had been shifted into their animal forms. Books had fallen from bookshelves, and towels spilled out of the linen closet in her hallway. The place stank of coyotes, wolves and bears, all the different scents muddling together.

Lana stopped behind him, resting her hand on his back as she leaned in. A breath caught in her throat. "Guess the place needed some redecorating anyway." She curled her fingers into his shirt, her grip tight enough to slice through as her nails shifted to claws.

Lucas scanned the room for any sign of movement, but based on the silence radiating off the wreckage, they had rushed in and out in the span of an hour. "You're coming with me," he murmured. "We'll work on cleaning up the mess later."

He turned around and didn't say anything else, just drew her into his arms. She leaned into his chest, sagging against him as though the air had been deflated from her. He could have stood like that forever, the cycle of their breaths echoing in the ragged air. She fit against him like his favorite saxophone, and he didn't want to let go.

The sight of her home in ruins like that made his tiger rage, lashing around in his chest. He burned with the urge to slash and strike at any Landslider to cross his path—hell, at anyone who even blinked at him wrong. *She. Doesn't. Deserve. This.* The injustice burned in his veins the same as it had back then. The same as it always did every time he stumbled upon scene after scene of shifters brutalized by the monsters among their kind.

"Let's head out to meet Sierra," he said, reaching for her hand. She gripped his tight, and together they headed for his car.

* * * *

By the time they reached the Red Rocks' cabin, two cars had already pulled into the driveway. In the golden light of late afternoon, the dark wood gleamed, and a stream of smoke piped out of the chimney, creating a picturesque, inviting scene. *Way more comforting than the trashed state of Lana's home.*

Lucas pulled to a stop before turning to look at her. "You need a minute?" He could feel her simmering from where he sat, like they shared a direct connection.

Lana shook her head. Her forest eyes burned. "I'll take every step forward to destroying these bastards. They've terrorized this region enough." She forced a grin that even he didn't believe. "Besides, I can navigate Ally and Drew while you make actual progress with Sierra."

He snorted, and he hopped out of the car, the slam of the door echoing in the brittle air. Lana kept pace, tugging her peacoat tighter as they stepped to the entrance. The murmur of voices sounded inside and when he opened the door, heat blasted him in the face. A fireplace crackled on the opposite side of the cabin where Sierra sat with someone new.

"About time you showed, Diaz," Sierra called. "Lana, good to see you. Come meet Ava Patel, the shaman we mentioned."

Ava Patel squinted at them from behind her thick glasses, and she wrinkled her nose. "Are these important-to-meet people, or are you just being polite?" she asked Sierra. "Sorry, but there are a metric fuckton of you with the combined packs."

Lucas couldn't help the laugh escaping him as he stepped up to offer a hand. "I'm East Coast Tribe, so, probably a good idea to remember me."

Lana waved a hand in front of her face. "The name's Lana, but you can call me Susie, Alanna, whatever strikes your fancy. I'm not picky." The scents of cinnamon and allspice wafted through the room, coming from the small French press and two cups set out.

"I brought an army's worth of tea if you want some," Ava offered. "It looks like all you folks drink around here is coffee."

"We just had said cups of coffee, but thanks." Lucas took a seat in the worn tan loveseat. Lana slipped in beside him, close enough that their legs brushed. Even still, she simmered with nerves, probably from the break-in. He hunched forward, focusing on the shaman. He'd been dealing with the elders his entire life, since they were the ones who'd tattooed him in the first place and merged him with the Great Spirit he was tethered to.

Ava Patel looked nothing like he'd expected. Her hair was pulled into a low ponytail, and she wore a hoodie with the Linux penguin on it as well as a couple of techie watches and black rubber bracelets. She sat with a hunch and a scowl, as if she would take a bite out of anyone who stepped into her space.

"Drew and Ally should be reporting in any moment," Sierra said. "We were scouting around Ricketts Glen after a couple of busts this morning, but I got the phone call that Ava had arrived, so I left early."

"Did you know Ganzorig?" Lana asked, switching her focus to Ava.

Ava picked up her cup of tea and leaned back into the couch. "I knew he was a douchebag, but that was about it. I've heard there's a device of his floating around the region? More misuse of his abilities?"

Lucas heaved out a sigh. "Yeah, we're looking for it. Thankfully we went through Lana's house before they broke in."

Sierra's gaze sharpened, and the woman surged from her seat before realizing she had the extra weight to go with her. Her hand circled around her stomach. "They got into her house?"

"While we were out today," Lana said, tugging at the end of her ponytail. "They would've at some point, honestly. Wherever Greg hid this thing, he sure as hell didn't want it to be found."

"Well, where is Greg? We can throttle the answer out of him," Ava asked. Lucas winced, and Sierra opened her mouth, but Lana's laugh burst through the room, acidic enough to melt metal.

"Try six feet under. If you start digging now, you might get to him before nightfall."

Ava readjusted her glasses. "Oh, that's awkward. Do you have anything connected to the device? Tracking spells don't even cost me a yawn." The woman seemed to be unflappable, moving past the situation as if she hadn't stepped on a claymore.

Lana glanced at Lucas. "Do you think Drew might?"

He nodded, his elbows digging into his thighs. Lucas rested his chin on his hands. If they could find Greg's device, the Landslider threat would die down. Yet on the flipside of the equation, he needed them to stay long enough to track Ganzorig. The shaman remained elusive and Lucas wouldn't let that monster roam free any longer. His gaze settled on Ava. "What about people? Can you track them?"

Ava grimaced. "I mean, I can track dead folks, but it gets kind of grisly. Spirit versus the body, all that jazz."

Lucas shook his head. "Not dead. Ganzorig is the one who's causing a lot of this mess right now, and if we could figure where he's hiding out, getting rid of him would eliminate the need to even find the device. At least, for now." He had known Mackey for too long to believe the bastard would give up on anything.

Ava nodded. "Yeah, I can swing a tracking spell no problem. I'm getting a nice big bonus for traveling down here and helping, so I'm on retainer for whatever you folks need right now."

"You're welcome to stay here as long as you need," Sierra said, patting the couch even as she glanced around the cabin.

"Hopefully not too long," Ava muttered into her tea cup. "How you folks live out in the boonies and don't go crazy is beyond me. I mean, I get the whole attuned to nature thing, hello, but it's just trees for miles around here."

Sierra bared her teeth with her grin. "I think you need to be on four paws to understand."

Lucas jostled Lana's leg, causing her to look at him with a grateful smile. He couldn't get enough of her warmth if he tried, and yet a pit began to form in his gut. When this assignment ended, he'd set off to the next town, probably hundreds of miles away. And she'd still be here, living in that big, empty house by her lonesome, at least until some regular Joe Shifter from the area swept her off her feet. Jealousy curdled in his stomach.

A car engine rumbled outside, and tires screeched to a halt.

A moment later, Ally and Drew burst into the cabin like they'd been set on fire. The door smacked against the wall with a resounding thud.

Lucas scented the blood before he caught the gashes up and down their legs, a deep one running along Drew's arm. Their eyes were wild and their shoulders heaved as the breaths escaped them. Lana shot up to bolt for the kitchen, EMT training in action.

Ally staggered forward a couple of paces, all eyes on her. "We found out where Joe Ganzorig's been hiding."

Chapter Eleven

Lana woke up to an unshakable sense of dread.

She rolled her shoulders, trying to banish the jitters as she cracked her door open. Lucas had already cleared out, though last night she'd heard him settle in place as he'd slept in his tiger form outside her door. Spirits above, she was smitten, even if her love for Greg hadn't faded despite the mess he'd dragged them into.

Ally and Drew's arrival had set things into motion. Words became plans, which would be executed today. She had cleaned their cuts before they started healing, and when their group stealthed to Ganzorig's hiding spot later, the two fighters would be ready for action again. Lana reached the bottom of the stairs, scanning over her foreign surroundings. The clutter on the tables had been her clutter, the mess of books and papers all hers.

They'd cleared what they could last night, stuffing crushed papers and scattered pens into drawers, but their hasty desperation couldn't erase the violation of having her house destroyed.

It couldn't change the fact that Greg was never coming home.

Lana shuddered when she approached her coffeemaker, getting the machine going as the first pale beams of sunlight filtered in through the window. Ally and Drew had run afoul of some Landsliders in Rickett's Glen, but they'd followed the scent to a cave entrance with enough covered prints to make it clear those weren't the only Landsliders roving around that spot. So now, they were going to investigate the lair.

The dark sludge hissed behind her while the machine set to work, and she pulled out two mugs, a habit she'd never shed, even after Greg had passed.

The slightest of creaks alerted her to Lucas' arrival. For such a massive man, he moved with the silent grace of his tiger. The pale gray T-shirt he wore might as well have been glued on, as the thin fabric clung to his ridged pecs and the abs she wanted to sink her teeth into. His umber eyes lit when his gaze rested on her, causing her heart to twist like a wet rag. She'd be lying if she said she wasn't falling and fast.

"Ready to stop Ganzorig today?" Lucas asked, prowling into her kitchen. Where there had been space before, he engulfed it—and not because he loomed over her. Even as Lucas spoke with a confidence as stark as the temperature, none of it settled past her skin.

"We'll be storming the gates in mere hours," Lana responded, pouring coffee into a mug before handing it over to him. "So, you'd be best off with some fortification."

Lucas closed the distance between them to grab the mug, skimming his palm over her hand. The slight touch made her shudder, since she craved him like the first breeze of spring.

Lana wanted him, but he would only ever be a temporary thrill.

"What are you going to do after we handle Ganzorig?" she asked, taking a step away from the temptation of those corded arms, of his sinful smile, of his heat. "Do the Tribe even get vacation?"

He flashed a lopsided grin and leaned back against the counter. "Shockingly, yes. Great health benefits too." His eyes darkened for a moment, but he ducked his head to sip from his mug. "I'll be on the road again, wherever Mackey is stirring up trouble. With his fixation on this region, though, I might be back."

Their gazes snagged like loose thread on wire, and the searching in his broke her heart. They were both stuck in stasis, banging on the walls to break free. Lucas was the first bit of shelter after endless rain, but maybe she'd left her marks too without realizing.

His careful touch, more so than anyone would expect from a big guy like him, his protective streak and the tilted way he grinned, how the motion caused his scars to crease – she wasn't ready to give him up yet. She had just begun to place the pieces to the puzzle of this gorgeous, beguiling man, and she wanted to know so much more.

Lana's feet carried her forward unbidden, the inexorable draw to him too powerful to be denied. He rested his hand on her hip as he drew her closer. The heat between their bodies was seconds away from combusting, and his touch left a permanent mark, like the first strains of a favorite song. Lana reached up to brush her thumb across those sensuous lips, memorizing the shape, as if his kiss hadn't already imprinted on her for life. A single breath escaped him, and time paused.

For this single moment, she could exist here with him. For this single moment, she wasn't a widow or the wife of Greg Bennett. For this single moment, he wasn't one of the Tribe. For this single moment, he could stay.

Her gaze landed on his lips, but Lucas pulled away first, shattering the fragile, quavering ray they'd clung to. Lana stepped back to grab her coffee, as if the heat from the mug could dispel the way her fingers tingled from mere touch.

"So, taking down Ganzorig?" Lana said before snagging a quick sip. It wasn't like she could evade the heat in Lucas' eyes or the way her body flushed.

He nodded. "Yeah, we're taking down the Landsliders."

Even as their mouths formed different words, Lana recognized them for what they were.

Goodbye. Goodbye. Goodbye.

* * * *

The car engine rumbled beneath her feet while they raced across the highway she'd traveled a million times in the direction of Ricketts Glen. Any awkwardness got amplified a thousand-fold after they picked up Ally from her apartment and Kyle from his place. Raven was covering his shift at Beaver Tavern so her packmate could run with them tonight.

Lucas had been quiet for most of the drive, and were they both buzzed as though they'd downed more than a single cup of coffee that morning. It didn't help that Ally kept leaning forward to flick her in the ear with a mischievous grin on her lips. Her blue eyes danced every time Lana met her gaze, and Ally would aim a pointed stare at Lucas while he drove the car. Lana's heart pounded in double time. She hoped Kyle hadn't taken notice of the tension thick enough to choke on that had descended in the car.

"Don't suppose you found a hidden side entrance to approach from?" Lana turned around in her seat to face Ally. The sinking feeling in her gut hadn't left, and with every road sign they passed bringing them closer to Ricketts Glen, her nerves increased in volume until they deafened.

Ally tugged at the bandage on her arm that would fall right off the moment she shifted. She wrinkled her nose when she looked up. "Don't worry, Lan. Ganzorig didn't spot us when we approached. We'll get the jump on his Landsliders."

"About how many do you think are in there?" Lucas asked, his rumbling voice filling the car. It thrummed deep in her bones, whether he was serious, joking or warm—he had one of those resonant voices that lingered.

"A whole kitten corral," Ally shot back, quick draw on the snark. She began picking at her nails, brimming with as much nervous energy as the rest of them. "In all seriousness, though, the cave wasn't large enough to house an army, and the narrow entrance seems to stretch far. Anyone attacking will have to form a single-file line."

The dark brown signs emerged into view for Rickett's Glen, and the sunlight sparkled past the bony limbs of barren oaks. Fallen leaves formed a tan carpet across the ground, the breezes skittering the withered husks across the highway.

"One by one is perfect," Kyle growled. "I've got some frustrations to vent."

"Don't we all," Ally muttered. A weary sigh escaped Lana's throat.

Even though his focus never drifted, Lucas spared a glance for her, the ever-present concern clear in his eyes. Lana pasted on a smile she didn't feel and curled her hands into fists. Whatever came at them here would be better than pacing through her home, waiting for their next attack.

Lucas pulled in to park beside a Jeep, one she recognized as the Red Rock beta's. Jer waited outside with Betty from the Red Rock pack. Drew leaned against the car, his aviators on and his mouth pressed into a thin line. Ally smacked Kyle out of the way and launched out of the car first, and Lana hopped out to follow, a puff of loose dirt billowing with the motion. Lucas loped up to Jer.

The Red Rock beta flashed a charming grin. "If we waited any longer for you lot, I was going to force these guys into a singalong."

Lucas smiled, his white teeth exposed. "Who says the opportunity is missed? I never pass up on a good team-building exercise. I can contribute to the baritone department."

"He's not kidding," Drew chimed in. "Those assholes forced me to sing round after round of showtunes with them."

Lucas grinned even wider. "Knock off the whining. You were having fun with me and Jess by the end of it."

Lana's mouth quirked at his comment, but she could feel Ally's gaze on her, so she nudged her best friend. "You ready to sink your fangs into some Landsliders?"

Ally lifted her eyebrow before she burst into laughter. "Sorry, babe. It's like a kitten puffing up against a lion. I know you're used to being the clean-up crew, not in the thick of the fight."

Lana tugged on her ponytail. Already, Lucas had taken the lead, heading toward the entrance of Ricketts Glen. Drew and Jer slunk close behind, and her feet carried her forward even if her mind was racing a million miles away.

As they veered in the opposite direction to the main trails and approached the thicker woods, Lucas turned around to face them.

"Listen, crew," he announced, his voice carrying. "We'll be shifting here, so this is where the vocal communication ends. Follow my lead. If you can't, you'll face the consequences later."

The command in his voice was undeniable, as were the sharp arch of his eyebrows and the firm lines of his mouth. Like that, she witnessed the formidable East Coast Tribe member who made shifters all over this side of the country quake in their boots. Even like this, though, her heart still twisted in relief at his presence. Even like this, he didn't scare her.

Ally leaned in close. "Does he use that tone in the bedroom?"

Lana elbowed her in the side, though she couldn't help her smirk. Spirits above, she'd be lying if she said she wasn't dying to find out. Ally might be using distraction on purpose—she knew her best friend too well—but it did help settle her nerves.

"Let's go." Lucas gave the order, and they all followed him deeper into the woods, past the cragged oaks until they came to a quick halt in the grove ahead. Lana's heart jackhammered. She'd gone on patrols before, but nothing where a fight was a guarantee. It wasn't as if she couldn't tear into another shifter, but the thought made her stomach flip. She preferred to be on the fixing end of things.

At once, their crew began stripping to shift. Even though Lana lingered near Ally, her gaze never left Lucas. She yanked her cargo pants down, dropping them to her shoes, and began to pull at the hem of her shirt. When she looked up, she licked her lips on reflex. Lucas' gaze settled on her, turning molten. He'd already stripped his shirt off, revealing lickable, defined muscles and the dark tattoos wrapping around his skin that glowed bronze in the sunlight.

She sucked in a deep breath and tugged her tee over her head before she sank into the shift. Her mountain lion had been clawing in her chest from the moment the problems had first arisen, begging to be out, to fight.

Her bones mutated as she changed into her wild form, pale fur sprouting across her arms, her teeth lengthening to fangs and her nails sharpening to claws. No more fragile palms—she had tough pads as she sank to the ground on all fours. The birds whistled, the sound piercing and more complex in this form, and the dappled sunlight cast fractals onto the forest floor. With her heavy layer of fur, the cold didn't affect her nearly as much, and Lana stretched, getting her muscles limber for a run.

All around her, the others in their crew shifted into mountain lions and wolves, with the massive Siberian tiger leading the charge. Once Lucas launched into the woods, the others followed. The dry earth flaked beneath her pads, and she kicked up leaves that had begun to mulch into the ground. In this form, the brown shades of the bark grew deeper and the brittle scent of decay even crisper. The loam from the ground invaded her senses as well as the chilling tingle in the air that meant snow loomed on the horizon.

They leaped around trees and launched over skeletal bushes with ease, none of their crew making a sound while they raced through the woods. Lana sank into the exhilaration of the run, letting go of the worries, the grief and the fear in the wake of racing along with her pack. Her heart pounded to the same beat as her paws, and her determination sharpened with every step forward.

Drew surged ahead to match pace with Lucas. He guided them in the direction of the cave he and Ally had found. Even though she'd run through these woods many times before until the grays, greens, and browns blurred around her, now her senses ran on overload with the alertness of a hunt.

A scent caught on the breeze. Shifter—not theirs. Lana perked up at the same time Ally did. Lucas slammed to a halt, everyone else sliding and skidding to follow suit. He turned his head in the same direction, the gold of his tiger eyes gleaming. Lana tuned out the whisper of the breeze through the branches and the rustles of squirrels in the underbrush, until she could hear the deliberate *thump, thump, thump*. Landsliders roamed through Ricketts Glen.

Lucas glanced to Drew then back at them. He tilted his head one way, and Drew leaned the other. The rest of their crew caught the directive, splitting down the middle. Lana and Kyle loped behind Lucas while Ally, Jer and Betty followed Drew. They crept through the woods with utmost care to keep as silent as possible.

Any snapped twigs or heavy footfalls would expose their presence.

Lucas led them away from the sound of those footsteps and the foreign scent while Drew headed in the opposite direction, as if they were both circling around their obstacle to meet at the same end point. The run slowed while their group wove through trees, focused on caution rather than the fast churn of mud and free abandon from moments earlier. Lana could feel the presence of the Landsliders in these woods, as if the trees, the leaves and the trickling streams were all coated in an oil slick.

To her far right, she caught a flash of dark brown fur. Lana froze beside Kyle as they waited behind a large oak. Lucas crouched lower to the ground to blend with the brush.

A bear shifter padded through the woods, but he hadn't glanced their way yet.

She didn't dare let out a huff of breath.

A big grizzly lumbered close behind the black bear as they roamed through the forest like they owned it. Kyle buzzed beside her, ready to lunge at the mere sight of them. Lucas, on the other hand, slipped into a meditative stillness. Lana focused ahead, watching, watching, watching. The silent tension skimmed the air with each brush of their feet forward, close enough that a clash could erupt with a single glance.

One glance.

Lana crouched in her space behind the tree, ready to spring once those gazes flickered their way. The moment the Landsliders discovered them.

The bears had almost passed their stretch when one of them stopped, the black one tilting his nose to the sky. He searched around the clearing, confusion in his dark eyes. Lana lowered even closer to the ground as if she could mask her scent with the rotten leaves. A sharp bark from farther away snapped their attention forward.

The black bear bolted. Even though the grizzly trailed a couple of paces behind, slowing to cast one more glance around the clearing, seconds later, they both raced in the direction of the parking lot to chase the sound.

Even still, their group of three remained planted. Lana cycled through her breaths, counting one, two, three, again and again. Lucas waited until the hush returned to this section of the woods before he straightened from his crouch and caught their gazes. He didn't offer any further direction but just plunged deeper into the thick of the forest.

Lana raced behind him, Kyle keeping pace with her. They hurtled through the towering pines and over the beds of desiccated leaves. The wind whistled past them, but the closer they got to the trickle of water, the more the scents cleared until the stench of the foreign shifters dissipated.

Lucas led them up a hill, weaving through the trees as if he'd been born in this place, as if he knew it with the surety of home. Lana managed to close the distance between them until she lapsed a pace or two behind. Her heart slammed when they got nearer to one of the falls ahead. The crystalline water splashed into a meager pool, the sound echoing like breaking glass in the cold air. At the base of the falls beside the pool lay a yawning void of an entrance. The pawprints churned into the mud were visible from here even though scratches had been gouged into the surface, as if that could hide them.

From the opposite side of the hill, two mountain lions and two wolves emerged. Lana tensed on instinct at the sight, even though the scents were the familiar ones of pack. Her claws sank into the mud around this area, which was hardened from the cold. This wasn't just a run through the woods—the time to take Ganzorig down had arrived.

Lucas took the lead, prowling toward the entrance of the cave. He lifted his head and sniffed the air before tilting it to the side, gesturing them to follow.

One by one, they entered the Landsliders' lair.

Chapter Twelve

Lucas hated caves.

The moment Ally and Drew had delivered the news that Ganzorig was camped out in a cavern deep inside Ricketts Glen, dread had taken residence in his bones. Even in his tiger form, the inky darkness of those places infiltrated like cyanide. Yet he was East Coast Tribe. He was supposed to lead fearlessly and remain in control at all times, but with every step toward the void, his insides unraveled.

The stale, metallic tinge to the air greeted him in the cave, like rock dust accumulated in every corner, but beneath that, Lucas caught the scent of other shifters, of coyotes, bears and wolves. Already, his eyes adjusted, working better in his tiger form, yet the gray shapes and narrow ridges of the rock walls ahead didn't offer comfort. In fact, the one thing keeping him moving forward was the weight of Lana's presence behind him. He could feel it like balm on a wound, a steady, grounding thing.

His heart thundered, but he ignored the infernal pulse while he tried to focus on sounds from deeper inside the cave. He caught residual scrapes and plunks, but with the way the tunnel echoed, direction was impossible to gauge. *One step at a time.* He laser-focused on approach, trying to ignore how his mind squeezed tight and his chest followed suit. All he could think of was walking into *that* room back then.

In the darkness, the memories always encroached.

He couldn't shake the feeling that they'd missed some massive hint. That Ganzorig and the Landsliders were a step ahead. They'd all felt that way from the moment Mackey had first struck. His betrayal had blindsided every single member of the East Coast Tribe, as one of their own began using his powers to terrorize the region. Guilt dripped from his fingers like the blood of all the innocents Mackey had killed while trying to achieve an objective eluding them all.

And Ganzorig had only followed in his leader's footsteps. Lucas retracted his claws before unsheathing them again, as if he could rid himself of the sight of that innocent blood spilled. As adults, most shifters met on an even footing in their inevitable clashes, but those cubs hadn't stood a chance.

The lure of answers had him moving faster through the tunnel as the ground sloped, bringing them deeper underground. At this point, Landsliders could emerge ahead of or behind them, and his muscles tensed for the imminent fight.

From deep inside, the echo of water dropping into a pool multiplied, the *plink-plink-plink* growing louder with their approach. He prowled forward, ignoring the way the chill increased with every step as if they weren't striding across granite but ice. Parts of the tunnel grew so narrow he needed to squeeze through, the rough rock scraping against his fur.

Up ahead, the tunnel widened, even though the gray and black gradient remained just as deep and impenetrable. Lucas hummed with tension, enough that the slightest movement would set him off. He was a firework ready to explode, and he planned on unleashing all his fury on Ganzorig himself. At least, if the bastard showed.

Drew slipped beside him, the tunnel wide enough to fit both of them at this point. The former Landslider's presence had fast become a source of stability. Ever since they'd apprehended Drew and started working with him, Lucas had been the main point of contact, and as he'd come to understand the guy more and more, he'd found he trusted Drew.

Even though the murkiness ahead made it tough to distinguish, he caught the sloping of the rock faces into a cavern. They followed the path to a slight turn. The first glimpses of amber light—the rays of a lantern— spilled from the entrance.

Lucas felt a jolt to his paw, a hesitation he pushed past.

The light flickered on.

Crimson drops trailed across the carpet.

The stench, that rotten eggs and copper.

Bile rose in his throat. He was here. In a cave, heading to face off against Landsliders. Not in that room. Lucas let out a huff of breath to push himself to keep going as Drew passed him. He felt a nudge against his other side. Lana prowled beside him, and understanding flashed in her amber eyes. A brief glimpse was all he needed. Her touch had become a grounding force he hadn't thought could even exist for him.

And yet, once they defeated Ganzorig, he would be leaving this place.

Lucas leaped to outpace Drew with ease, heading to the entrance of the cavern, the tawny light the same shade as his fur.

He slowed upon approach as he caught those foreign scents — not just of other shifters but the one that made his nose twitch, the stench of the magic surrounding shamans. They hadn't been off the mark. Ganzorig was here.

Lucas prowled to the entrance, standing on the far right to peer out at the cavern spanning before him. His heart amped up to a steady thrum in his chest. Lanterns hung from juts in the rock wall, lighting the massive expanse. He was on what appeared to be a lower level. A cragged path carved into the sloping stone led to higher ground, overlooking the rest of the space. Stalactites the color of burnished copper clawed for the earth, the same as the groping tendrils of the stalagmites fighting to dominate. Water dripped into small pools that collected in the dips and divots of the limestone and shale.

"You can keep huffing and puffing down there, but we heard you the moment you entered." Ganzorig stepped out of the shadows onto the elevated expanse of stone. The middle-aged man didn't fit the appearance of someone hiding away in caves, with the pressed button-down and fancy black slacks he wore, as if he'd popped out of a business meeting to pay them a visit. He didn't look like someone who could've mixed meth to turn shifters to berserkers or the sort to slaughter families.

Ganzorig focused his gaze in their direction, so Lucas emerged from the entrance. *Not like we have the element of surprise on our side.*

Two wolves slunk from behind Ganzorig toward the sloping trail that led to where they'd entered, their shadows stretching along the walls. Another coyote and a bear emerged onto the higher platform out of a tunnel that led deeper into the caves. Jer slipped past Lucas, his teeth bared and a growl slipping from him. For the Red Rock beta, this fight against Ganzorig was personal — the shaman had used to supply his meds.

Ganzorig didn't budge from his perch while he watched over them like some lord or king. Lucas' chest strained with a rage he hadn't realized he'd been pinning back. All he could see was the shamans who'd held him down and marked him as a kid during the ceremony where they'd tattooed his skin, tying the Great Spirit to him permanently. Then the images of the house they'd found slammed him in the gut.

The bloodstains on the carpet leading to the couch.

The shifter children who lay dead on the ground, blood pooling around them, roots somehow plunged through their chests.

One tiny hand outstretched, pale as fallen snow.

The sneer on Ganzorig's lips and his dark, impermeable gaze like the depths of this cave all fueled the heat combusting inside Lucas.

"Attack them," Ganzorig commanded, sweeping his hand out. The bear and coyote separated from his side to launch down the sloping rock, kicking gravel and dust. They raced in the same direction as the two approaching wolves.

Lucas crouched as Drew and Ally slunk up beside him. They had the numbers on their side, no matter how much confidence Ganzorig exuded. His rage percolated inside him until it rose up his throat, and he opened his mouth. A roar escaped, one that quaked the stalactites of this cavern, sending bits of stone tumbling.

The two approaching wolves leaped forward, but Jer launched to greet them in a flash of russet.

Lucas bolted after him, crossing the short distance in a few lazy leaps. He soared through the air. Drew loped past the wolves, making a beeline for the bear that thundered down the slope in their direction. Ally tagged close behind him, the two taking cues from each other as though they'd been doing this their whole lives. Kyle, Lana and Betty prowled in the back, all three shifters tensed to lunge.

The ground reverberated beneath him as he landed in front of one of the wolves, causing pebbles to tremble. He could feel them vibrate, waiting to be whipped around at his bidding.

The silver wolf took one look at him and lunged to the side, joining the other shifter in attacking Jer. Lucas moved with the swiftness of a striking missile, and he zoomed forward, teeth bared. Before the wolf could sink her fangs into Jer's haunches, Lucas snagged his jaw around her back leg. He planted hard on the ground, using his heft to whip his head to the side. He brought the wolf shifter with him until he opened his jaw, releasing his grip. The wolf tumbled across the rocky ground.

Kyle churned up gravel, launching in to join them. The mountain lion slashed out at the silver wolf before she could even rise. Lucas whipped toward the other wolf who'd tackled Jer. The two rolled around on the ground in an almost indistinguishable blur. Jer's russet coat was a stark contrast to the pale white of the Landslider's. Lucas bowed his head and charged.

His dense forehead thudded into the flash of white with a resounding thump that sent them both tumbling. Before he could follow through, he caught the glimpse of the coyote's mottled fur as it snuck around the opposite side. Those umber eyes fixed on him.

He hadn't taken a step forward before Betty and Lana lunged toward the coyote in unison. The Red Rock wolf darted in first, and Lana looped around, baring her teeth. Lucas fixed his gaze on Ganzorig. Enough messing with his peons. He would take down Mackey's right-hand shaman.

Ganzorig murmured, his hands clasped around an object, and he took on the meditative focus of a shaman performing a spell. He wasn't the only one with magic. Lucas focused on the stalactites above the shaman, reaching out with the abilities innate to him, ones he'd practiced with for years. The massive spikes trembled, and he gathered his energy into focus. If he chased after Ganzorig, the man might have a chance to bolt for the other tunnel.

This route left little margin of escape.

Lucas lifted his paws as he reared, and he slammed them to the ground. The stalactites snapped, the sound cracking through the cavern. For a fragile moment, the structures hummed mid-air. Then they descended.

At least six stalactites dropped, their jagged points heading for Ganzorig at top speed. Grit rolled through the area in billowing sweeps, and the shaman disappeared behind the clouds. Lucas stepped back a pace.

Ally and Drew had almost taken the bear down, and Jer was winning his wrestling fight against the other wolf, based on the red streaming across the pristine-snow coat. Betty's muzzle dripped with crimson as the coyote's head lolled to the side in her grip.

Lana prowled toward the opening they'd arrived through, tilting her ears as if she heard something.

If the Landsliders they'd passed in the woods had looped around, they'd be fast outnumbered.

She took a few tentative steps then leaped forward, disappearing into the tunnels.

Lucas' heart slammed so hard it pulsed in his throat. *Fuck.* He should be chasing after Ganzorig and hammering the final nail in his coffin. The bastard didn't deserve to take another breath. Yet what if more Landsliders emerged? He couldn't forgive himself if something happened to her.

He'd sworn years ago. *Never again.* Like it or not, in the short time they'd known each other, Lana Renoir had managed to leave a permanent mark.

The dust hadn't quite settled around Ganzorig. Lucas let out a low huff and burst for the tunnels. Grit churned beneath him and pebbles flew behind as he raced toward the opening leading back out to the forests of Ricketts Glen. Ganzorig had appeared too calm throughout the fight for there not to be a trap. Lucas kept waiting for the floor to fall out beneath him. He plunged back into the tunnels.

He caught sight of Lana, who was prowling with purpose. In seconds, he'd leaped beside her and aimed a gentle headbutt to her side. Her muscles tensed, but she nuzzled him before her ears flattened at the slight click of claws on stone echoing through the tunnels. That wasn't just one set of paws approaching either.

They needed to alert the others. The rest of the Landsliders had arrived.

He nudged Lana forward, and she dipped her head in a nod. Together they whipped around in the direction they'd come from. They hadn't gotten a few paces before the ground began to tremble.

A boom quaked from the cavern, one that reverberated all the way to where they stood.

Panic clawed at his throat, and he lunged forward. *No, no, no.* The shifters from the Red Rock and Silver Springs packs had followed him in here — he should be leading them. Lucas outpaced Lana, the pads of his paws barely hitting the ground. He flew through the tunnel to emerge back into the cavern.

No one stood on the platform, nor the lower section. The shaman wasn't among the shifter bodies littering the cavern floor either. Ganzorig had disappeared from the place.

Jer stepped back and forth, letting out a howl of irritation that echoed through the cavern. Already, Ally loped to where Ganzorig had last been. The tunnel that Ganzorig and the other Landsliders had emerged from was now filled. Stones piled in front of the entrance, shaken loose from the ceiling or ground floor with an evenness that suggested magical influence.

He must've escaped through the tunnel, leaving them stuck there to face the Landsliders who marched in behind them. Betty paced alongside Drew, who crouched beside the bear they'd mauled, an anxiousness brimming in the air.

A breath of relief rushed out of him at the sight of the Red Rock and Silver Springs shifters pacing across the cave. No one was hurt. He let out a sharp growl, drawing their attention to where he and Lana stood in the entryway.

Ganzorig might've escaped, but more Landsliders were coming. They needed to be prepared.

Two wolves and a grizzly bear stepped into view from around the bend.

Lucas bared his teeth, expecting more to emerge from behind, the veritable army that he'd seen run rampant through these regions. Except no one followed. The three Landsliders caught sight of them and froze. They stared at each other in perfect stillness for the span of a breath — until the first wolf bolted back through the tunnel, the other two following behind.

Confusion tangled in his chest as he bolted after them. Why were they running away? Surprise had flashed in their gazes, as if this hadn't been a planned attack. He leaped through the winding tunnel at top speed, the stone face scraping against his fur and grit spraying with his heavy footfalls. The other Red Rocks and Silver Springs members thundered behind him, their steps echoing through the expanse as if a militia bore down on these remaining Landsliders.

He churned up the stones while he ran, gaining on the three Landsliders. In the distance, the sunlight beckoned from the opening. Out there, the tightness would dissipate. Out there, he could take a full breath again.

The wolves burst free from the tunnels first, springing out in opposite directions across the clearing. The grizzly bear raced off in a third direction, making it impossible to follow all three. *Not like any of them were the real target.* The real target had sealed himself deeper inside the cave.

It shouldn't have been this easy. Sure, Ganzorig had escaped, but no elements of the confrontation stacked up.

Once he emerged into the sunlight and the bright rays soaked in through his fur, the tension inside him uncoiled. Being in the cave had smothered him, like being held underwater. Lucas bolted into the woods, leading the team through Ricketts Glen. Instead of following the rogue Landsliders, he headed in the direction of the parking lot. They needed to regroup and discuss a new strategy.

The raw earth churned under his paws and he welcomed the cool breezes, sharp and clear, unlike the stale air in the cave. Frustration scorched his throat like spice. Ganzorig had been right in his grasp. He should've never relented, yet he'd run off and given the bastard a chance to escape. *Again.*

The race to the parking lot passed in a blink compared to their slow, methodical approach. Lucas prowled toward the trees near their cars where they'd left their clothes, the scent easy to distinguish. He began to shift to his human form even as the tiger sank his claws in stubbornly. The transition took him over with the smooth liquidity of the waterfalls around there, his fur diminishing until the skin emerged and his claws retracting as they morphed back to nails.

Within seconds, he'd returned to two feet and was tugging on his clothes. He hadn't slipped on his sneakers yet when he noticed the only other shifter to make the change back to human form was Lana. Jer pawed at the ground, a whine splitting the air, and Ally paced back and forth across the earth.

"Guys, shift back," he called over to them. "What are you waiting for?"

Drew padded to him and shook his head, a stark seriousness in his gaze.

Betty let out a low growl and slammed her paws down in frustration.

"Oh, fuck." The words escaped him. He sank to his knees in front of Drew, the full weight slamming into him like a high-speed train.

Ganzorig's chanting, his quick disappearance — he hadn't escaped to save his own hide. He and Lana were the only ones who hadn't been in the cavern when the boom sounded.

The shaman had lured them there on purpose.

Whoever had been in the cavern when Ganzorig had cast the spell couldn't shift.

They were trapped in their animal forms.

Chapter Thirteen

By the time they pulled up to her house, Lana was ready to crawl under a blanket and never come out.

They had dropped Ally, Drew, Jer and Betty off at the Red Rock cabin in the hopes Ava could whip out some shamanic mojo to fix this mess. The entire foray had been a disaster, from losing Ganzorig in the caves to not realizing he'd planned this spell for them. The pleading look from Ally's mountain lion when she'd stomped around, unable to shift back, would haunt her for some time to come. Lana swallowed hard, her throat tightening.

Lucas turned the engine of his car off and seemed to deflate. He sank forward to rest his forehead against the steering wheel.

"Fuck," he muttered, tightening his grip on the wheel. "Fuck, fuck, fuck."

The anguish radiated off him so thick she could taste it in the air. Those dark eyes glowed with loathing and his mouth formed a thin line. He couldn't even look at her.

Even with the air of 'don't fuck with me' around him, Lana could feel the way he grieved, a visceral thing between them. What had happened today was a devastating loss, and he was bearing the brunt of it. She reached out and slipped her hand over his.

"Hey," she murmured, her voice softening. "Today sucked, and I'm not going to try to convince you otherwise. But you don't get to shoulder the weight alone. None of us had any idea Ganzorig would try something like that."

"I should've," he said in a near growl. "Instead of running him down and making sure he was fucking dead, I was diving after you through the tunnels. Hell, I would've taken any excuse to get farther out of the cave. I'm a fucking coward and don't deserve to call myself Tribe."

Lana had buzzed with her own distress ever since they'd left Ricketts Glen, but the moment Lucas opened up, hers melted away. The way he ripped himself to shreds lanced right through her heart.

"Okay, well that's some bullshit," she responded, "but instead of sitting out here in the cold, there's a house right in front of us. We can chug this self-loathing train to there."

Lucas' mouth twisted as he nodded in response. She hopped out of the car first, and the echo of his door slamming resounded through the crisp air. A shudder rolled down her spine, but whether from winter's breath or the events of the day, she couldn't tell. A couple of flakes drifted to tickle her nose and cheeks and melted there. She looked up to witness the swirling wonder of the falling snow, as though the stars themselves had descended from the skies.

Lucas was about to stride past her, but she reached to slip her hand into his. He whipped toward her, a broken ferocity flashing in his eyes. He was hurting like she'd never seen him before. But he trusted her enough to let her see, and that—that meant so much.

Even with the cold seeping past her peacoat, when their eyes met, heat blossomed inside her anew. It licked her from the inside out, the long-stoked flames turning into a blaze with a single look.

Her feet brought her forward before she even realized, closing the space between them. Lucas wrapped his hands around her waist and slammed his mouth on hers. They crashed together like a meteor to earth, like the inevitable. Lana kissed him with a hunger that had been building from the moment he'd first stepped through her door. Flakes of snow drifted to her hair, melting on her cheeks and vanishing as they hit their lips.

Her chest squeezed so tight she might break. His pain filtered through in every brush of their lips together, the burden he shouldered alone. For tonight at least, she needed to take it from him. They both needed to heal.

His mouth was hot and demanding, and the way he brought her body flush to his had her forgetting that they stood on her front lawn in the middle of January. She sank into the melody of their motion, the heat of his palms and the feeling of weightlessness when he held on to her. All the worries, the concern and the grief just disintegrated. His tongue caressed hers, coaxing out a moan. The flakes of snow accumulated in her hair brushed away moments later when he grabbed a fistful of her strands. Her body sparked to life at the possessive touch and his firm grip.

"Let's head inside," Lucas murmured against her mouth. Lana barely had the chance to nod when he scooped her into his arms to carry her the rest of the distance. A breathless laugh escaped her. The snow swirled above, blinding brilliance against the velvet sky, yet she'd never felt safer or warmer with the way he clutched her tight.

She passed him the keys as they reached the door, and they jingled as he one-handedly got it open. Lana couldn't help but trail her fingers down his neck while she wrapped her arms around it. "You sure you don't want to just keep on making out in the freezing snow?" she teased with an amused smile. "I'm sure the Arctic temps do wonders for the libido."

Lucas brought the door closed behind them after he carried her inside. Already, her ears stung from the heat indoors and her eyes had begun to water. He leaned down to brush his lips against hers again.

"Absolutely sure," he murmured against her mouth. "Because the neighbors don't need to see the things I'm planning on doing to you."

The satin voice traveled straight to her core, and she squeezed her thighs together. She was soaked for him, and all he'd done was carry her inside. While they'd been outside, she'd been able to lose herself in the moment with him, blinded by the thrill of the snow, of the starched air, of his big body bracing hers. Inside her house, the memories of Greg tugged at her heels like the tide, even as she remained present here with Lucas.

She didn't question where this was heading—where they both wanted it to. However, the bed wasn't something she thought she could handle.

"Down here," she murmured before sinking her teeth into his corded neck. He glanced to the steps, which was where he'd been heading, and came to a direct stop. She bit harder, eliciting a groan from him. "I don't want to wait."

His gaze rested on her, a knowledge there brushing through her like a paint stroke. She didn't need to say anything—he knew. For a moment, the hesitation tripped her. Maybe she'd fucked things up for good—after all, who wanted to be with someone haunted like her?

Except then he swept his lips against hers in a kiss that was pure, honeyed possession, the sort that dripped through her insides as slow and sinuous as molasses. He loped forward in a few massive strides then lowered the arm bracing her legs. Her boots had barely touched the floor when he crushed her against the wall, his mouth meeting hers with the same insistence she felt in the *thump-thump-thump* of her heart.

This close, she couldn't help but trace the ridges of his chest through the thin fabric of his gray tee. He leaned in, brushing the thickness of his erection right between her legs. Lana let out a sharp breath, the desire to have him thrust inside her turning to exquisite agony.

Lucas broke away from her lips to meet her gaze. "Are you sure you're ready for this?" he asked, the sweetness suffusing her insides with whiskey warmth.

"Tonight, we need this more than ever," Lana murmured, tracing the firm lines of his jaw before she slid her fingers down along the column of his neck. She slipped them beneath the hem of his shirt. His body was scorching, a heat she needed to feel pressed against her. Hunger roared under her skin, a demand that sent her reeling. She looked him in the eyes, pure seriousness emanating from her. "I need you, Luc."

The words galvanized him to action. One second, they were staring at each other, inches apart, and the next, he crashed his mouth to hers again. Lana moaned into his mouth, overloaded by his firm body pinning her against the wall and the way his erection thrust against her drenched core, which was so, so ready for him. Her skin grew so sensitized that even the thin layers of fabric between them were too much.

Lucas swept his hands along her body, along her waist, and her hips, until he grabbed hold of her thighs and lifted. She twined her arms around his neck, leaning up to press a kiss to his lips. He took the couple of paces forward and crouched to set her down on the steps. When he knelt before her, Lana's mouth went dry. She sucked in a breath when he brought his callused fingers to the hem of her pants. Her core pulsed in response.

She tugged them down, even though warmth swept across her cheeks at the hunger in his gaze when he scanned across her bare legs. He nodded to the useless scrap of fabric between her thighs. Lana bit her lip and brought that down too.

"I've been wanting to taste you for far too long," Lucas murmured, his dark eyes gleaming.

Her heart pounded. They'd reached the point of no return, but the fear didn't grip her any longer. She wanted to plunge off this precipice with him.

"Likewise," she responded, sliding her tongue across her lips as she looked him over. The tiger flashed in his eyes, bright gold, and he prowled forward with languid grace. When he settled his palms on the insides of her thighs, all the nerves vanished. His touch tamed the way her mountain lion paced inside. His touch felt right when nothing else lately had. From this vantage point, Lucas Diaz was an unforgettable sort of gorgeous, light scruff on his angular chin and brown eyes that radiated warmth like a hearth.

When he lowered his mouth to her drenched folds, Lana forgot everything else. His tongue slipped out, and the moment he glided it against her clit, she dug her elbows into the hard wood of the steps. Her head tilted back, and she surrendered to the sensation. His palms were hot on her thighs, and he dug his nails into her skin with a delicious bite. The feline way he lapped at her clit, lazy swipes at first that quickened to a crescendo, had her panting within seconds.

Sweat pricked on her forehead as his tongue performed pure magic, and her thighs tensed with each ensuing stroke. The breath caught in her throat, and she indulged in how damn good he felt. The relief of being touched, of letting go. She surrendered to the rhythm, to the way he devoured her. Her elbows burned against the hardwood as she dug in harder, her whole body tightening in anticipation.

Lucas nipped and sucked and licked until she grew delirious. Until her moans filled the empty halls of the house, echoing back.

She twisted like a rag, tighter, tighter, tighter, until the steady, pulsing rhythm of his tongue to her clit pushed her over the ledge. Lana released, a cry ripping from her throat before she sagged against the steps, her thighs loosening and her arms growing lax. Her gaze blinked white and hot from the fury of the orgasm he'd wrung from her. With a shaky breath, Lana forced her head up to meet his eyes.

The sight of Lucas between her legs wrenched her with need. She wanted the ache inside her to be filled by him. His dark eyes gleamed with a desire that weighed heavy in the air between them.

"Spirits above, you're beautiful," she murmured, reaching to run her fingers across his glistening lips. Even as her mind soared and her limbs grew loose and easy, her heart thundered.

"I think that's my line," he rumbled, prowling overtop her. The heated way he looked her over made her feel wanted. She missed that, so much. Lucas brushed his lips over hers, and she kissed back hard, scraping her teeth over his lower lip. He circled his hands around her waist again, and in seconds he'd lifted her off the steps. The way he carried her around as if she weighed nothing made her insides clench tight. She wanted to feel his power driving into her again and again and again.

She gave him a pointed look. "I think you're a bit overdressed, gorgeous. Clothes off. Now."

A blinding grin spread on his face, his eyes sparkling with mischief. "*Ay dios mio*, woman. Could you be any sexier?"

A flush heated her cheeks when he lowered her to the couch. She bit her lower lip, offering a coy glance before she tugged her top off to hit the ground, her bra following suit a second later. "Challenge accepted," she responded, her voice heating. She sprawled on the couch, spreading her legs open wide. Her chest thrummed in anticipation as she lay bare before him.

Lucas pulled off his T-shirt first in a fluid motion, exposing muscles that made her mouth water. The man was fucking exquisite, from the dark patterns of his Tribe tattoos across his bronze skin to the tight V that trailed down to the pants he was now unbuttoning. The *snick* echoed around the room when his zipper descended. All their dancing around ended there as he slipped off his jeans.

He towered over her, his cock heavy between his legs, and the mere sight made her core throb.

The tiger gleamed in his eyes while he prowled forward, bracing himself on top of her. He sank his palms into the couch on either side, and her entire body trembled in anticipation of the skin to skin contact, of the moment he'd lower himself into her. This was the predator she should've been afraid of all along. The one she was willing to go toe to toe with.

He brushed his arms against hers, and she sank her fingers into the tight, smooth muscle of his shoulders, the heat undeniable. He pressed against her, the back of the couch scratching against her bare skin while he brushed the silken length of his cock across her drenched folds. Lana shivered in response, desperate for him like she was mindless in heat.

She dug her nails in, drawing him closer as she pressed her lips to his. Need burned between them like asphalt on a summer's day, a languid slowness to their movements, and a careful deliberateness. She understood the free dive off the cliff they were taking. She drank in the taste of him, memorizing the curve of his mouth, those rough lips against hers. He nudged the tip of his cock against her entrance, and Lana couldn't help but wrap her thighs around his, guiding him in.

He lowered himself into her inch by inch, and a breath escaped her with each one. Her chest squeezed tight at his possessive grip on her hips, and she bucked to bring him deeper, deeper. He was so thick she strained to pull him inside, steel encased in velvet. Still, Lucas' mouth never ceased as he kissed her lips, her neck, her collarbone. He glided his hand up to encircle her breast, the rough tip of his thumb swiping across her nipple.

She gasped into his mouth, and he swallowed her moans while he continued to tease her. Her core ached around him as he plunged deeper until he slid in the whole way. Lana bit his neck, tasting the salt of his skin, a delicious thrill running through her. When he began to move inside her, that was when her nails dug in. He settled his palms around her hips again, gripping tight. He rocked into her with enough force to make her toes curl.

Her back scraped against the fabric of her couch, and his weight pressed on her until she was engulfed by him, the scent of sage and rosewood surrounding her. Lana rocked with him, their bodies finding each other like an old, familiar melody. Her sensitized nipples brushed against his chest, his skin warm, rough and utterly delicious. She couldn't stop sucking and licking the expanse before her, driving her teeth into his traps, his deltoids and the corded muscles of his neck.

They moved together slowly at first, seeking, but once they found their rhythm, it grew wild, frenetic. The desperation that gripped both of them tight leaked out of every coiled movement, every thrust as he drove into her. They became a tangle of teeth, of skin, of measured touch. She dug her heels into his firm ass, and he slammed into her so hard the breath flew from her.

Their hips met again and again. Her moans filled the room and his heated breaths burst across her skin. This might've started as incendiary attraction, as a way to unleash the stress and pressure dominating them both, but it fast transformed into something primal, something she felt in her bones. Lucas was only supposed to be a distraction, but every time they clashed together, she fell more and more.

He bit the soft point between her neck and shoulder, the tender motion causing her core to pulse even tighter. Sweat beaded across her forehead, and her breath hitched as they seemed to race against each other. His thighs tensed between hers. He was close. Lana dug her nails in tightly, guiding his lips to hers. She drank in the taste of him as she bucked forward to greet his thrust.

They collided together with a smack that resounded through the room, the sting almost as delicious as the way her lips stung from their fevered kisses, keeping her present here with him even as the pleasure had her feeling weightless, boneless. She bit down on his lip and when they separated again, their eyes met.

The look seared her, the desire, the adoration, as though he were staring at the stars or the sea or the snow.

Lana swallowed, hard. Whatever she held on to released in that moment. As he slammed back down into her, she clenched tight around him. His cock pulsed inside, heat spilling through her, and she came with him. Her gaze flashed, the heat scorching and the bliss radiating through her from the inside out to her fingertips and toes. Ragged breaths tore from her throat, and she sagged into the couch, resting her hands on his broad shoulders.

Their harsh breaths cycled through the quiet of the house, and she couldn't have torn her eyes from his if she'd wanted to. Lana yearned to stay in this moment for as long as she could, to memorize the sheen on his forehead, the stubble on his chin and the thick eyebrows released in surrender.

The realization sank claws into her chest. She wanted more than a single night with him. She had been tipping forward for so long she hadn't realized she'd fallen for the impossible, for a member of the East Coast Tribe.

For Lucas Diaz.

Chapter Fourteen

They had fucked on the couch, the floor and against her kitchen counter.

Lucas couldn't get enough. Of the way she tasted, the way she moaned and just how perfectly their bodies fit together.

Somehow, after everything, they ended up curled on her corduroy couch, a wool blanket loosely covering them while they drank piping hot mugs of tea, because Lana had insisted that they needed some hydration. He tugged her closer to him, and she nestled in, the rose and orange scent of her an addiction. Heat emanated between them despite the snow falling outside the windows, and his insides twisted tight. This was a perfect moment, a perfect memory.

One that would haunt him when he left.

Lana leaned in against his chest, and she'd flipped his palm over to trace his callused and beat-up hands. Her soft and sweeping touch cracked him right open.

"We'll find a way to fix the others," Lana murmured. She stared at his hands, worn and beaten from so many fights. "Ally and the rest. We've got Ava on our side, and I don't think Ganzorig will vanish. He's still after the device Greg hid." At that, she lapsed into silence, those green eyes turning darker.

He didn't have to question the discomfort flickering through her gaze. He was the first person she'd slept with since her husband had passed. If guilt twisted in his chest at the thought, it must pale in comparison to what she felt. And yet, he didn't want to let her go.

A shaky breath escaped him. Now that he had some space from the situation, he realized Ganzorig had planned the spell from the start, whether he'd killed him or not. He and Lana stepping out of the cavern had been a blessing from the Spirits—otherwise, they'd have been trapped too. Yet he couldn't help the pulse of shame marching at a rising beat in his chest every time he failed to stop these monsters.

"I just wanted to be able to save them." The words cracked when they fell from his lips, and he hated that. Lana threaded her fingers through his and squeezed tightly, the action bolstering him. "I wasn't able to save her."

The simple fact had chased him ever since.

"Who was she?" Lana asked, nuzzling in closer to his chest. He pulled her in tight, the skin to skin contact and the heat between them beneath the blanket somehow giving him the grounding to voice the words that had remained stitched to his lips for so long.

"My baby sister, Josefina," he said, as if saying her name out loud was so easy, as if it hadn't become an oppressive silence in his family ever since. "We didn't live in the best neighborhood, but hey, when I was around, no one wanted to fuck with Tribe." He stretched out, the knotted scars along his arms clear despite his tattoos.

"My folks stepped out for the night, and Maria and I were supposed to keep an eye on the younger two. I was fifteen." The thrum in his chest grew louder and louder, as if he were still back in the broken-down first-floor apartment. As if the *drip, drip, drip* echoed every night, like he hadn't found a way to move his family out of their neighborhood as fast as he could after everything that had happened.

"Josie went to bed early while the rest of us stayed up watching a movie. We heard the breaking glass and bolted for her room." A sharp breath escaped him, and Lana squeezed his hand again, as if bolstering him to keep going. "Her room was dark, and when I flicked on the light…" His mouth dried at the memory, the one that sank claws in past flesh even after all these years. "Some anti-shifter assholes in the area had been scoping out our place for months, like the Coalition around here. They wanted us out of town, so they shot my baby sister with a silver bullet."

When Lana looked at him, her eyes were glassy. "I'm so sorry, Luc." Tears slipped down her cheeks, and he reached to brush them away. The expression on her face, the tears in her eyes, mirrored everything he kept coiled inside. His tears wouldn't flow—they already had, years earlier—but he felt bare, more exposed than he did lying here naked on the couch with her.

Yet he needed her to know. Whatever developed between them had grown too immense to contain, to define. One taste of Lana Renoir and he'd sworn off all other women for the rest of his life. He just wanted her, more than anything.

She let out a shaky sigh and offered a soft smile. "You've been holding on to that a long time, haven't you?"

He nodded. She understood when so few did. She understood, whether he said the words or not. "When you're Tribe, everyone looks to you for the answers. We're expected to lead from an early age, which doesn't leave a lot of room for weakness."

Lana shook her head and jabbed a finger to his chest. "That's not weakness. That's your strength, the gigantic heart of yours that wants to protect people in need. Your sister's death might've cemented that in your mind as a bad thing or a failure, but the fact is, you've seen a lot of ugly shit on the road, yet you still care. People like you are so, so rare."

His insides melted at the earnest look in her eyes, the determined ferocity he recognized as her own strength. He couldn't help but dip down and brush another kiss to her swollen lips, as if he might communicate all the words that wouldn't come. As if he could tell her that he wanted to keep her. For once, he wanted to stay.

"You're the rare one," he murmured, gliding a thumb across her cheek. "You've survived all this and you're still able to see the best in people."

She tugged at the blanket in front of her but didn't move from his side, even when her gaze distanced. "How the hell am I supposed to shake this guilt?" she asked, but the question seemed to be more to herself. "You're the first person since Greg who's even sparked my attention. I didn't know I could have these feelings again, and one part of me is so, so relieved, but the other part hates myself."

"Have you tried talking to him?" he asked, holding her tight, as if somehow he could leech away her pain.

"I used to go to Josie's grave and talk. It felt like she could hear me, even if she couldn't answer back."

Lana shook her head. "I should. I just didn't have the solid ground to stand on until now." She glanced to him. "At least, as solid as this can be."

His mouth dried, but he couldn't stay silent about how he felt. Even if he was being selfish. "I don't want this to end."

"Me neither," Lana murmured before she looked at him. Her eyes were as green as bottle glass, and hesitant. "But how would we even do this? You're always going to be on the road, and I'm part of a pack — I've got my jobs, my family, my house here."

Lucas licked his lips, wishing he held the answers. Most of the time, he doled them out whether they were the truth or not — as Tribe, he couldn't afford to sit in silence. Yet here with her, he wasn't Tribe. For the first time in so long, he was Lucas Diaz, and with her, he could be honest.

"I don't know," he said. "All I know is that you're the first bit of light in a long stretch of darkness, and I want to try to make this work. Whether it means me stopping here as much as I can, talking on the phone, whatever we need to do." Long distance was folly. Those relationships fell apart every time. He knew that. He also knew he'd regret for the rest of his life if he let Lana slip through his fingers.

Lana intertwined her fingers through his. "That's all we can ever do. Try," she responded, her voice hushed. "Try to hold on to those moments that flicker like candlelight with the people we care about. You and I both know they don't always last."

He pressed a kiss into her silken hair, and her words sank in deep. She was right. However, if he could have one wish in his life, one hope to grasp, he wanted to hold on to her for as long as possible.

* * * *

Today, Beaver Tavern was opening early. With members of both packs unable to turn, they needed enough space for them to all meet, including their shaman friend Ava, in the hopes of being able to form a new plan.

Lucas' brain had been revving into overdrive from the moment they'd exited the cave, so the time he'd spent with Lana last night had been the break he needed. They'd both fallen asleep on the couch, and when he'd woken in the morning, the path had stretched out as clear as the daylight streaming through the windows.

At least, until he'd gotten a text from Dax bright and early, one that had ignited his guilt and fears anew. Based on Ava's examination, the spell wasn't just some temporary deal—if they didn't find a way to undo it and fast, the shifters would eventually be stuck in their animal forms.

He turned the music up a little louder in his car, as though the sound might drown out the way they were both buzzing.

Lana wrinkled her nose. "Are you listening to smooth jazz? That shit is like nails on a chalkboard."

A laugh escaped him while he raced down the highway. "I play sax and do some freeform with bands when I can jam."

The heated look she passed him almost had him swerving on the road. "I might be willing to give it a second chance to watch you in action. My musical preferences veer toward electronica."

Lucas let out a groan. "*Dios mio*, of course I'd end up with someone who hates real instruments." A second later, Lana jabbed him in the side, and he couldn't help the grin rising to his lips. No matter what troubles they faced, for once, he felt good. Supported, even. Shit, after the marathon sex and the emotional outpouring that had happened last night, he'd been reborn.

Beaver Tavern cut its mark along the side of the road, the inch of snow on the roof adding to the cozy appearance. The interior lights were on even though their OPEN neons remained off. The snow piled around the edges of the gravel parking lot, a scraped-together clean-up after the sudden fall they'd had last night. He spotted Dax's car among the mix, as well as a few he couldn't identify. While he wheeled his car over the gravel, his nerves paraded in at a marching beat.

Even though this was a pack problem, he'd been the lead on this mission. He hadn't anticipated Ganzorig's moves, and now the Red Rock and Silver Springs packs had suffered because of his bad call.

Lana placed a hand on his arm. "You are a good leader, Luc. Even if the answers aren't clear right now, I trust you'll make the best choices possible given the situation. You have instincts and experience on your side."

He shook his head. "How do you do that? You seem to know what I'm feeling at any given moment."

Lana shrugged. "Gift and curse, I suppose. Blame yourself for being so easy to read."

A grin tugged at his lips as he slipped out from the driver's side of the car. Lana snagged the pile of papers she'd brought along with her and followed suit. They headed for the entrance. He'd spent so long bolstering himself that he'd never realized the blissful relief of support—maybe even he could lean on someone.

When he stepped inside Beaver Tavern, the sounds of a full bar washed over him, low murmurs, loud shouts and the clink of glasses. Except this wasn't the usual regulars enjoying a night out—this was preparation for war.

Amidst the shifters from both packs striding through the place in their human forms, Ally and Drew were curled up by the fireplace in the back while Betty prowled through the aisles. Kyle slumped in the corner of the room, fast asleep. Josie, the part-timer from Red Rock, had stepped in to cover his shifts behind the bar. Jer sat beside Raven, who kept reaching down to run her fingers through his russet fur. Everyone brimmed with the same bucket of nerves they were all saddled with—at the looming deadline that could spell the fate of these shifters.

Ava perched on one of the tables, her legs dangling over the wooden edge as she flipped through stacks and stacks of books around her. Sierra sat at one of the cleared tables next to Dax, hunched close in deep conversation. As the door clicked shut, a couple of gazes flickered their way. Lucas nodded at the familiar faces before heading toward their in-house shaman.

"I'll be there in a minute," Lana said before she passed him the papers. "Give these to Ava and see if they help. They were those notes of Ganzorig's we pulled from the boathouse."

He clutched the papers tightly while Lana jogged over to where Ally and Drew were curled up. She slammed to the floor in front of them and circled her arms around the mountain lions, drawing both of them in for a hug.

The rift between her and Drew seemed to have dissolved in the wake of everything that happened, and he couldn't help the twist of admiration in his chest. After what had occurred between them, he wouldn't blame Lana for hating Drew for the rest of her life, but the woman held an immense capacity for healing in all regards. Lucas strode to where Ava sat mid-table, concentrating, her glasses sliding so far down her nose they were an inch from falling off.

"Have any idea what sort of mojo Ganzorig pulled?" Lucas asked upon approach.

Ava's head shot up so fast she almost tumbled off the table. "Spirits, the lot of you sneak around way too quietly. I'm going to make you all start wearing bells to announce your presence." She resettled at the edge of the table and began swinging her legs back and forth. "The what was easy to figure out, but I'm just stuck on the how. Shaman spells each have their own imprint, and this wasn't one he pulled out of his ass. He must've spent a fair amount of time crafting it. Based on my estimation, we've got a week before our furry friends are stuck that way for good."

His gut clenched at the reminder as he handed over the research Lana brought along. "Maybe this'll help."

Ava scanned the papers over and hummed. "This is good. Now, shoo. I'm not going to get anything done with the way you guys keep interrupting my focus."

Lucas let out a snort at the brazen balls on this woman. Few talked to the Tribe like that, yet she didn't even seem to register who stood before her. He headed over to where Lana was talking with Dax, needing to do something. Ganzorig was out there in Ricketts Glen still, but he wouldn't be leaving until he found the device he'd come here for. Guaranteed, he was hiding out in the cave, so they needed to find an alternate route inside.

He stepped beside Lana, resting his hand on her shoulder on instinct.

Dax's gaze followed the motion, and his eyes flashed. The Silver Springs alpha didn't even pay attention to him, focusing on Lana.

"Greg hasn't even been buried a year," Dax murmured, his voice low and filled with biting judgement. "And you're already moving on? You know he's Tribe. He can't stay."

A growl ripped from Lucas' throat, loud enough that the rest of the bar silenced. Rage burned deep in his chest, the match lit. Lana's shoulders deflated, and his teeth turned to fangs. A deep, primal anger gripped him, bred from the connection that had emerged between them, stronger than any he'd felt in his life.

Dax's gaze flickered to his, but the Silver Springs alpha didn't look away.

Lana straightened, even though she didn't move his hand from her shoulder. She glanced to him. "It's okay, I've got this," she mouthed, a cool fury radiating from her. She faced her alpha with her chin lifted. "What am I supposed to do, Dax? Live in solitude and wither away more and more every year? I've been dying ever since Greg did, and Lucas has been the first person to offer a breath of life."

He swallowed hard at the way her words echoed through the room, at the truth they'd both danced around. He hadn't realized how much he'd desiccated until she'd suffused him with the feelings he'd long buried.

Dax opened his mouth and shut it. He let out a short breath. "We need you both focused. Distractions are how shit like this happened. We might lose some of our most important pack members because of this misstep." He gestured around the room to Ally and Drew, who were locked in their animal forms, potentially forever if they didn't find a fix. Sierra pushed herself from the table with some effort, her gaze darkening as she approached her mate. Before anyone could say anything, Dax ran his hand through his hair. "I'm going to take a beat." He headed for the back room of the tavern, and Sierra followed close behind.

Lana turned to Lucas and placed her hand on his chest, even as everyone's stares burned into them. The sheer strength she'd displayed had him wordless. Not just anyone would go toe to toe with their alpha.

"Dax is hurting." She kept her voice low, so others couldn't hear. "He was being a dick, but Greg was his best friend." She shrugged, attempting to be cavalier even though her gaze swept the floor. "I knew someone would have a problem. I'm going to drive home and do what I can to keep sorting through the files we got from Greg's office. You do your big bad Tribe thing, okay?"

Lucas passed her the keys to his car, trailing his fingers across the pulse of her wrist. "I won't be long," he murmured. "You call me if you need anything."

"I think I'm going to take your advice," she said. "Maybe make a detour on the way back."

His heart twisted in his chest when she left, like she'd taken it along with her. With the way he'd fallen, maybe she had.

As the door creaked shut and Lana left, murmurs broke through the room again, though he collected more than a couple of curious looks.

Lucas sucked in a deep breath, trying to get his tiger to settle. Part of him wanted to race to the back of the bar and slam Dax's head through a wall. His claws kept trying to prick out. However, he'd come here to rally what remained of their troops to face Ganzorig. He might've let the shaman get away once, but he wouldn't again. While Ava raced against the clock to find a fix for their pack members, he had another solution in mind—the spell might not hold if the shaman was dead.

"Okay, crew," Lucas called in his Tribe voice, the sound booming through the enclosed space. "Gather around. We have an attack to plan."

Chapter Fifteen

Lana sat behind the steering wheel of a car that wasn't hers, and if that didn't just sum up her life right now, she didn't know what did.

She raced across the asphalt, the sun flickering through the overhead trees and glistening on the fresh coat of snow spanning either side of her. A year ago, this hadn't been her life. A year ago, she'd been happily married with simpler plans of starting a family with Greg, nights out at the bars with Ally and throwing herself into her massage practice and EMT shifts.

She'd been changing from the day Greg died, and when Lucas had crashed into her life, she'd veered onto a different road altogether. Those old dreams belonged to someone else, and her chest burned with stoked coals threatening to set fire to something brand new.

Her grip tightened on the steering wheel the closer she got to the cemetery. Dax's words echoed in her head again and again and again. They were the same ones she'd repeated from the moment she'd begun to feel something for Lucas, since the first flash of attraction had filtered through her veins. Yet it wasn't until she'd heard those words out loud from her alpha's lips that she realized how ridiculous they were.

Greg had died, and a part of her would always belong to him. But if she didn't find a way to move on, she'd be sentencing herself to an early grave. From a young age, she'd always needed closeness and touch. She'd needed people, and Lucas had been the first person to bridge the gap. He didn't look at her with sad eyes, or like she might break. He let her be.

Her heart thundered in her ears as the sign for Hook Cemetery came into view, white letters on battered metal.

The gravestones lay a short walk away from the beaten patch of grass that had become the parking lot, covered in snow. Lana pulled into place and shut the car off, but her limbs weren't moving.

Her mouth tasted tart, like the cranberry vodka Ally had given her a shot of before she'd exited the car on the day of Greg's funeral.

There had been so many tears.

Hers, his parents, the members of the pack. Their emotions had crashed over her like a tidal wave until she was drowning, drowning, drowning. The entire day remained a blur for her, her limbs numb while Ally and Dax had tugged her around like a broken doll. They'd lowered her husband's body into the ground. Covered his casket with dirt. And she'd just watched.

Lana sucked in a sharp breath. Her entire body shook. If she didn't get out now, she never would. She unclicked her safety belt, the sound echoing through the car, and exited. The snow crunched beneath her boots, and the chill iced her cheeks that were already numb. Her eyes pulsed with phantom tears as she headed down the beaten trail covered in pure white. Her muddy boots sullied the path as she approached.

She bypassed the other tombstones in differing shades of gray, heading for the one she could identify even if she were blindfolded. This trek was seared into her memories. Greg's tombstone had been a square, modern one, black-colored granite. She made her way over to the grave by powers unknown, because she was half a shade sure her mind had departed several miles back. She stood in front of the grave then sank to the ground, unable to keep herself upright.

Her knees dug into the slush of snow, but even the cold permeating her bones didn't come close to the cold she felt at seeing the name printed on the tombstone, every damn time. She'd been avoiding this journey, because she knew no matter how many secrets emerged about Greg, it didn't tip the scales of the years of good he'd done in her life.

"Hey, baby," she murmured, digging her fingers into the snow before her. The ice sent a shudder through her that felt a lot like a sob. "You left a big mess behind, you know? I wish you could've told me some of this — any of it really." She paused, staring at the granite. *Not like I'll get a response.* Wind whistled through the tombstones.

"And I want to be so mad," she continued, spearing the snow with her fingers. "But I fucking miss your laugh so badly. I miss making coffee for us every morning because you were always shit at waking up. I miss the dinners at your folks' and going to sit and talk at Zip's for hours to argue about zombie survival plans or what new gossip was going down in our pack."

Lana opened her mouth, knowing what she needed to say next, but the words wouldn't come. She needed to. She needed to do this. Tears broke free at last, the familiar heat stinging her eyes. "Baby, I found someone." She leaned forward to stare at the ground, her breaths coming out in rasps. "And he's a good, kind man. I think you would like him a lot."

She looked up, her nails forming claws when she dug them deeper into the ground, as if somehow she'd be able to reach in and pull him out. As if somehow she'd be able to speak to Greg one last time.

"Is this okay?" she asked, her voice breaking. The tears ran freely down her cheeks at that point, heat that froze in the wake of the bitter cold of the place. "Can I move on?" was all she managed before lapsing into silence as the sobs racked her body. She trembled, from the wind, from her tears, at the sight of Greg's tombstone before her, as permanent and forbidding as the day they'd installed it.

She curled forward, sinking to the ground until her forehead touched the snow, the blinding cold brushing against her skin. Her shoulders shook and all she could do was surrender to the grief she'd never left behind. Not truly. Silence reigned in the lonely cemetery. The sun beat on her hair, her back, even while the cold, barren ground greeted her. Harsh, ragged breaths escaped her throat as she waited.

For an answer.

For a sign.

Except nothing answered back. The wintry winds continued to curl around her and the morning sun pounded down, unceasing. Because they didn't stop for tragedy. Even though her world had shattered last summer, the seasons continued to turn. The leaves

Katherine McIntyre

crumpled in autumn and they were hidden under the winter snows. Everything had continued moving after Greg died.

Even she had, though slow and unsteady at first.

Her throat squeezed tight when she pushed herself from the ground. She reached out to run her fingers along the tombstone, as if she could touch him.

"Baby, you're still with me," she murmured, needing him to somehow know that. "I might have found someone, but you're always going to be a part of my life." She could never forget his warmth, like the sun, and how he'd thrown his whole body into hugs. His confidence had infected her when they were kids and led her to chase after dreams, whether starting a horror club in high school or becoming a massage therapist because she wanted to help people.

He had been a large part of the beginning of her life, and he would always be with her, every time she sang rock songs off-key or smelled the forsythia in the spring. But she couldn't end here. Not yet.

A car door slammed from over where she'd parked, but she couldn't bring herself to look behind her. The footsteps pounded through the area, someone moving at a light jog. Her nails turned to claws and she tensed. The steps were growing louder in her direction.

"Lana," a familiar voice called out, but she didn't relax.

Instead, she straightened from where she knelt, rising to a crouch. "Come to make sure I'm properly flogging myself, Dax?"

Her alpha stopped in front of her, his shoulders heaving. His cap was tipped down, and sweat glistened on his neck since he must've done some running. His normally smiling eyes were as serious as the stones

166

surrounding them. They stood in perfect stillness, staring at each other in the hushed quiet, two predators unwilling to budge. At least, until Dax closed the space between them and threw his arms around her. He drew her in tight with a ferocity that conveyed everything.

"I'm so sorry, Lannie," Dax murmured into her shoulder. "I was out of line."

Some tightness in her loosened at hearing those words. Dax had always been closer to Greg back in the day, while she'd confided her deep darks to Drew and Ally. But he was her alpha, her childhood friend. He meant a whole damn lot to her, and part of her needed them to be okay.

"You were. Out of line, that is." She somehow found her voice, even though they were standing in front of Greg's grave like they had back on that day. "Dax, if I don't move forward, you might as well bury me now. I've been so alone in my house that I've been withering away."

He pulled away from her and tugged at the brim of his cap, a sheepish look in his eyes. "I know, I know. And you have every right to move on. It was just— seeing you with Lucas, when it had always been you and Greg... Everything's changing so much right now, and I snapped." He slipped his hand through Lana's and squeezed tight.

She passed him a look. "You're going to be an amazing dad, Dax. I wish Greg could've been here to meet your little one too." Her throat tightened. Greg would've adored the hellion Dax and Sierra were going to raise.

He gave her a nudge in the side before he rubbed at his nose, glancing away. "I swear, every time. How did he ever get anything past you?"

She shrugged, a shiver of sadness rolling through her. "Obviously he did, between working for the Landsliders, stealing their Doomsday device and hiding the fact that his business was failing."

Dax let out a low whistle. "I know. If he were here, he would've gotten a fist to the face, and we could be done with the drama. Instead, I'm left with this tangle inside. Part of me wants to forgive him so bad, but every time I broach the idea, my issues with Drew crack wide open."

Lana tugged back on his hand. The sunlight soaked into her skin even though it ached from the cold. "Maybe that would be a good thing. There was always more going on under the surface between him and your dad. But that's a conversation for the two of you to have."

Dax let out a shaky breath. His blue eyes grew glassy while he stared at Greg's grave. "I don't want to let him go."

Lana leaned against her alpha, her old friend, lending him her strength. "You don't have to. I'm not. Greg will forever be a part of our lives and our pack."

Dax offered a sidelong glance. "You tell the others I choked up, and there'll be consequences." He dragged a finger across his throat, and the ghost of a smile rose to his lips.

She snorted. "Like that'd be a shocker to anyone. Remember, we were all there when you bawled your eyes out watching *Braveheart*. Or *Die Hard 2*. Or any other action flick we put on at movie night. Seriously, man. Get it together."

The droll tone was pure Greg, the way they'd always ribbed at each other, and Dax's grin wavered for a heartbeat. At least, until laughter exploded from him, as vibrant as sunlight. His shoulders shook, and she couldn't help but lose it too. The laughs choked in her throat until she wheezed, leaning forward and slapping her frozen palm to her sodden thigh.

Their laughter filled the empty air, echoing through the solitary cemetery as if the sound sliced through the crowds of ghosts. Her mirth permeated her with warmth the way he always had, as if he roamed between them, a glint in his eyes and a quick joke on his lips. Greg's legacy would live on through them — through the stories they'd tell, the old quirks and their treadworn jokes.

Lana lifted her chin to stare at the broad horizon, the sun casting stark rays over the spindly trees and the sparkling fields of snow. For the first time since her husband had died, her path stretched before her again, waiting to be walked. The road might be difficult, but even though she'd lost her best friend and her first love, she wasn't alone. Not only did she have a family she loved and the promise of a new adventure with Lucas, but Greg was still with her along the way.

Lana squeezed Dax's shoulder. "We'll carry him with us."

Chapter Sixteen

Lucas had managed to wrangle members of the pack into a reputable search team to scan the perimeter around Ricketts Glen where they'd found the cave. Burning his irritation with a run through the woods had done him good, even if they weren't closer to finding another way in. Ganzorig couldn't have disappeared inside, so the tunnels had to lead somewhere—they just hadn't scoured enough of the territory yet. Regardless, he wouldn't stop until he'd found a way to undo the spell trapping the Red Rock and Silver Springs members as mountain lions and wolves. They only had a week before they got locked in their animal forms for good.

He stepped out of Beaver Tavern to where Lana had returned his car earlier—she'd caught a ride back to her house. Lucas had settled into the Explorer when a text from her pinged on his phone.

I've got a lead on the device. Meet me at the Phoenix Lodge.

Lucas floored it across the highway in the direction of the lodge. He left his window cracked so the cold air filtered through, cooling the sweat on his skin and clearing his clouded mind. After everything that had happened in the past week, he hadn't taken a second to sit and breathe with the events. A mere text from Lana had him grinning like an idiot. Despite the chaos, the setbacks and the nightmare of the spell Ganzorig had cast, he had fallen hard for Lana.

He tapped his fingers on the steering wheel. Even if they weren't mates, he'd fight for this newborn relationship. She was the plummet out of a plane into oblivion, yet at the same time the steady earth he landed on. The fascinating woman consumed his thoughts, and he treasured every second they spent together. He couldn't predict the future—his life had always been as wild and capricious as a tempest—but he didn't want one without her.

The sun began to set, hazy smears of crimson and indigo across the sky. Already, the moon watched overhead, a delicate orb that would intensify when night fell. His heart pounded faster as he drove nearer to the lodge. Each second brought him closer to her, and he craved the peace and the thrill like he craved the summer in January.

The music on the radio washed over him, sweet notes that hit with a deeper resonance than before. His fingers itched for an instrument, whether the sax or a guitar, even though he kept his good saxophone at his folks' place in Arizona. Most instruments didn't travel well—not when his car could get ambushed by enemies and he'd be toting them in and out of their rotating motels.

His stay in Lana's home had been his first respite in far too long.

In the distance, the carved wooden sign for the Phoenix Lodge came into view, a facility used outside of town by humans and shifters alike — he'd caught the pamphlets plastered all over Dusty Pines Motel. A winding road traveled into the shadows of tall, towering trees, and he took the turn, plunging down the beaten path.

A massive lodge of lacquered pinewood stood out at the end of the path, the windows lit by single candles casting cozy rays. A long, elevated porch stretched out across the front, framed by a balcony railing of more polished wooden beams. The coating of snow overtop made the place look like it had been plucked out of a catalog. All it needed was a smokestack puffing charcoal into the air and an old lady knitting in one of the rockers out front. He veered up the drive to where a parking lot sprawled out, half-filled with cars.

He pulled in to park and hopped out of his car, tugging the lapels of his coat tighter to shield out the breezes painting his skin with ice. At the end of the driveway, he caught a familiar figure leaning against the back end of her car. The mere sight of her lodged his heart in his throat.

Even with the thick peacoat wrapped around her, Lana's curves couldn't be disguised. He could still feel the glide of his fingers across her silken skin. She'd pulled her hair into a loose chignon and her eyes lit at the sight of him. He loved that she didn't even bother to hide how she felt, her excitement plastered all over her expression.

Lucas crossed the space between them and circled his arms around her. She leaned into him, and he brought her close, basking in the sheer relief. The wintry breezes sharpened her scent of citrus and rose, one he was fast coming to treasure.

"I missed you," she said, as if affection could be so easy, as though they'd stumbled on something true and real. The simplicity of her statement humbled him, the words profound after a lifetime on the road.

"Every second since you left the tavern," he murmured into her hair, squeezing her tighter to his chest. A hushed awe clung to his words, that he could admit them out loud. Ever since she'd unlocked him, he spilled out for her to see, terrifying and exhilarating all in the same breath. He leaned in to brush a kiss to her lips, trying to tamp down the hunger that swept through him at the mere touch.

She skated her fingers across his neck and returned the kiss with an intensity that made him want to bend her over and take her against the hood of her car. Lana pulled away, trailing her tongue over her lips.

"On task, Diaz," she teased him, her eyes glittering with the same desire. She sucked in a breath, and her gaze darkened. "I visited his grave earlier. Dax showed up too, and that's what gave me the idea."

He leaned against the hood of the car beside her, his full attention zeroing in on her every movement, every word from her mouth. Spirits above, he had it bad.

Lana pulled out a small clay dove that fit in her palm. "They were the favors for our wedding, which we held here. Greg kept this in his desk along with his papers, and I'd nabbed it when we'd gone to his business. I was so mad at him for keeping so much from me that I didn't even think of the hiding place we had here, back by the woods."

His heart wrung tight. The love she felt for her late husband was warm in her words, clear in her eyes, and yet she still leaned in against him with her hand clasped over his.

"Well, what are we waiting for?" he said, pushing up from the car. "Let's go check this spot out."

Lana nodded. She slunk past him, heading toward the edge of the lodge which opened to a broad field silhouetted by the woods, tall pines standing like guardian sentinels. He kept pace with ease as they reached the fringes of the snow-covered field, his boots crunching down on the solid sheet. Lana glanced to him, and her lips quirked with a grin.

"Tag, you're it." She smacked him in the arm and bolted off.

His jaw dropped. *Is she really — yeah, yeah she is.* A second later, he tore after her, a laugh ripping from him unbidden. He kicked up a spray of snow while he chased her, his tiger lunging to the surface. Even in the thick of the night that fell, stretching the shadows to sprawl across the field, she became pure sunlight.

He darted after her, reaching forward to tap her on the shoulder. She let out a startled noise and whipped around, shock flashing on her face. Another laugh escaped him as she dove forward, and he sidestepped with fluid ease. His heart felt lighter than it had in years while he spun circles around her, closer and closer to the woods. She kicked a spray of snow at him, and he lifted his hands to block. Flakes flew past, pinpricks of cold along his cheeks and chin. His shoulders shook with laughter. This was the sort of play he'd never gotten to experience. Not only had he been an eldest brother, but he'd run missions for the Tribe even at an early age.

He skidded back, and she lunged again, reaching out to grab him.

Lucas drew her closer to the woods, to the rich pine wafting their way, carried by the crisp winds. Lana slowed for a moment, stalking with a predatory gleam in her eyes which was pure mountain lion. She prowled forward, one step, then another, changing direction each time.

He wove back and forth too, following the same principle to never let her know which way he'd be going.

Her lips twitched with that damnable smile. She didn't care about winning in the slightest — she was simply having fun.

She sprang forward, all muscles and poise.

Lana launched for him, but he didn't want to move out of the way. Lucas reached and caught her as she descended, slipping his hands around her waist. She thudded against his chest, and he stumbled back even as he tightened his grip on her. He dipped down to claim her lips again, crushing his mouth to hers.

Lana slipped her tongue in to caress his and melted against him.

He let out a rumble of a groan while he pulled away. "We've got to get to the woods, and if this continues, I'm liable to take you right here."

She bit her lip, her eyes gleaming like fire against glass. "Tease," she said, before she slunk forward, stepping into the shadows of the forest. Based on the pendulum swing of her hips, he wasn't the only one teasing. He followed her into the forest where patches of pine needles and parched earth peeked out. The trees had blocked the snow from coating this section, and as they prowled deeper in, the rich loam and the crisp juniper threaded through the air.

"Would he have just placed the device somewhere in the woods?" Lucas asked, his voice echoing in the winter quiet.

Lana glanced back. "If it was a hole in the woods, no. Any animal could dig it up, and this is private property anyway. We're trespassing, Mr. Lawman."

Lucas rolled his eyes and quickened his pace to walk in line with her. "Shifter law governs pack lines, not human property. So, then, where's the hiding spot?"

Lana wrinkled her nose and crouched, sniffing the air as she tried to catch a scent. Even in this form, their senses were more adept than a human's. She thrust a finger to the right. "That way." She wove through the trees with a grace that had him alert to follow, and after they'd walked several more feet, she crouched again in front of a massive conifer surrounded by dried pine needles and cones.

"It's here," she said, lifting her fingers. "Get ready to dig." Her nails shifted to claws, and she sent the debris flying behind her. Lucas crouched, changing his own nails to claws as he helped. They hadn't dug more than a couple of inches before his tips clanged against a flat pane of metal. Lana nudged him out of the way and lifted the remaining handfuls of dirt to brush the metal top of what looked like a box.

"So, you did just bury stuff in a hole in the woods," Lucas said, resting his elbows on his knees.

Lana pursed her lips. "Yes, smartass. But Greg placed the box out here to keep the gift he'd gotten me safe. He had wanted to surprise me. So, over the years, we ended up using this for other special occasions." Her hand paused on the latch.

Lucas met her gaze, understanding at once. "If it's not here, we'll keep searching."

She sucked in a shaky breath. "Yeah, I know. I guess part of me is hoping even while Greg was mired in all of his Landslider bullshit, that our relationship still meant something to him." She glanced away for a second to blink, hard, but then her fingers found the latch again.

Lana flipped the lid open.

Inside lay a rectangular platinum box, wires looped around it with an array of smooth buttons on the side and a black switch on the end.

A laugh escaped him, followed by another one, until his chest squeezed tight and his shoulders shook. Lana looked at him, forehead creased, and he cackled like a lunatic.

He managed to gasp in some breaths to settle himself. "I'm realizing now, the one person who knows what this device even looks like is trapped in his mountain lion form."

Lana's confusion melted into amusement. Her eyes crinkled as she reached down and pulled out the box. "Ace planning on our part. Well, just in case it is said Doomsday device, I promise not to press any buttons or flip the big switch."

He pushed up from his crouch and offered a hand to Lana until he realized hers were both full carrying the box. "Let's head to the house. If we've got the device they're searching for, we have the exact lure we need to drag Ganzorig out of his lair."

Chapter Seventeen

After her back and forth bumper-car day, Lana latched on to Raven's *'Grab a drink?'* text like a lifeline. Lucas had driven to the Red Rock cabin to show Sierra and Dax the potential Doomsday box they'd found, and she was buzzing far too much to focus on anything at home.

Lucas was determined to draw Ganzorig out, but some of their best fighters remained trapped in their animal forms. And if they didn't hurry and Ganzorig escaped again, the others could be stuck that way for good. Her throat pinched at the thought of never having another conversation with Ally.

She pulled up to Beaver Tavern, which had cozy amber beams glowing out of the windows. At this point of the night, only a few cars remained in the lot. Lana tugged on the end of her ponytail as she approached the bar, the rich scents of smoke emanating here from where Gene and a couple of others liked to sneak out and grab a cigarette. Guilt plucked a chord inside her —

she should be doing something, anything, but right then, she didn't know how to help.

Lana opened the door and strode inside. Josie leaned behind the bar, but Raven wasn't sitting in any of their normal spots by the stools. Before she could look elsewhere, a mountain lion she'd have recognized anywhere prowled over to nudge her in the leg. Lana ran a hand through Ally's fur, her chest tightening at the sight of her friend trapped in this form. She couldn't imagine the terror gripping them right now at not being able to shift with ease.

Ally led her over to the round table in the corner of the room where Ava and Raven were parked with a pitcher of foamy dark beer and so many notebooks and textbooks that the surface couldn't contain them all. Raven looked at Lana and mouthed '*Help.*'

"I saw that," Ava said, pushing her glasses up her nose even though she didn't look away from the book she was skimming over. "You offered to research with me. Just because we changed venues to the bar doesn't mean it's going to be all suds and smiles."

Raven snorted and reached down to pat Jer on the head, who slept curled by her feet. "Don't have to tell me that twice. I'm normally all about silence to focus, but these spell books are half-chicken-scratch, half-angry Greenpeace rants. I called in Lana to offer vocal assistance."

Ava cast them both a librarian's glare from above her glasses. "If you two start jabbering away over pints, I'll put all this shaman power to the better use of a muzzle."

Lana grinned and took one of the open seats, reaching past a stack of old papers tethered together by electronics cables. Betty lay fast asleep in the corner of the tavern while Kyle prowled from table to table, filled with the same restless energy that buzzed through all of them. Drew paced across the weathered planks as well, and his umber gaze flared when he glanced at her. Lana sucked in a sharp breath. She needed to find a way to free them. Somehow.

Ally stepped up to Drew and nudged him in the side. He stopped pacing and rubbed against her, his hackles lowering as he seemed to calm a fraction. Lana understood all too well how touch grounded in the wake of grief or fear.

"Before I dive in blind," Lana started, pouring herself a pint from the pitcher, "why don't you explain to me how this spell works? Otherwise, I'm going to be pulling out my hair in minutes."

Ava looked up from the book she was scanning, and Raven let out a groan.

"Her explanation's going to be all shaman-babble mixed with techno-geek. You're not going to understand a second of it," Raven warned. She pursed her lips before offering a coy wink to Ava. "Which is why we love you oh so much, Ava."

Ava crooked an eyebrow. "Quit flirting, gorgeous. I'm already committed to the cause by the lure of cold hard cash." She closed the book over her finger to save the spot. "From what I've been able to tell so far, it's not like Ganzorig eliminated their human side—it's just blocked."

"Well, the shamans created the original spell binding animal spirits to humans, the ones that created humans. What triggers the shift if not conscious choice?" Lana asked. Curiosity took the wheel. As a massage therapist and EMT, she had plenty of experience working on humans and shifters alike, and the differences in physiology were still being explored.

"What about fear? Extreme emotion?" Raven jumped in. "You know, when we're in a heightened situation and our nails shift to claws without prompting?"

Ava passed Raven an arch look. "Well, yes, the animal is connected intrinsically to the human and those base impulses. Since it's a protective force, any threats will push the animal side to the fore." She pursed her lips and heaved a sigh before picking up a pint and taking a sip. "All right, Takahashi, you've got my attention for some chatter time."

Lana took a sip of the creamy porter, the liquid calming her nerves as it slid down her throat. Her mind was racing a thousand miles a minute, but like this, she felt useful at least.

"He could be amplifying the stress response to keep them in their animal side, at least until his spell takes hold for good," Ava mused, placing her pint on the table. She tossed the book she was holding to the ground, and it hit with a reverberating *thump*. Ava tugged a different textbook from the stack, this one on physiology.

Lana chewed on her lip. Stress response was her forte—she'd been calming people down for years with massage. "Would the opposite turn them back?" she asked, running her fingertips across the papers in front of her. "A sedative or a way to place them into the parasympathetic?"

Ava glanced at her, those dark eyes sharp as a shiv. "Well now, there's a suggestion."

"You think that might work?" Raven asked, the urgency in her voice spurred by the desperation that must have burrowed deep. Her mate was one of those stuck, and Lana could grasp quite clearly the bone-deep fear of loss Raven must be going through.

Ava pushed a notebook into Raven's hands. "You're going to be jotting things down. I was thinking about this in terms of spells, bindings, enchantments, but I think we might've found ourselves a tail to chase."

Lana's heart thumped in anticipation, hope sinking claws into her chest. "What can I do to help?"

Ava handed her a pharmacy textbook. "Since you seem to have some basic medical training, you're going to look up the sedatives. I brought a stash of supplies with me, so we'll be able to at least try."

Lana had begun flipping through once the weight of the hardback sank into her palms. The mostly full porter lay forgotten next to her on the table, and she focused on the print lining the pages. Anticipation dried on her tongue. After the helplessness that had sliced her to ribbons in the wake of Ganzorig's spell, she sped into action.

She cast a glance to Ally and Drew, who had settled side by side along the corner of the room. Her heart squeezed tight. For a moment, the years melted away like sunlight on the snow. All the damage and hurt faded in the wake of the warm memories of the adventures they'd gone on, the dumb arguments, late night horror movies and drinking shitty vodka in the woods together. Lana swallowed hard.

She would find a way to break them free from this spell.

* * * *

The next morning, a knock sounded on the door, bright and early.

Lucas rose from his seat in Lana's kitchen and placed his cup of coffee on the table with a clink. She still lay asleep upstairs, and after the late hour she'd arrived home from her visit to Beaver Tavern, he wasn't about to wake her. Ava had banished her from the bar when she'd fallen asleep over a book for the dozenth time, especially after she drooled on the pages. Vigilance filtered into his veins as he strode to the door, the sort driven into him at a young age. He slunk up and peered out of the peephole.

A grin rose to his lips, and he flung the door open.

Drew stood on the doorstep, on two feet, with his hands jammed in his pockets. He wore his aviators, and his blond hair glinted gold in the early morning light. "Sorry for the unannounced arrival. After Raven and Lana left, Ava managed to come up with the right cocktail to turn us back. I paid Dax a visit, and he filled me in on what's going on."

Lucas took two paces forward and threw his arms around the man. Drew froze, as if Lucas had tossed a mean right hook, but a moment later he relaxed and squeezed tight.

"I'm sorry," Lucas said, the words coming out in a rough scrape. He hadn't realized how much he'd gotten used to running through abandoned houses and investigating spots with the ex-Landslider until this had happened. They worked well as a team, but more than that, over the late nights grabbing a beer and shooting the shit, the long car drives talking about nonsense, they'd formed a real friendship. For Lucas, those were rare.

Drew shook his head as they separated, and he clapped a hand on his shoulder. "You've got nothing to apologize for, man. I needed some quality time with my mountain lion anyway, and Ava's been hard at work since she arrived. She's started putting together a way to separate the blood compulsion from the Landsliders' mark."

Lucas crooked an eyebrow and leaned against the door frame. "Do you mean you might be able to resist Mackey's compulsion?"

The steps creaked as Lana approached, rubbing the sleep from her eyes. In her off-shoulder sweater and yoga pants, with a drowsy look on her face, she was pure sex. Lucas couldn't help the way his pulse sped or his libido kickstarted at the mere sight of her.

"Who's here?" she asked before stepping next to him. She blinked in surprise. "It worked? Ava got you guys turned back?"

Drew leaned against the doorframe, a grin sliding onto his face. "Thanks to yours and Raven's help. Ava's bunkered away in the Red Rock cabin now, snoring away in the guest bedroom. She threatened pox on the first person to try to wake her up."

Lana nodded even though her enthusiasm retreated to caution, and Lucas slipped a hand on her shoulder, needing to connect with her somehow. Needing to show he understood.

Lana drew a shaky breath. "Both of you are letting all the cold air in. Come on inside, Drew. We can put a pot of coffee on."

Lucas didn't miss the careful way she phrased her words or how she looked expectantly at him. This was a big deal, an olive branch offered after everything that had shattered between them.

"Thanks, Sunshine," he said, offering a tentative grin—a rare sight on the normally guarded smartass. He stepped in, bringing the door shut behind him.

"Ally's heading over here soon too. She wanted to swing home to water her plants first."

Lana lifted an eyebrow. "You two looked cozy at Beaver Tavern." The way she talked had an ease to it, despite the tension in the air, as though they'd stepped into a past dimension. Even as an outsider, Lucas could feel it brimming between them. After everything that had happened and all Drew had done, Lana was trying to forgive him as best she could.

Lucas led the way to the kitchen, letting go of Lana's shoulder. "I already brewed a pot, so help yourselves." He couldn't ignore the accelerated thump of his heart. Lana's gaze rested on him, those eyes glowing with a warmth he couldn't imagine life without.

Drew swept past her to pluck a mug from the cabinets, knowing the spot without question. He glanced her way. "You know Ally's done with me. She was done before and is especially done now."

Lana poured herself a mug and blew at the surface of her piping hot coffee. She shrugged. "I don't think Ally even knows what she wants, Drew. I wouldn't count her out unless she finds her mate."

He didn't miss Drew's near-imperceptible glance away before he reached to pour himself a mug. Lucas leaned in beside Lana and grabbed his cup of coffee. He wrapped an arm around Lana's shoulders and let out a sigh of relief. After his initial plans had crumbled in the cave, he hadn't known how he would sort out this mess.

However, the pieces were coming together. The players were back in place.

Drew cast a glance at the two of them, a genuine smile rolling to his lips. "I see that finally happened."

Lana's forehead creased and she tensed. After Dax's response, he couldn't blame her.

Drew's grin softened. "I think Greg would've approved. You've got a knack for picking the best people, Sunshine."

Lucas could've reached out to hug the man again. After their hesitation moving forward and all the minefields of her husband's passing, encouragement from someone who had once been a close friend meant all the more. Her eyes grew glassy and she nodded.

Lucas squeezed her shoulder. "I'm going to grab the device. Let's hope this is the one we've all been searching for." He stepped away from the loaded silence in the room, letting Lana process those feelings as he jogged to the trunk in the living room where they'd kept it since last night. He lifted the platinum box out, careful not to bump anything. This item would spell their demise when activated. If he wasn't worried about the backlash, he would have smashed the thing right here and now.

Drew approached on quiet footsteps. He let out a low whistle. "Yeah, that's the box these bastards have been searching for."

Lucas met his eyes. "Hope you're ready to bait Ganzorig." As their gazes met, they both understood the real target. They had a chance for this nightmare to all be over, if they could lure out Mackey Kendricks.

Chapter Eighteen

Dax's crew found the other entrance.

She and Lucas had found the device.

A confrontation was looming, and Lana couldn't help the fear coating her insides like tar. Lucas had planned and planned ad nauseum — he'd sent the challenge out to Ganzorig. They had the device and would bring it with them to the original entrance tomorrow morning. No one questioned if the shaman would respond, but Lana was worried because he wasn't the only one they were baiting.

Based on the shared glances between Drew and Lucas, they would use the lure of the device to draw the real monster out from the shadows. The man who'd been behind all the assaults to this region, from the bombs on their homes to the Coalition attack. The one who'd forced loyalty on her husband and Drew through compulsion. The one who had ordered Greg's murder.

Lana had walked about a hundred circles inside her house the moment she'd headed in for the night. The creaks were comforting, since she knew they came from her and not an outside source—not the Landsliders hunting down the device. Dax and Sierra were protecting it that night at the Red Rock cabin—her house would be too obvious a target.

Her mountain lion paced back and forth in her chest, working itself into a frenzy. She didn't catch the scent of another predator on the breeze, but she kept circling roundabouts on the same thoughts and tapping her fingertips along her forearms as she walked. Tonight was a powder keg. They'd lit the fuse and stepped back, but an explosion was imminent.

Lana headed for her kitchen, which was closer to her back door. As she strode forward, she couldn't ignore the prickle across her skin as if she was being watched. Déjà vu flashed through her, to the night Lucas had first arrived. Except this time, she didn't catch the scent of any shifters or hear the infernal scratching. She balled her hands into fists and summoned her courage, even though her imagination reeled into overdrive.

They just wanted the device. Not her.

Yet it was hard to use consolation logic when Greg had been murdered over this thing. Lana's mouth dried as she approached her porch. A thickness descended in the air around her, one that couldn't be natural. She stepped barefoot out onto the wooden planks, her toes numbing from a cold so deep it stole her breath. The screened windows displayed the length of her backyard, but no glowing stares returned hers. She didn't catch the flash of fur, even as she searched the woods through her mountain lion's eyes.

She lifted her leg to take a step back.

A creak sounded.

She hadn't moved yet.

Lana whipped around. The middle-aged man in her kitchen was average height, dressed like a city slicker with his thick inky hair carefully combed. A man she'd last seen in the cave at Ricketts Glen. His mouth moved with whatever incantation he kept in his arsenal.

These fuckers need to stop breaking into my house.

She didn't hesitate. Her nails turned to claws, and her skin began to mutate, the fur pricking to the surface. The shift overtook her. Switching into her other form was as simple as stepping into a bath. One moment, she stood on two feet, human, and the next she'd submerged into her mountain lion form. She bolted for the still-open porch door.

Ganzorig wandered through her house, alone. Guaranteed, he was searching for the box.

The moment she sailed through her door, those dark eyes focused on her. Ganzorig lifted his hands, and the floorboards trembled beneath her. Lana didn't care. Her rage burned fierce after the threats they'd left, after the way they'd broken in and destroyed her house and after they'd left her paranoid and violated. Her paws barely hit the ground while she raced for him, teeth bared.

Ganzorig's eyes widened when he realized she wasn't stopping. He scrambled toward her front door, kicking up the decorative carpet as he ran through her living room. *Not like he has a horde of Landsliders to hide behind now.* Lana chased after him, the pulse of the hunt a rising thrum within her. He wouldn't get an easy out from this confrontation tomorrow. He wasn't going to get his hands on the device Greg had died over.

Ganzorig raced for the door and yanked it open. She closed in on him, the distance between them growing shorter with every pace forward. While she was in this form, he didn't stand a chance of outrunning her. His boots slammed onto the porch out front, and he rattled down the steps. Lana sailed right by him with a snarl.

He threw his hands up, indistinguishable words flying from his lips in a sanctified stream. Her paws hit the withered grass right when green vines emerged from the ground and coiled around her limbs. A growl ripped from her as she yanked at the stubborn vines. Ganzorig didn't stop, bolting across the lawn at a speed she didn't think possible. She threw herself to the ground, using the force and momentum to tug the vines off her paws.

Once she broke free, she continued her chase. If she could end this here — if she could stop Ganzorig now — maybe the people she loved wouldn't be out there risking their lives tomorrow.

He vaulted into the silver Maserati parked farther down the street. She had made it halfway across the asphalt when the headlights flashed on and the engine rumbled to life. Even in her shifted form, the Maserati would win. Lana leaped to Marcy and Rick's lawn right as Joe Ganzorig rumbled forward, aiming the big metal beast right at her. His tires screeched when he veered through their circle at destructive speeds, the squeals echoing through the stark air.

Lana panted, rising to her feet again. The mixture of adrenaline, anger and fear had her needing to fight or tear into something. Ganzorig disappeared down the street and she headed home, padding across the withered grass and snow comprising her front lawn. Her door hung wide open.

The rumble of a car engine sounded again from down the street before Lana entered. She whipped around, her teeth bared in anticipation. The headlights were higher up, the sort belonging to an SUV she recognized the moment the Explorer came closer to pull into her lot. Lucas skidded to a halt and almost leaped out of the driver's seat, the slam of his car door reverberating through the air.

Some tether uncoiled inside her at the sight of him. She padded deeper into her house, the heat soaking past her fur. Lucas' footsteps echoed through the crisp night as he raced toward her—the man seemed to have a preternatural sense for when things went wrong. Either that, or he smelled the way magic reeked through her yard now.

She shifted to two feet, her bones transitioning and her eyes returning to normal. In this form, her senses dulled from the sharpness of her mountain lion. Her fur morphed to skin and her hair drifted down her back to brush against her shoulders again. Lucas didn't stop moving. He loped across the room until his hands were around her waist and he dragged her into a fierce embrace.

"What happened?" he asked, murmuring into her shoulder. He dipped his head to press a kiss to her chilled skin. The sheer relief she felt in his arms sometimes made her want to cry. It saturated her cold bones with warmth and suffused her beaten spirit with hope. Her feelings for Lucas were a raging blizzard and a hearth fire all in one breath.

"Ganzorig was snooping around to see if he could nab the device," she responded, collapsing into his arms. The heat he emanated was enough that she melted from the core out, her fingers and toes tingling. "Obviously, he left disappointed."

Lucas' shoulders sagged with relief. "Tomorrow," he whispered against her skin. "This will all stop tomorrow."

Lana wove her fingers through his thick black hair and gave a light tug. The motion caused a deep rumble in his chest, one that reverberated through her. She'd been so relieved to see him that she hadn't given a single thought to her nudity. But the sensual sound, his hands on her waist and his mouth on her skin sparked her libido to life. All the pent-up irritation and adrenaline soared through her, waiting for an outlet.

As if he could read her mind, he sank his teeth into her traps, and Lana let out a moan, sagging into his arms.

"Bad," she whispered, her voice husky with need.

"Come on now," he murmured against her skin. He continued to trail kisses up the column of her neck. "You didn't think you'd tamed the tiger, did you?" His deep voice made her thighs squeeze tight. Already, she was a chord begging to be plucked, and he strummed all the right notes. She wanted to see him unhinged. Raw. Unfettered.

Lana's fingers found the button of his jeans, and in seconds, that was unsnapped and she slid the zipper down. Lucas kicked his pants off, needing minimal encouragement to tug his shirt to the floor as well. He stood bare before her, all bronze skin and scars, the Tribe tattoos along his arms and legs a testament to what he'd survived and endured. His dark eyes gleamed with the same molten desire pooling between her legs, and she couldn't help but sink to her knees.

His cock stiffened as she stroked her fingers along the length. His thighs tensed and his breath hitched in anticipation. Lana loved how responsive he was, how the big, burly man became a bundle of nerves, feelings and pure expression waiting to be tapped. She leaned forward and traced her tongue along his impressive erection. A moan escaped him, one of those deep, guttural ones that traveled his entire body.

She licked her lips, anticipation welling between her legs. Lana lapped at his cock, the long strokes making his thighs tense, then she took his whole length into her mouth. Lucas' fingers wove through her hair, and he tugged tight as she began to find a rhythm. He smelled like the earth, and the salt of his pre-cum lingered in her throat as she sucked harder. He rocked into her, pure possession in his hold, and Lana reached up to sink her nails into his thighs.

Lucas let out a moan, his cock stiffening in her mouth. She traced her tongue along his length and sucked him harder, pushing him closer to the brink. His hold on her hair tightened, the sting delicious as she moved faster and faster along his length. She sank her nails in deeper, and his thighs tensed.

His cock pulsed, the salty liquid spurting into her mouth. Lana swallowed it down before she pulled off him. She wiped the side of her mouth with her thumb as he sank to his knees in front of her. Lucas leaned in and pressed a kiss to her lips with a force that radiated through her whole body.

Lana pulled back and drew in a breath. "Want to take this to the bedroom?" She met his eyes, searching them to see if he understood what she meant. How much he meant to her.

His gaze softened, and he reached forward to trace her face with his fingertips. "Are you sure?" The gentle touch made her shiver. They'd fucked across every other surface in this house, but the bedroom had been off limits. She'd shared the room with Greg, an undisturbed, sacred space. Yet something stirred deep within, a confirmation her mountain lion echoed. She was ready to move on.

Everything about Lucas Diaz was perfection—his kindness, his strength and the gentleness he exposed. She wanted to know so much more, to see his imperfections and weaknesses—already, she could see the stubbornness and control freak tendencies emerging ones guaranteed to lead to spats down the line. And she couldn't wait. She wanted to share the highs and lows with him. He'd proved he could handle both.

Lana nodded. "I'm in this for keeps, Luc."

He let out a shaky breath, explosive in the tense air between them. Then those dark eyes transformed from softness to depths unfathomable, to something wild, pure and beautifully real. "Good," he responded, his voice raspy. "Because I can't imagine returning to a life without you."

Lucas pushed himself from the ground in a fluid movement, his muscles working in perfect symmetry. He reached down and, before Lana could react, hoisted her into his arms. A giddy laugh escaped her throat— she adored the easy way he picked her up and tossed her around.

"I'm going to fuck you until you're screaming my name," Lucas murmured, his husky whisper tickling her ear. A shiver rolled down her spine. Within seconds, he was striding for the steps, which creaked under his powerful tread as he carried them upstairs.

"Not too much of a challenge," she responded, her lips quirking with a grin. "I mean, you barely have to touch me and I'm ready to come for you."

"Spirits above, you're fucking sexy." Lucas dipped his head to claim her mouth. They reached the second floor, and his footsteps echoed through the hall. He carried Lana toward her room. Her heart hammered in her ears, a deafening sound the closer they got to the end of the hallway.

Lucas nudged the door open. She thought she'd freeze at the sight of her bedroom, but the heat from his bare skin pressing against hers, the feeling of being in his arms and his earthy scent grounded her. He carried her over to the bed and lowered her down. Her back hit the smooth sheets, but with an inch between them, he was all she could see. Those dark eyes burned with desire, and she reached up to trace the scars along his cheeks. On their first night together, they'd immolated, the sort of flame that could burn quick. This was the steady blaze of a hearth building between them, something real. Something lasting.

Lucas closed the gap between them to kiss her hard. He grazed his fingers over her hood, then he slipped two between her soaked folds. Lana gasped into his mouth, but he devoured the breath. He began to move his fingers inside her, the sensations causing her toes to curl. Her back arched when he quickened the pace, gliding in and out of her. Her need increased with every breath until it grew into a painful pulse.

His mouth was rough and sweet while he kissed her neck and licked her skin. Any thoughts were obliterated under his skillful guidance as he coaxed her closer and closer. His massive legs settled on either side of hers, and she ached to have him fill her to completion. His erection slid against her thigh, silken steel. Her nipples brushed against his chest each time she arched under his touch, and the sensations pushed her into overload.

He pressed his thumb against her clit while he stroked it in time to the way he thrust his fingers inside her. Yet it wasn't until she looked up into his striking face to see the concentration in his umber eyes and the way his lips parted with his entire focus on her that she hurtled over the edge. She was a ship careening to the edge of a waterfall, and she'd accepted oblivion.

Lana let out a ragged gasp as the orgasm rocked through her. Her lids shuttered and her core pulsed in response to his touch, bliss radiating through her. Lucas slowly pulled his fingers out, but she didn't have the chance to even sag against the bed. He nudged the head of his erection inside her, and Lana bit her lip. She wanted him to ram into her until she lost where he ended and she began.

He slid the whole way in, filling the ache inside. Lana lifted her hips to greet him and wrapped her arms around his neck.

"*Dios mio*, you're everything," he whispered in her ear while he rocked inside her. Lana swallowed hard, the emotion heating in her eyes and causing a lump in her throat.

Lana reached up to run her fingertips along his face, down his chin, to brush against his lips. "You saved me, Luc," she responded, barely able to get the words out.

His breath hitched, but he didn't respond, just kissed her hard enough for her to feel it in her toes. He thrust deep, and a moan escaped her. Lucas began to rock inside her, a rolling force she'd grown familiar with in such a short time, one she'd surrender to in a heartbeat.

Lana thrust her hips to greet his again and again, a dance they both knew on instinct. His hands traveled along every inch of her body, and his lips were on her mouth, her neck, her breasts. She radiated in the incendiary sensations, the way her toes curled at his hot touch and how her back arched every time he drove deep inside her. The scent of him enveloped her and sweat beaded on her forehead, a drop tickling as it trickled down her neck.

Lana bit on his deltoids, his traps, tasting the salt of his sweat on his smooth skin. His muscles flexed while he moved, almost as mesmerizing as the way his mouth caressed her lips, coaxing the moans from her. He thrust into her again and again, a delirious dance that sent her reeling. Each time her sensitized clit smacked against his skin, the breath stuttered in her throat and she came closer to the edge.

"Come with me," he murmured against her mouth.

Lana nodded, and she gripped tight to his shoulders, matching the desperate pace he set. Their limbs were slick with sweat, and her skin stung as they crashed together in unmatched fury.

Her mind floated away until all she could do was feel, feel, feel. The way his heated breaths puffed against her skin. The deep sound of his groans that traveled straight to her core. The taste of him, salt, earth and potential.

He brushed a kiss to her lips, this one light as a feather and as loaded as a promise.

Lana screamed his name when her core clenched tight. Her senses reeled, her vision blanked and her head dug into the mattress. She thrummed in the wake of her orgasm. His cock pulsed in response as heat flooded her insides. He sagged, crushing her into the mattress as he pinned her down. His kiss deepened, and he dipped his tongue in to stroke hers.

Her entire body trembled, but the solid weight of him kept her from floating away.

"*Mia, mia, mia,*" Lucas whispered in her ear, a reverence in his tone like a prayer.

That was when Lana felt it.

Something that had been brushing against the surface all along clicked inside her, like a tether that had been forming solidifying in the air between them. *Mine.* Her gaze sharpened when she locked eyes with Lucas.

"We're mated." The words came out near breathless.

He nodded, his lips pressed tight. Hesitation overtook his gaze as he stared at her, searching.

Heat pricked her eyes, and she threw her arms around his neck, drawing him to her. A watery laugh escaped her. "You're my mate, Lucas Diaz. You're mine."

Chapter Nineteen

Lucas had been up since five that morning, but he didn't want to move from the bed. Lana lay fast asleep still, the hesitant rays of the early light deepening the golden glow of her skin. Her lashes were impossibly long, and her perfect mouth parted with the gentle cycle of her breaths. He couldn't look away. She was the most beautiful thing he'd ever seen — and she was his.

Pride thrummed in his chest, warmth suffusing through his entire body as he draped an arm around her to keep her close. His mate. He couldn't stop smiling. He had traveled all over the States, but it had taken a lot of years, a small town in central Pennsylvania and the biggest threat they'd ever faced to find her. She was worth all of that and more.

He dipped his head to press a kiss on the top of her head. Lana let out a soft noise and began to move, her lashes fluttering.

She looked up at him with those arresting green eyes. He brought her even closer, needing to feel their bodies skin to skin. Lucas breathed in her scent, one that had become as safe as a placid lake in such a short span.

"G'morning, beautiful," she murmured. Her eyes crinkled. "You're smiling."

He traced her cheek with his thumb, unable to help the giddiness pounding inside him. "Because I'm happy. I never in a thousand years thought I'd get to wake up next to my mate."

Yet in a few short hours, they'd be throwing themselves into danger again, risking their lives. Lucas tugged her a little closer.

"We're going to take Ganzorig down," she said, knowing in her gaze. "There's no other option."

The unsaid weighed heavy in the air. That they'd just found each other. That they had so much to explore. That this connection was one he'd dreamed of, and now after he had it, he would slaughter anyone who tried to take his mate away.

Lucas wrapped his arms around Lana to draw her tight to his chest. She brushed her fingers along his skin in a soothing sweep. He'd savor this moment for as long as he could, the canary yellow beams filtering in to highlight the dust motes dancing through the air like fairy lights, the warmth from the heater thrumming through her house, and the feel of her silken skin against his.

He'd stay here for as long as he could because in a few short hours, they'd be facing not only Ganzorig, but—if their plan worked—Mackey Kendricks.

* * * *

The entire car ride to the Red Rock cabin brimmed with tension. He and Lana exchanged casual conversation, but he could feel the lingering press of her gaze and the weight of the unspoken desires and dreams drowning the air. He raced down the strip of asphalt, chasing the sunlight. Barren trees flickered past on either side.

"If you're not going to say it, I'll ask," Lana broke another quiet spell. "What do you and Drew have planned? Don't think I haven't noticed the conspiratorial way you two have been whispering."

Lucas heaved a sigh. The less she knew, the better she'd be, yet part of him hated withholding anything. "Do you trust me?"

"Yeah, I do," she responded, suspicion ringing her tone. "But if you're attempting some suicide mission by luring Mackey Kendricks here, I won't forgive you. I need you alive, Diaz."

He let out a low whistle. "Perceptive as always. We're hoping to bait the big guy, yeah." His gaze flickered her way. "But trust me. If it's life or death, I would let him run free over leaving you alone, *mi amor*."

The winding drive to the Red Rock cabin peeked into view down the road, and Lucas slowed. He could feel Lana's glare on him and couldn't help but grin. She was annoyed, sure, but he loved that he'd found a mate who cared so fiercely, one who gave a damn if he came back or not.

He drove down the long driveway to pull in to stop behind a mess of other cars from the rest of the pack members who had arrived. Lucas leaned back in his seat and looked to Lana, who still stared at him, her lower lip jutted and worry flaring in her eyes.

"I've spent my life putting the Tribe first," he said, his insides coiling tight. Brushing the surface of those memories Taser-shocked his system. Yet he couldn't leave the car without telling her. Not this time. "Before my family, before my friends and before myself. They've taken more than I ever realized, until I met you. Every moment I spend with you, I'm not the East Coast Tribe. I'm the man I forgot existed, one I didn't even know I'd lost. They've taken enough from me."

He reached forward to brush his thumb across her lower lip, eliciting a shuddering breath from her. "You come first to me. Before my duty to the Tribe and before all the countless missions I'm going to be on, because that's the life I'll always be leading. Trust me when I say that none of them will come before the life I want to spend with you. The road might get dangerous, but I will fight fang and claw to make it back to you, every damn time."

Lana sucked in a sharp inhalation and nodded. "I'm not big on the rough and tumbles myself, but you can bet your ass I'll patch you up any time. My skill set's in healing, not destroying."

"You have no idea how much I need someone like that," he said, a grin on his lips.

She winked as she scanned the scars along his arms and his face. "I might have a bit of one." Lana squeezed his hand tight before she cracked the passenger door open. "Let's do this."

He hopped out of the car, his heart hammering. Their plan was risky, and he didn't like the conquer-and-divide aspect. Lana would be running with the other group, and he'd be leading the charge. He couldn't fuck up again.

Voices emanated from inside the cabin, which teemed with plenty of shifters if the cars were any indication. He cracked the door open, and the heat blasted him. The fireplace had died down, but a few errant flames glimmered there over the mostly charcoal logs. Sierra sat on the couch, her hand on her stomach while she shouted something over to Jer, who waited in the kitchen beside Raven and Betty. Dax and Drew stood in the far corner of the room, engaged in deep discussion. With the two brothers beside each other for once, the family similarities grew even more apparent.

Ally strode right up, flashing a grin to him then Lana. "Well now, don't you two look cozy?"

"Should we have arrived baring our teeth and soaked in blood?" Lana drawled beside him as she threw her arms around her best friend. Ally's nose twitched, and she stared at both of them, her eyebrows furrowing.

"Something's different between the two of you," she murmured. Her eyes widened, and she squeezed Lana tight. "Lan, did you? Is he?"

She nodded, her eyes gleaming in excitement. Lucas couldn't help the pride that thrummed through his veins, no matter that they were churning with adrenaline for the upcoming fight.

"I, for one, never expected to find my mate here." He kept his voice low, not wanting to alert the others. After all, Dax had given their relationship a less than pleasant reception in the first place. Right now, he needed to work together with the Silver Springs alpha and set personal problems aside.

Ally let out a squeal before clapping her hands over Lana's. "Holy hell. That was unexpected."

"About time you arrived," Drew called as he and Dax approached. "We're ready to head out, slacker. Already got the groups divvied up and everything."

"Who's carrying the device?" Lucas asked. He delivered a lazy smack to Drew's shoulder. Drew smirked and tossed a joke of a punch back, knuckles barely grazing his arm.

Ally raised her hand. "I am. After all, out of the lot of us, I'm the fastest."

As much as they wanted to keep the device away from Ganzorig, the lure would never work if they hid it. Based on the way he'd been searching for the device at Lana's place last night, he'd be able to sense if they hadn't brought it with them, and Lucas couldn't risk the shaman not showing.

"That's debatable," Jer called from the opposite side of the room. "I'm pretty sure I could outrun you any day."

Raven rolled her eyes. "Does it matter?"

"Yes," Jer, Sierra and Ally all responded at once. Lucas restrained his grin. He'd worked with a lot of packs in the past, but few were as close as the Red Rocks and Silver Springs. Their packs were bright examples of the communities shifters could grow into, the big families who celebrated together, lived together and fought together.

"You ready to do this?" Dax asked, extending his hand to shake.

Lucas clapped his against the Silver Spring alpha's and nodded. He understood a peace offering when it was extended. "I'll drive."

"I've got the rest," Jer called out, loping toward the door. As much as everyone joked around, a gravity descended upon the room as chairs were pushed in and mugs were placed on the countertop.

Sierra stood from her spot on the couch.

"Kiss my ass, babe," Dax said, standing right in front of her. "You're not coming along." Before she could argue, he leaned in to press his lips to hers. The tough Red Rock alpha ran her fingers through his hair, drawing him close by the collar of his shirt.

They pulled away, and Sierra's laser gaze traveled to Lucas. "Bring him back," she said. "Kicking, screaming, whatever. Just make sure he returns."

Lucas nodded, the promise forming a tight knot in his chest. He'd made a similar one to his own mate. "I swear it."

Lana slipped her fingers through his and squeezed, since the woman was apparently omniscient. "Time to stop Ganzorig."

At her quiet command, everyone headed for the door and Sierra followed. The Red Rock alpha watched by the door as they all piled into their cars, Lucas slipping back into the driver's seat. He caught Sierra's vigil — she watched even when their engines roared to life and they drove farther down the dusty track.

Ally leaned up from the back seat to whisper with Lana, and Drew and Betty brimmed with silence as Lucas pushed on the gas. His car flew down the highway toward Ricketts Glen, mere minutes away. The winter wind howled outside the car from the intense breezes buffeting around, but the sun gleamed on the stretches of crystalline snow still there from the fall nights ago.

He cranked up the smooth jazz that blared from his speakers, earning a groan from Lana. Spirits above, the sound of her voice resurrected a thrill in his chest, every time. The familiar stretch of the road reared into view, the spidery oaks marring the landscape to the right, thick brambles and heady pines marking the deep forest that stretched as far as the eye could see, all part of Ricketts Glen State Park.

"You keep making promises we're going to jam sometime," Drew called up from the back seat. "I'm beginning to think you were lying about playing sax."

"Next time I visit my folks I'll bring it with," Lucas promised. "We'll see how well you can play guitar." His skin buzzed with anticipation, with the thrill of a fight. His tiger stamped back and forth in his chest at the thought of looking Mackey Kendricks in the eye and tearing out his throat.

The brown signs for Ricketts Glen stood out, and Lucas drove down the route he'd come to memorize. This was one of the longest stretches he'd lingered in an area apart from Phoenix, where he'd grown up. His tires crunched gravel when he pulled up the drive into the almost barren parking lot. Not like this was a popular spot mid-winter. He parked next to Jer's Jeep, offering him a hefty dose of déjà vu to the last time they'd attempted this. However, they had the device and the other entrance at their disposal.

Lucas prayed it would be enough.

A hush fell through the car as he switched the engine off. Drew hopped out first, followed by Betty. Ally squeezed Lana's shoulder before she stepped into the cold winter air. Lucas let out the breath he'd been holding.

"You're coming back to me," Lana affirmed with a steadiness that didn't reflect in those eyes, the shade of sunlit meadows.

"I am," he responded, even though a lump formed in his throat. He leaned across the seat to cup her face. He lowered a kiss to her lips, a soft whisper fast leading to something deeper, furious and fearful. She tasted like coffee with too much cream, like lazy Sunday mornings, like his light in the darkness. Lucas poured all of himself into the kiss, tightening his grip around the back of her neck.

"Everything I have, everything I am, is yours," he whispered against her lips, his heart so full it could break.

"You have my heart," Lana murmured, which meant more than he could ever express.

If he didn't make it back, if something happened to her—a thousand worries tightened his chest and quickened his breath, but he couldn't give them weight. They both had jobs to do. So instead, he pressed a kiss to her forehead. "*Te amo*," he whispered before he let go.

Lucas hopped out of his car before the crash of emotion tugged him under and he lost the drive to keep hurtling forward. His heart raced, but he didn't betray an ounce of fear, slipping into professional mode.

"Ally, Jer and Dax, you'll be following me." He barked out orders to the other shifters who milled between the two cars.

Drew stepped beside him. "Lana and Raven, we'll be infiltrating their cavern while they're stepping out to play." He smacked Lucas on the back, and their gazes met. "Best chance we're going to get. Stay safe, brother."

Lucas clapped a hand on his shoulder. "You too." His gaze slipped to Lana and Drew followed it. The mountain lion shifter nodded. No words were needed for him to understand. Drew stepped past him and tipped his fingers for them to follow.

Lucas took a few paces forward in a different direction but paused to cast a glance over to Lana.

His mate strode with a feline grace, her chin lifted and her jade eyes blazing. She met his gaze and the air evacuated his chest. Understanding reflected in her eyes of what they could never communicate through words. No matter what happened today, he didn't regret a second of the time they'd spent together. Of coming to Red Rock and Silver Springs territory. Of falling in love with Lana.

They stepped onto different paths, both heading for the woods—both heading into different dangers.

Both too terrified to ever whisper goodbye.

Chapter Twenty

Each step farther away from Lucas squeezed her heart a little tighter.

Lana tugged at her jacket, as if the prickle sweeping across her skin had to do with the cold. The sun shone bright, as though those pristine rays hadn't caught the memo that today blood would be shed.

"What are we expecting to find in the cave?" Raven asked Drew while they wove through the slender trees. Even with the thick matting of pine needles and dry twigs, they barely made a sound. "Ganzorig is going to show for the meet-up, not hang around inside the cave."

Drew didn't glance back as he hiked forward, his gaze steady on the trail he was carving through the forest before them. "Three reasons," he said, lifting his fingers to tick them off. "One, we're going to make sure our crew won't get ambushed by reserve Landsliders. Two, if Ganzorig tries to pull another shaman trick, we're there to stop him. And three, this is the best chance we'll have to get our hands on whatever Mackey's planning. If we take Ganzorig down first, I can guarantee they'll destroy whatever's in there before we can get to it."

Raven let out a low whistle. "Pretty clever for a Landslider, Williams."

"Ex-Landslider," he corrected, passing her a pointed look.

Lana's chest burned and the words leaped to her lips. "How did you and Greg get involved in the first place?" The question had haunted her more fiercely than ever since she'd found out her husband's secrets. In the distance, the crash of falling water mingled with the rustles of critters and the whistling wind. The cold air pasted against her cheeks.

Drew hunched and jammed his hands into his pockets. His gaze darkened. "You can thank my pops for that. The old man got entangled with them years ago, and as his designated heir, he dragged me into the 'family business'." Drew's voice grew as brittle as the surrounding branches. "When Greg's business fell on hard times, he approached my father. You can imagine what dear old dad suggested."

Regret twisted in her chest like a sodden rag from the hurt their old alpha had caused Drew and Greg, and from all the things she wished she could've heard from her husband's lips, not secondhand.

"I understand," she said, the sole words that made sense right now. The only ones that mattered. Drew had caused damage, whether he'd been at the helm or not, and it would take time for her mind to disassociate him from her husband's death. They couldn't just resume the close friendship they'd had, if it ever repaired.

However, she'd known of his conflicted relationship with the former alpha. She and Ally alone knew the weight on his shoulders and the brunt of what he'd dealt with to save Dax from his father's bullshit. In her heart of hearts, she saw the goodness in him, and she understood.

Drew bobbed his head, his lips pressed tight. He forced his gaze forward even though she caught the sheen in those sky-blue eyes. "We're closing in on the entrance," he said, his voice gruffer than normal. "When we get close enough, we'll shift. Follow my cues."

Even though Raven's jaw clenched, she didn't argue. Out of the three of them, Drew was the one on the team who'd scouted the location already. Besides, after witnessing his hatred for Mackey and knowing what the ex-Tribe member had made him do, she understood he would die before helping the Landsliders again.

They approached a fringe of trees, the trunks thick enough to hide behind and the spindly webs of branches casting intricate shadows onto the ground. Water burbled around this area from the stream that rushed through, the sound growing louder and louder with each step forward. Lana's heart hammered. Her nose twitched with the conflicting scents in the air. They were nearing the trails humans traveled, farther from the wild expanse of brambles and tumultuous waterfalls their packs roved through, so it was no wonder this spot had taken a little extra time to find.

Drew approached a cluster of thicker oaks and stopped. "Time to switch forms."

The words had barely left his lips by the time he shunted his clothes to the ground, pushing the pile to the base of the tree. Lana sucked in a breath and followed suit, tugging off her jacket then her clothes, ignoring the icy breath of the wind on her bare skin.

The shift overtook her fast. Her mountain lion emerged as if she'd been waiting for years, not a mere day, and her claws pricked out, the fur bristling across her skin. Her hands turned to padded paws and her bones began to mutate until she settled on all fours. In this form, the muted grays and browns of the forest floor grew brighter and more varied. The sounds that had seemed so intermittent before turned more noticeable, and the scents she'd struggled to distinguish in her human form changed to clear pathways.

Coyotes, mountain lions, wolves and bears all muddled here, the trails leading in the same direction as the running water. None of the scents were familiar. None of these shifters should've been roaming through Red Rock and now Silver Spring territory.

Drew's form was taller than hers, the massive mountain lion a darker shade of tan. Raven shifted as fast as them, her wolf the sleek color of her namesake, with several silver streaks throughout her coat. Drew tilted his head to the side and prowled past the veil of the trees.

A clearing lay ahead, a winding stream slicing through the layered shale. Foamy crests formed on the turbulent water that burbled past. A large hill stretched out before them, several straggly trees and threadbare bushes growing on the surface. Crags of rock protruded and several fissures at the base soaked in the darkness, inky openings that beckoned them. In this form, Lana didn't need to look to know which one led to the other entrance. Even with the crisp scent of water dispelling some of their stench, she could smell the trail of other animals leading to the dip at the far right.

She bristled with tension. Even though nothing leaped out at them, she couldn't shake the sensation that they were being watched.

Drew didn't head straight toward the entrance, instead loping in a far circle to approach from the side. She and Raven maintained a distance of several paces behind. The crisp wind rifled through her thick coat, the chill not bothering her in this form. Icy water coated her paws when they waded through the stream, freezing enough to send a shiver through her. They approached quickly and quietly, worries and fears fading from her mind as she focused on the hunt.

Her predator instincts took command, and she scanned the fissure in the shale. Her nose twitched from the barrage of scents, but she waited for a sign of movement or a sound to indicate any oncoming threats. Drew skulked in the lead, his umber eyes focused while he crept closer and closer.

Her heart pounded fast as the hunt consumed her, each footstep measured, each breath silent.

Drew slipped inside first, and Raven second. Lana approached the entrance, stale air thick and heavy from more than rock dust. This place oozed with the same magic Ganzorig had wielded against them last time they'd entered from the other side.

Lana stepped into the inky darkness. Her eyes adjusted after a couple of blinks. She padded forward, caution buzzing through her veins. A *drip-drip-drip* echoed from deeper inside the cave, but she strained to catch any rustles or breaths that might give away Landsliders roaming deeper inside.

The three of them padded through the narrow pass, traveling over weathered ground. The dips and divots in the stone were similar to those of the first cave entrance they'd found. Her nose twitched at the stench of other shifters which mingled with the acrid metal from the rocks around them. *Thump, thump, thump.* Lana almost halted in her tracks, when she realized the main sound she heard was the beating of her heart.

Up ahead, an amber light filtered in through the darkness, something that had to be manmade. Drew slowed when he reached the edge of the tunnel, where it spilled out into a larger cavern.

Unlike the massive one they'd stumbled onto before when they'd found Ganzorig, cozy lamplights decked this one out, illuminating the white markings covering almost every spare surface along the rock face. While uneven areas dipped in and out of darkness, the primary section of the cavern spanned flat and wide, forming an elevated platform in the center.

Those lantern lights illuminated the mottled colorations on the surface of the platform, most of the pigment concentrated in the middle. The coppery scent was too familiar.

That wasn't the coloration of the stone.

The shamanic crystals, the herbs sprinkled in a circle around the platform and the splatters of the brownish red across the tan, even stone—Ganzorig was performing blood sacrifices.

The soft scrape of shifting pebbles was the one alert they got.

A bear lumbered out from the sheath of shadows. This wasn't an average black bear or even a shifter-sized one. This creature had been warped into a massive brute, almost unrecognizable. Its eyes bulged wider, bits of stone crusting around them, and mottled patches of rock traveled up and down its back like a disease, protruding through the dark fur. It limped forward on uneven feet, the natural grace stolen away in the wake of what this shifter had been turned into.

And it hadn't arrived alone.

What had once been a coyote emerged, teeth bared. Roots twisted around its limbs, twigs jutting out from its fur in sharp points as if the beast had merged with a porcupine. One of its eyes was missing, a spindly branch protruding through the hollow socket. Its growls echoed through the cavern, higher pitched with an eerie whine to them. Two normal shifter wolves emerged beside the coyote, nudging it forward as if they were herding the two mutations.

Whatever had been done to those creatures, Lana could guarantee they hadn't signed up to become the monstrosities crawling before them. The stones whirled at her feet. She was going to be sick.

Drew crouched low to the ground, baring his teeth, and Raven's growl reverberated to the ceiling. Lana dug her claws into the film of dirt and dust, settling on the immovable stone beneath her. Ganzorig had committed atrocities here. The filthy residue of his magic formed a thick film in the air, crawling down her throat with every inhalation.

For a single moment, the Landsliders stared at them while they glared right on back, muscles tensed and teeth revealed. Both sides were matches ready to ignite.

The coyote burst forward, shattering the standstill like a rock through glass.

The beast was massive, each step worth three of theirs. Drew whipped his head to them, his umber eyes glowing in the dark. His gaze snared on Raven, and she dipped her muzzle, taking the directive. The Red Rock bartender surged to greet the monster.

Drew didn't give Lana any cues. Instead, he seized the distraction, bolting in the direction of the mutated bear, which left her facing the two wolves. Even though she felt more than outmatched, with their attention on Drew, Lana took the chance.

She raced forward, heart thumping so loudly that the *thud-thud-thud* drowned out any other noise. Her nerves were on fire, alight with the adrenaline of the hunt, one she'd denied her mountain lion time and time again. She bared her teeth.

The bear let out a ground-shaking roar, one that sent dust filtering down from the stalactites above. Drew leaped for the beast, unleashing his claws.

Lana kicked up pebbles as she raced forward. Two wolves, one mountain lion. She ignored the throb in the back of her mind—desperation left no room for doubt. One wolf glanced her way, pivoting to face her. His muzzle dipped, and sharp teeth emerged. *Side of the neck's open. Front legs too.* Those muscles tensed as the wolf prepared to spring forward.

Lana didn't choose either.

She veered close, close, close. The brown wolf snapped, the jaws swerving an inch away from her, but she whipped around him. Instead of diving down, she launched herself up in the direction of the white wolf whose back was turned.

Lana landed smack on the beast's back, claws extended. She sank them in past fur, past skin with a squish. The force of her landing crushed the wolf to the ground, and Lana raked her claws down. Crimson spurted with the stroke, the color bright against the snow-white coat, but she ignored her inner protest, her predator taking the helm. Movement surged behind her before she caught the motion.

The brown wolf leaped for her. At the last second, Lana hit the ground and rolled. The wolf collided with his brethren.

Lana sprang forward, unrelenting, driven by the desperation of the darkness, the smaller space and the twisted sense of wrong radiating through this cavern. She rammed headfirst into the brown wolf, sending him skidding into his friend again, who whipped around, teeth bared.

Drew let out a low growl. The bear's paws to the ground were stone on stone, emitting a grinding noise that reverberated through the cavern. This would be a fast and furious fight — it needed to be — she wouldn't survive long against these two, nor would Raven and Drew against Ganzorig's atrocities.

Where Drew charged in against the bear, Raven took a different tack.

She raced around, using her nimble speed to her advantage. The coyote had become tough, grizzled and covered with roots that began to shift inside it like a living creature, but the extra baggage slowed the beast down, seconds that cost. Raven loped back and forth across the cavern floor, never staying in the same spot twice.

One of the wolves near Lana crouched, tensing those hind legs for a leap.

Lana paced, trying to keep from broadcasting her moves.

The brown wolf lunged for her, snapping gray teeth. She waited until the heat from his breath burst across her muzzle before slamming to the ground. He landed on her back, but she'd been preparing for that. Claws sank in past her fur, pinpricks of pain hitting before she bucked back, sending the beast soaring off her. As he tumbled to the ground, her gaze met Raven's. The Red Rock wolf's eyes flashed silver. Lana caught the cue.

Raven charged in her direction, leading the mutant coyote their way.

The brown wolf in front of Lana didn't even see them coming, while he revealed his teeth and focused on her. Raven swerved at the last second, her movements fluid. The coyote did not.

It rammed straight into the wolf, who pivoted around to face his attacker.

Lana had sidestepped out of the way, her paws churning up the dust on the cavern floor. She couldn't let this chance pass them. Raven surged beside her, the sleek wolf moving with finesse while they headed for the other Landslider. The white wolf growled and charged for her. *Fine.* Lana crouched, fangs at the ready. The Landslider closed in on her when Raven lunged out.

The Red Rock sank her teeth into the beast's back leg, slowing her down. Lana let her mountain lion instincts take over. She snapped out, sinking her fangs into the shifter's throat. Blood gushed, hot and wet as it dribbled out her mouth and into her fur. She whipped her head back and forth until the Landslider stopped resisting and went slack. Lana opened her jaw, and the wolf crumpled to the floor.

The scrape of the coyote's steps gave it away.

The other Landslider extricated itself from the coyote's grasp. Now both were pissed and rushing for her. Raven nudged her in the side, dipping her muzzle to the left where the Landslider was charging. Lana didn't need to ask—she trusted Raven's cleverness.

Lana took the lead this time, surging across the platform to meet the brown wolf midway. Raven snuck around the other side, her teeth glinting in the low lamplight. The wolf's breath blasted her in the face. She ducked her head, the beast's jaw snapping over. She might've dodged the wolf, but the mutant followed close behind. Too close to escape.

The coyote rammed into her at full force.

The breath flew from her lungs when she tumbled to the ground. A loud whine came from behind them as she smacked against the cavern floor. Dust and grit clouded her nose. *Not like I can shake myself off.* The coyote leaped overtop her, claws sinking deep. Her teeth clacked together, but she tried not to cry out in pain. Drool dripped from the creature's muzzle, hot and slimy as the liquid soaked into her fur.

The tendrils of branches began to move. The tip of one of the roots slithered toward her, the sharp edge sinking in like a claw. More of them twisted forward. The beast pinned her down, slathering and gnashing its teeth. Those eyes stared at her, filmy, listless, with a distant, deranged light to them. The sight dosed her like Novocain. Lana rolled her weight to the side, trying to tip the coyote off.

It leaned down harder, so she bucked under the weight, sending them both tumbling. The branches jabbed into her, piercing like needles through her fur while she rolled around with the beast. Lana closed her eyes to protect them, trying to lash out on feel alone before she raised her claws.

A low whimper sounded from behind her, and Lana's stomach bottomed out. It couldn't be Raven.

The coyote sank its teeth into her shoulder. Lana howled out in pain, lashing forward. The movement dug the branches in deeper. She needed to find a way past them. One swipe. A tendril wrapped around her paw, the root protruding from around the creature's front legs. The connection flashed in her mind like a warning light.

Lana stopped fighting the beast and sank her fangs into the root.

The coyote let out a shriek that radiated through the cavern. She swung her head to the side, tightening her grip on the root curled around her paw. Using the leverage, she yanked it. The coyote surged with the root, stumbling forward. The root loosened from her paw, going slack.

Lana didn't give the creature a chance to recover. She charged headfirst for an open spot along the flank. The coyote flew back, landing on its side.

Raven surged past her, an inky blur. The Red Rock wolf leaped onto the mutant coyote in a blur of fangs and claws. Lana wove around to the opposite side, bounding onto the beast's leg and biting the roots twined around it. She hefted her entire weight onto the rest of the coyote, ignoring the errant branches protruding from the fur as they pierced into her flank.

Raven's teeth flashed, and she bit and yanked on whatever exposed fur she could find. Blood stained her teeth, dripping from her muzzle, and the coyote let out a loud rumble, deep from its throat. It surged up, snapping with its teeth, its front legs flailing, but it didn't find purchase. Raven was too fast, and Lana held tight on its back.

Its struggles grew weaker and weaker as Raven continued her assault, each bite drawing more blood until a mottled pool collected beneath the beast. Lana tugged with her teeth, biting harder into the roots, which drew a feeble yet unearthly scream from the creature. It wheezed, those breaths ragged.

Until it stopped moving.

Lana let go of the root as the final twitches racked the creature. She couldn't help the pang of sympathy for the beast, mutated beyond anything the shifter had originally been. Her own husband had been victim to Kendricks' horror show, given shamanic fuel by Ganzorig.

The scrape of the bear's feet echoed through the cave. *Drew.*

He snarled before charging the bear again. Blood streamed from several cuts along his flank, deep enough to send spatters to the cavern floor. His chest heaved from the effort of taking the biggest guy on by his lonesome. The bear lumbered forward with formidable heft and speed, covered in so much stone it looked like it had emerged from the rock face.

Lana glanced at Raven, who dipped her stained muzzle in a nod.

They both raced toward Drew as fast as they could.

Lana's paws pounded against the gravel and the bumpy stone floor. Her heart thundered as she sucked in the stale, thickened air. She surged across the platform to come to her friend's aid. Raven veered to the far right in an arc, moving faster. Lana remained steady, charging head-on toward the bear's flank.

She lowered her head. It was time to check which was harder, stone or her thick-as-hell skull.

The bear hadn't noticed their approach, those glazed, crazed eyes focused on Drew alone. *Good.* The space closed between them.

Lana rammed full force into the bear's side. Her head rang from the strength of the collision, and she stumbled. A patch of stone scraped her ear, the abrasion stinging like most of her body did at that point. The beast let out a bellow, but not before Raven swept in from behind, snapping at the creature's legs.

Drew took the chance they offered him.

He leaped, sailing right for the mutant's throat. His teeth sank in, more crimson staining the already blooded ground.

The growl cut off, and the bear swayed on those massive paws. Lana backed away. The bear took another step forward. Another. Drew's fangs were bared, stained in the beast's blood. Raven's grip on its back leg hadn't faltered. She yanked her head to the side, sending the mutated bear crashing to the cave floor.

The ground shook with the fall, as though they'd dropped a boulder from above. The abomination shuddered one final breath.

Except the ground continued shaking, grit cascading from overhead and a couple of pebbles pelting her skull. All the white markings painted on the rock face began to glow brighter and brighter. The shakes turned to full-fledged quakes, and the cavern lit up like a Christmas parade.

Drew let out a roar that emanated through the cavern, whipping his head in the direction of the exit.

The cave was going to collapse.

Chapter Twenty-One

Lucas stalked in the lead across Ricketts Glen, cutting through the familiar path they'd traveled days before. Their group dripped with tension, as if he were leading them to an execution. His heart quickened with every step away from Lana. He might've taken the riskier job, but hers wouldn't be cocktails on the patio. Ganzorig wouldn't have brought all his Landsliders to this exchange.

"So, what's the chances Ganzorig has a trap planned for us?" Ally called out from behind.

"That's pretty much a guarantee," Dax drawled, a step or two away from Lucas.

"You focus on keeping the box safe," he called. "And the moment we make sure Ganzorig's there, if there's any further trouble, run." His gaze hadn't left the forest in front of them. He half-expected Landsliders to come springing out from every shadowed dip in the path or to launch from behind the monolithic oaks they strode past.

"Leave the wolves to get the job done," Jer teased Ally while they hiked through the wilderness. "We all know you feline folk get lazy." Betty snorted in response, and Dax shook his head, pushing past to stride neck and neck with Lucas.

"Diaz, care to share your expectations?" Dax asked, his perceptive gaze slicing like a switchblade. It wasn't a far leap to surmise they'd be attempting to lure bigger fish than Ganzorig.

"This item's important," Lucas said, weaving past another pine, frozen sap staining the sides. His boots sank into the dried pine needles and mud but barely made a sound. "Important enough that our real target might make an appearance. If he does, leave him to me."

"You won't be tackling him alone," Jer growled, the burn of old wounds in his voice.

"Yeah, I will," Lucas called. "Unless you're packing some secret mojo to defy Tribe compulsion you haven't shared with the rest of your pack."

Jer let out a low snarl but didn't continue arguing. The cold wind whistled through the skeletal tree limbs as the pale sunlight turned the gray bark to silver. In the distance, the hushed trickle of water infiltrated with every step closer to the falls. Lucas couldn't help the wires tightening around his heart, the way they squeezed tighter and tighter with every step closer.

He couldn't fuck this up. Too much rode on them pulling this off. A drop of sweat cooled as it traveled down his neck, and he licked his dry lips. They wound through familiar trees, closer to the cave entrance where they'd last found Ganzorig. His nose twitched with the scent of foreign shifters coming from the same direction they were heading in. As if he needed further convincing that Ganzorig was waiting for them with an army at his back.

"Ready for this?" Dax asked. The sound of water grew louder from the falls where they'd found the cave entrance last time.

Lucas shrugged. "Take down a psychotic shaman, keep everyone alive and get the damned device out unscathed. The whole thing sounds like a breeze. Are you sure you don't want to go back to the cabins?"

He snorted, tugging at the brim of his baseball cap. "I wish. Sierra's probably going out of her mind right now."

Lucas' throat tightened. Out of everything on his list, number two was by far the most important. Some of the Tribe might be ruthless, but he'd never caught the memo. Their steps slowed as a familiar hill rose into view. Leaves matted into brownish sludge, accented by the fringes of pearly snowfall slipping through the overhead trees, and to the right, the falls churned up foamy water that spilled into a crystalline pool.

The cave entrance lay beside that, a void swallowing the light.

Except their targets weren't waiting inside the cave.

A familiar form stood on the top of the hill, the shaman waiting with his arms crossed. He wore a green sport coat and as he checked his watch, the gold glinted, catching the sun. *Like we're late for some business meeting.* Lucas restrained his growl at the sight, even though his tiger surged in his chest, wanting to tear the man's throat out.

This shaman had plagued them for months. He'd wreaked havoc on this town and so many others without a care as to who got killed in the process. Shame had flooded Lucas when he'd stumbled onto those cubs murdered just like Josefina had been, and a helplessness at looking at those broken bodies, unable to rewind time or stop that horror.

No more.

Ganzorig would die, today.

Lucas continued forward, each step purposeful as he waited for Ganzorig to look up at them. The second the man lifted his hands, snapped his fingers or tried anything that might indicate a spell being cast, he'd act. Their crew quieted in the face of the immediate danger lurking before them.

The shaman wasn't the only one on the hill, even though he stood by himself. The scents of other shifters were strong here, meaning they were either hiding behind the trees, along the other side of the hill or waiting in the entrance of the cave to launch out at them. Ganzorig dangled all by his lonesome like bait, but Lucas wouldn't let his guard down for a moment.

Lucas slowed at the base of the hill, not willing to climb the rest of the way until he figured out where the other shifters were hiding. "I half expected you'd be on the other side of the continent, Joe," he called, his voice echoing through the clearing. The falls thundered beside them, the thrum of water resonating through his veins.

Ganzorig stared at him with a wan smile on his face. Lucas hated his arrogance, so similar to the man who'd betrayed them. "I'm just shocked you managed to find my device. The lot of you do more navel gazing than actual work." His gaze flickered to Ally. With the box so close to its maker, the shaman would be able to sense the signature of his magic stamped all over it. That must be what he'd been attempting last night when he'd broken into Lana's house.

Lucas was sick of the way this bastard had tormented his mate. Sick of the fucked-up shit this man had already done, turning his kind to berserkers and murdering children. And he was sick of Mackey and the Landsliders leading them in circles over and over again. That ended today.

"Well, we've got your device, which means I'll hold you to leaving these packs alone," Lucas called out. He crossed his arms over his chest and kept his gaze on Ganzorig, all while searching his peripheral vision. For anything. Any sign.

"Once you give it to me." Ganzorig nodded to where he stood on the hill, not budging in the slightest. He wanted them to come to him. *Why?* He glanced over the length of the hill covered by matted leaves and broken twigs. He almost missed the breaks in some of the leaves, the streaks across their surface of a dark substance the color of charcoal.

A trap, of course. If they started up the hill, chances were something would explode, or snare them. *Screw him.*

Lucas tilted his head to meet Ganzorig's stare. "Right. We're not going to traipse up the hill. You can come to us, or we'll walk away." Dax snorted beside him, the alpha's shoulders tensing. The man prepared to attack at the first sign of trouble.

Ganzorig's mouth quirked in a grin. "It was worth a try." The shaman settled his gaze on him. "You know, we could always use another Tribe member among the Landsliders, Diaz. Don't tell me you buy the myths they've been feeding us from birth about destiny and duty. Freedom's worth far more than that."

"Not the cost you've paid," Lucas intoned.

Ganzorig lifted his fingers to his lips and let out an ear-piercing whistle.

Jer stepped closer to him and Ally flanked Dax while Betty hovered behind them. Where before the hill had lain empty, shifters now emerged beyond the crest. First another mountain lion slunk into view. A black bear approached next, followed by a wolf. Then three coyotes trotted up to join the others, standing behind Ganzorig in a defensive position.

The shaman closed his eyes and lifted his hands, murmuring something quick beneath his breath. The words held the weight of a spell. He lowered his hands and gave a flourish. "There. We'll come to you, then."

Ganzorig and the Landsliders strode down the hill to greet them. His footsteps echoed through the clearing, the sound mingling with the burbling river while the shifters approached. Lucas tensed. The moment the Landsliders reached the bottom, they'd expect Ally to hand over the device. He hadn't missed how Ganzorig's gaze had rested on the pack slung over her shoulder. He couldn't risk the shaman getting his hands on it.

He glanced to her, and their eyes met.

Any second now.

His claws threatened to emerge, his tiger smashing against his chest with increasing urgency at the nearness of these predators. However, Mackey Kendricks wasn't among them. The gray of the mountain lion's fangs gleamed, and Lucas didn't miss the white marks painted up and down Ganzorig's arms. No mistake about it — they'd arrived to fight.

Feet away.

"Ally, run." The command flew from him.

Dax and Betty stepped in front of the Silver Springs beta. Ally's blonde hair flew behind her as she bolted in the opposite direction, deeper into the woods. Jer shifted into wolf form, his limbs contorting and fur emerging.

Lucas hunched, teeth bared as his fangs emerged. Here, they'd hold the line.

Except none of the Landsliders gave chase.

They should've been rushing for Ally as fast as their paws could carry them. Ganzorig's chin was lifted, the damned knowing burning in his eyes like stoked coals. Lucas' skin prickled and nausea swept over him like the flu.

"Stop." The voice came from behind him with the undeniable timbre of a command. The powerful resonance of one of the Tribe. Bile rose in Lucas' throat as slowly, slowly, he turned.

A man strode through the woods behind them, one whose approach had been so silent they'd never heard him coming. Two grizzly bears lumbered from behind, but they were docile compared to the man they walked after, tall enough to tower with dark, handsome features—dense eyebrows, the jaw of a leader and an aquiline nose. He'd barely aged a day since Lucas had last seen him years ago. The Tribe member who'd gone rogue, the one who'd been building the Landsliders in secret for far longer. The one responsible for so many deaths, for tainted drug infestations and for attacks on shifter families.

Mackey Kendricks.

'We have these abilities for a reason beyond all this,' Mackey had insisted.

Their last conversation had replayed in his mind for years now. They'd been patrolling through a forest in

New Hampshire and set a campfire in the woods. The battling packs had worn them both to the bone. Situations like those made him question why they even did this in the first place.

Lucas had shrugged. *'We were chosen by the Great Spirits. This is thankless work, but it's needed. Governing our kind, keeping them from going out of control – that's the exact reason we were given these powers.'*

The firelight had reflected in Mackey's eyes, and he'd crossed his arms, staring into the blaze before them. *'There's got to be more out there than this life of forced servitude.'*

After what they'd dealt with that night, Lucas couldn't help but agree. If he'd known what Mackey had meant back then and what the man had planned, he would've torn out his throat then and there.

After all those years of them chasing after him, Mackey Kendricks appeared before them.

Ally froze at the command, her legs ceasing to work. At the same time, Mackey crossed the distance, his gaze as dark as a night with no moon and his stride steady. The man moved like an earthquake, leaving destruction in his wake. The two bears prowled behind him, readiness in their stances. Her eyes widened when she tried to jerk her arm, her leg, the small twitches unable to counteract the command Mackey had given.

"Ally," Lucas called out again. *"Run."* This time, he pushed his will into the word, the compulsion descending. Mackey's eyes met his. In his gaze lay madness. The man had always been charismatic to a fault, but a single scratch beneath the surface revealed the haunted halls of his youth, an ugliness that had broken him long before he'd begun running with the East Coast Tribe.

The spell shattered. Ally surged forward again, stumbling as she was freed from the restraints. She was outnumbered — he needed to step in. Lucas strode to close the distance between them.

She didn't make it three paces before Mackey appeared before her, moving like a strike of lightning. His arms shot out before she could react, and he wrested the pack from her shoulder.

"Thought I told you — don't move," he said, a coolness in his tone. The wintry woods paled in comparison. Ally's body froze again, her arms outstretched, mid-grasp. Mackey closed the space between them, crushing his lips to hers. Ally's blue eyes widened in horror even as she didn't budge an inch. He pulled away, slinging the bag over his shoulder. "Thanks, sweetheart." His gaze flickered to Lucas. "Been a long time, Diaz."

It had all happened in the blink of an eye, but his name on the bastard's lips triggered his instincts. Lucas charged.

His calves squeezed tight as he burst forward, slicing through the space between them. Moldering leaves flew in his wake when he charged, nails shifting to claws. His heart hammered and his throat tightened as he choked on the pure, volatile rage radiating all the way to his fingertips.

Mackey met his gaze head-on, but he didn't twitch or shift. He stood there with the device slung over his shoulder. Warning bells rang in Lucas' head. Always, always, the Landsliders were steps ahead. Mackey glanced past him. *Fuck.* Lucas halted mid-stride, his boots digging into the earth. He spun back around.

Roars split the air as the Landsliders charged Dax and the others. However, Ganzorig locked in on one person with his palms raised.

The glint of the silver stake under the sunlight was the one alert he got. The projectile zipped toward him faster and faster.

Lucas ducked on reflex. Too late.

The stake burrowed into his shoulder. His hands clamped around the length to try and slow the projectile. The breath evacuated him when the pain descended. The silver coating the stake made his body revolt, and he dropped to a crouch as he yanked it out as fast as possible. The metal scorched his palms when he tugged. The stake clattered to the ground, its tip coated in crimson. For a single moment, he felt nothing, then the pain descended with a viciousness that numbed his teeth.

"Better luck next time," Mackey called out and cast a glance to the grizzlies on either side of him. "Make sure they don't leave this clearing alive." Lucas glanced back to see the asshole retreating into the woods with the device slung over his shoulder. He'd already carved a fair distance away, running at top speed.

The pain racked through his body, the silver scorching where the stake had plunged into his shoulder. Lucas breathed the pain in, consumed it, converting it into focus.

For a single moment, he considered giving chase. He considered leaving the Red Rocks and Silver Springs to fend for themselves to run after Mackey and the device. After all, that was the top priority, the reason he'd been sent here.

Then he glanced toward the Landsliders. Jer snapped at the coyotes in his wolf form alongside Betty, who'd transformed too. Dax whipped around in his mountain lion form to face the bear racing for him. The two grizzly bears who had arrived with Mackey began their charge — they'd tear Ally apart. The numbers weren't in their favor, and with Ganzorig wielding the elements to his whim, they would die. None of them would make it back alive.

He'd made Lana a promise, one he intended on keeping.

Right now, he needed to deal with the immediate threat. He rose from his crouch to face Joe Ganzorig.

"Ally." Lucas straightened, his focus not veering from Ganzorig. This ended now. "*Move.*"

She grimaced, her arms collapsing by her side at his command. Lucas didn't wait to give orders. The shift overtook him, his limbs mutating as fur sprouted across his skin. His tiger emerged with an urgency that pounded through his veins — the ancient beast had been waiting all this time to burst free. His claws clicked against the hard earth while he settled onto the ground, his front limb sagging from the gash in his shoulder where the silver stake had plunged in.

Not like a little cut would stop him.

This place and these people had suffered enough. Ganzorig had done so much damage as Mackey's second-in-command.

The anger built and built and built inside him, so acidic it stripped him raw. Until all the crimson-spatter rage lifted into his throat and he opened his mouth.

The snarl grew, vibrating louder and louder, until his whiskers trembled and the earth shook. A deep-throated roar reverberated from him. The pebbles at his feet trembled in its wake and several of the shifters stopped mid-prowl to glance at him. His gaze never left

Ganzorig. If the shaman wanted to toy with the elements, Lucas could level the playing field.

One of the bears growled from behind, closing the distance between them. Both the sizeable bastards zeroed in on him, the biggest threat in this place. Ally bolted to catch up, already shifted into a mountain lion. They could come and get him.

He charged forward, slamming his paws to the ground. Lucas tried to ignore the shooting pain that lanced through him while his front paw dragged from the wound. With each step, the grit around him trembled. Lucas drew it in, pebble by pebble, stone by stone. The rocks rose from the ground as he passed them by, rising higher and higher under his control.

Ally raced behind him as they surged toward the clash.

Both bears lumbered forward, gaining speed.

Ganzorig lifted his hands again, murmuring something. Lucas wasn't stopping.

Brambles whipped out from the trees he bypassed at the shaman's command, and branches slithered like snakes across the ground, aiming for them. One of the limbs curled around Ally's paw, and she slammed to the ground, a hard breath escaping her. The other tendril darted for his hind leg, but he veered past it. He cast a glance back, but Ally dipped her head in a nod and whipped around to face one of the bears. The other continued charging after him, mere feet away.

He didn't give a damn if the beast slashed him in the back. Ganzorig wouldn't get away.

The pounding of footsteps echoed from deeper in the woods.

If Mackey Kendricks had brought more Landsliders, they were all fucked.

The bear wasn't halting, and neither would he. Ganzorig tried whipping another tendril toward him from a nearby bush, but Lucas vaulted over it, landing hard on his good front paw. The clatter from the woods grew louder, snapped twigs and crunched leaves.

Three shifters emerged at the crest of the hill. An ink-black wolf and two mountain lions.

The mere sight of Lana punched him in the chest. His mate.

The bear charged for him, but Lucas crouched, his back legs ready to spring. The moment it closed in, he sprang forward. He sailed overtop the bear, and when he hit the ground, he kept running.

Straight for Ganzorig.

All the rocks and grit he'd been collecting trembled in the air above him as he Pied-Pipered them from the ground.

Lucas slammed his paws to the earth.

Everything he'd collected rained down—targeting a single shaman.

Chapter Twenty-Two

Raven led the way through the woods, knowing the worn paths and bony bushes even better than Lana did, and Drew trailed close behind. Every step forward had her heart thumping harder and harder. Every step brought them closer to the confrontation against Ganzorig.

Lana was terrified of what she'd find.

A roar split through the air, deep, resonant and filled with rage. One she recognized at once. Her mate.

They raced up the hill that mere days ago they'd seen from the opposite side when they'd been exploring the Landsliders' cave. Blood stained her fur in stiffening flecks as she ran, and the wind whistled through the skeletal limbs around them. They reached the top of the hill overlooking the clearing below, sliced in two by the river.

Ganzorig stood at the base of the hill, his hands extended. He was commanding the branches and earth to obey his whim. Jer and Betty snapped their muzzles against a mountain lion and coyote, while two coyotes and a bear attacked Dax, who seemed to be wading in deeper water with every lunge. Ally's pale coat gleamed in the sun as she fended off a massive brown bear, and the other grizzly aimed in the direction of the tiger that had stolen her heart.

Lucas vaulted forward, his gaze flashing gold as he soared closer and closer to Ganzorig despite the tangle of roots surging up to trip him and the errant branches whipping out under the shaman's direction. Drew veered toward Dax, bounding over to help his brother while Raven raced in the direction of both her mate and packmate.

Lana headed for Ganzorig.

She hadn't missed the stones buzzing in the air around Lucas, so she loped in a wide circle around the shaman. Her tiger slammed his paws to the ground, and all those rocks weaponized.

The stones pummeled down overtop the space where Ganzorig stood, a miniature avalanche descending onto him. The rocks kicked up a clamor and dust rolled out in every direction from the force of the blows. She dodged around a couple of errant stones that dropped to the ground before her. Lucas wasn't stopping, a low snarl reverberating from his mouth as he leaped through the roiling clouds. Lana looped around to dart in behind him.

No way would she let him tackle this asshole alone.

She burst through the clouds, the grit stinging her eyes. Ganzorig should've collapsed under the stones that battered him, but instead, a tangle of branches, twigs and roots he'd summoned surrounded him like a shell.

The grizzly bear raced after Lucas with the same dogged determination as her tiger chased down the shaman. Lana needed to buy him time. She crouched low, waiting for the beast to pass. With the rolling grit settling to the ground, she blended in with the dust.

The massive bear launched past her, pitch eyes focusing on her mate.

Lana launched at him. Her claws sank into his heaving flank, and she yanked down. Blood welled to the surface, but she clung on, sinking her grip in deeper. The bear stopped mid-stride to rear back, bringing her with him. She slid with the motion, never detaching her claws. They dragged with her, causing the bear to roar in pain. Lana landed on all fours and the grizzly whipped around to face her.

Lucas bounded forward to leap onto the tangle of brambles Ganzorig hid behind mere feet away. A glimpse of the shaman from between the branches betrayed how much he'd exerted himself. A slick sheen of sweat glistened across the man's forehead. Magic came at a cost and the spell in the cavern alone would've drained the water from his canteen.

The bear's front paw zoomed into her peripheral vision before she could dart away.

A *thunk* rang through the air, and the breath left her body. She flew under the force of the blow to slam onto the hard ground. The pain crashed down seconds later. Lana's side ached as she scrambled to push herself from the beaten earth. Her breaths were shaky and her limbs buzzed with adrenaline, the dull throb of her muscles threatening to grow a whole lot worse. The grizzly charged for her, picking up speed.

Lana waited. She tensed her back legs, preparing to jump. The thunder of its footsteps echoed and heaving breaths sliced through the fragile-as-ice air. Lana dove to the side, weaving back and forth. Where the bear had far more power than she did, speed was in her favor.

Lucas let out another snarl, feet away from her. One of those tree limbs sliced through his front leg, right near the shoulder seeping with blood. Ice flooded her veins. *No, no, no.* She couldn't lose him.

All strategy abandoned her in the wake of terror. The fear that had frozen her for so long now turned as incendiary as a pipe bomb. Her paws started moving beneath her before she even realized she was loping in his direction faster, faster, faster.

The grizzly's heavy footsteps pounded behind her, the sound as isolated and distant as if a glass wall separated them. Her sole focus was the bastard who'd injured her mate.

Never. Again.

Lucas was snarling, surging forward again with his claws extended. Ganzorig stepped away pace by careful pace. She didn't even question it. He was going to run.

Madness gripped her bones, her heart jackhammering while she churned the earth beneath her. Until she sailed through the air.

Ganzorig's gaze flickered her way — too late.

Lana slammed into him with the force of a trebuchet before the man could even lift his hands. He toppled onto his back, but she didn't budge. She only had him pinned for a second when Lucas charged in. He sank his fangs into the man's neck, and he whipped his head to the side. The rip of flesh rent the air and blood sprayed.

The sticky substance coated her fur, drops spraying across her muzzle. Lana choked back the bile as she held steady. Ganzorig lifted his hand, grasping — for what, she didn't know.

A second later, it no longer mattered. His head dropped back and his eyes dimmed.

As much as she hated what they'd done and as much as she detested the Landsliders with all her might, she couldn't help the tug in her chest.

The spray of pebbles gave the grizzly away. Lucas snarled, his muzzle stained crimson and his fangs dripping. He whipped around to face the grizzly bear. The beast slashed down, and Lucas waited until its claws were an inch from him before he dipped deeper to slam his forehead into the bear's chest with a resounding thud. The ground shook beneath them, but not from any attacker.

Lucas split seams in the earth itself. The bear stumbled, and Lana took a tentative step forward.

Before Lucas could leap up to tear out the shifter's throat, a pale gold blur sailed in from behind. Ally launched herself onto the beast, sinking her fangs into the back of its neck and tearing stripes into the grizzly's flank. It roared, but that was when Lucas slammed his paws to the ground again, sending pebbles to thump into its chest. Lana darted in low, grazing her teeth into its hind leg.

The grizzly toppled.

The ground shook, and Lucas leaped at the same time Ally did, their muzzles snapping as they tore the shifter to pieces. Lana let go of her grip on its leg — the bear didn't stand a chance.

She stepped back a couple of paces. Jer and Raven trotted over to them. Betty crouched, her flank heaving with her shallow breaths. The mountain lion and coyote were barely recognizable on the ground. One of the coyotes that was attacking Drew and Dax loped away as both Williams brothers descended upon the bear. The other coyote already lay lifeless, feet away. The grizzly that had tried to tangle with Ally had met a grisly fate.

Not like we haven't taken our own damage.

Lucas limped, blood flowing at an even faster rate, and Drew and Dax wobbled on their paws, barely able to stagger over to her.

Lana began to transform back to human form. She needed to get them to the cars, stat. While she had joined in the fight, here was where her real work began.

* * * *

Lana emerged from the back room of the Red Rock cabin, her hands discolored from carrying yet another bundle of bloodstained rags.

"Taking on three shifters at once isn't 'playing it safe', dickbag," Sierra snarled as she stitched another gash on Dax's shoulder.

He flashed her a weary grin. "You call me the sweetest things, darling." All that earned him was a legitimate growl from the Red Rock alpha. Jer and Raven were in the shower and would probably be there for quite a while. Betty had crashed out in the bedroom the moment they'd arrived back.

Lana's heart stuttered while she stopped by the kitchen and ran her hands under hot water and soap to clean them thoroughly. She nabbed a couple of ice packs from the freezer and carried them over to where Drew and Lucas slumped on either side of the couch.

Lucas grinned, wide enough to show teeth, at something Drew said, and warmth suffused her at the sight of his amusement, even though his eyelids kept slipping closed, and his breathing had grown slower and more rhythmic as exhaustion sank in fangs-deep. Lana lifted an eyebrow while she leaned in front of him, setting an ice pack to his shoulder. The silver had done serious damage and the wound would take some time to heal.

"Glad you both think getting yourselves banged up is hilarious." Lana cast them both a glance. "We might've knocked Ganzorig out of the picture, but Mackey has the device. We failed."

The grin tugged at Lucas' lips again, and he placed a hand over hers. His eyes gleamed with a mirth that didn't stack with the loss. "I told you to trust me, right?" Lucas said, exchanging a sideways glance with Drew, who smirked.

Lana's forehead creased. "Don't tell me you wanted Mackey to get the device?"

"Ava cast a binding spell on it. He's got to untangle that before he can even hope to use the thing," Drew jumped in, pushing up from the couch only to wince and sink back down.

"So that buys us time," she said, watching their reactions. The situation didn't warrant their whole *nudge-nudge, wink-wink* routine.

Lucas gripped her hand tighter, drawing her gaze to him. His eyes gleamed. "Mackey's been two steps ahead this whole time, running from place to place, and we've been stuck chasing him. However, this device? It's important enough to warrant bringing back to his lair. If there's one thing I've learned about shamans through the whole nightmare with Ganzorig, it's that they're connected to their spells."

"You can home in on the location of his lair," Lana breathed, the giddiness rising in her chest.

A genuine smile split Drew's face. "The one he's kept secret from most of the Landsliders. This is the break we've been waiting for."

Lana sank onto the couch between them, wonder striking her dumb for a moment. And here she'd thought they'd suffered a major loss. "You clever, clever boys."

Lucas reached up even though he flinched from the pain of the movement. He stroked his thumb across her cheek. She could've sobbed at the sheer relief that flushed through her at sitting there beside him.

"It's a good thing you guys managed to retrieve some of Ganzorig's instruments from the cave too before the whole place crumbled," Lucas murmured. "Whatever he was cooking up in there, I guarantee we haven't seen the last of those creatures."

Lana wrinkled her nose even as she nestled closer to Lucas, skating her fingers along his forearm, though she was careful to not lean against his shoulder. Heat radiated off him and their eyes met. Drew slumped back and closed his eyes, probably to give them a few seconds of privacy.

Lucas' words before they'd separated echoed in her mind. *Te amo.* I love you.

She parted her lips, wanting to tell him back. Still, the words hesitated. It wasn't that she didn't feel the love. Every time she slipped her hand through his and every time their eyes locked, she did. His presence made it bloom in her chest as though she'd discovered the feeling for the first time. For so long, her 'I love yous' had belonged to Greg, and even though she'd accepted the change with all her heart, she still stumbled sometimes.

Her lips twisted with a grin, and a shaky realization cascaded over her. "*Te amo,*" she whispered. Those. Those were theirs alone.

Lucas' smile lit his whole face, his white teeth gleaming and his scars crinkling with the movement. His brown eyes glowed as though she was the first breath of warmth after an eternal winter. Lana swallowed but pushed up on the couch to press her lips to his. The kiss was as ethereal as a sunbeam, the heat soaking through her like a sip of coffee, and for the first time in far too long, she tasted hope.

Chapter Twenty-Three

"Are you ready?" Lucas called, leaning against the front door of Lana's house — or what had now become their house.

"I'll be there in a second," Lana responded from the kitchen.

A couple of weeks had passed since the fight with Ganzorig, and it had taken one phone call before Lucas' darling sisters had placed threats that if they didn't meet his mate at once, they'd slit his throat. His mama's request had him booking the flight out to Arizona to see them, as he'd already done the sit-down dinner with Lana's folks here.

Drew would be heading out on a stealth mission the moment Ava gave him the go-ahead that the device had stopped moving around. For now, Lucas would take the breath of reprieve as he did the unthinkable — introduced his mate to the Diaz family.

Even as the thought clunked around in his brain, his lips twitched with a smile. He hoped he never lost the squeeze in his chest every time he uttered the word.

"I promise, I'll keep the house from burning down," Ally said as she strode toward him from the kitchen. She lifted the keys. "Now that I'm the official caretaker, I have some vested interest."

Lucas and Lana had had a long talk after the fight against Ganzorig. Even though she'd be joining him on the road, they weren't going to sell the house. She'd made some compelling points. First off, he wouldn't be traveling in the Tribe forever, and it allowed them somewhere to settle down. Second, she'd need a place to crash when she returned home, and she planned on making some visits without him to see her family.

Lucky for them, Ally had been ready to ditch her apartment anyway, so Lana had struck a deal with her. Ally would pay a lower rent and keep up the house in their absence.

Lana strode in behind Ally with her backpack slung over her shoulder. She leaned in and squeezed her best friend around the shoulders. Ally brushed a kiss onto Lana's head.

"I trust you, Ally-cat," Lana said. "Call me if you need anything, and text me anyway. I'll need to vent about Luc's crazy family." She winked at him and his heart strained at the seams with how damn much he loved this woman.

With her hair pulled into a casual ponytail, her black yoga pants showing off those slender legs, and a burnt orange jacket that enhanced her green eyes, he was half-tempted to carry her back up the steps and have his way with her. The subtle citrus scent wafted off her, and his tongue traced his lower lip.

Lana closed the distance between them and slipped her hand in his. "Be good. We've got a flight to catch." Even as she said it, her eyes danced.

"Ew, guys. Do the nasty in your car, or somewhere well away from me," Ally called, leaning against the couch. Lucas cracked the door open and the cold winds bleached his skin.

"Might want to grab the Lysol wipes then," Lana called back as she stepped through the door. "We've fucked over every square inch of this place. See you soon."

The door clicked shut behind them and laughter exploded from his chest. Lana gripped her own, her shoulders heaving. Their eyes met and they barely made it five paces before the shakes overtook them again. Within seconds, he was gasping for breath, tears stinging his eyes as the amusement bubbled up like liquid joy.

"Want to bet we're going to come back to a sterilized house?" Lucas said, sliding into the driver's seat of his car. The engine rumbled to life, the reverberations traveling up his shins.

"Oh, guaranteed," Lana said, settling into the passenger's seat. The click of her door shutting dosed him with adrenaline. He pulled out of the driveway and set off down the road, her house growing smaller and smaller in the rearview mirror. She leaned forward, fiddling with the radio, a look of concentration on her face and his heart skipped a beat. Her presence soothed his tiger like nothing else, her proximity a balm to his soul.

He kept expecting to blink awake out of a dream, because this was more than he'd ever hoped for. He'd spent years on the road, years isolating himself and shouldering the burden alone. Yet he'd found someone who was his equal in every way, someone brave enough to face the challenges that would arise by his side.

She was the light that swept the darkness away.

Want to see more from this author?
Here's a taster for you to enjoy!

Tribal Spirits: Forged Redemption
Katherine McIntyre

Excerpt

Thanks, sweetheart.

Ally paused in the middle of brushing her teeth as bile rose in her throat. Sweat pricked her temple and she gagged the peppermint toothpaste into the sink. Mere minutes in Mackey Kendricks' presence and he haunted her nightmares again and again. And now she was heading out to stalk the beast to his own den.

A knock sounded on her front door.

Ally sagged over her sink, digging her palms into the cool porcelain. She knew who waited on the other side. Her heart lurched in response, a reflex she couldn't help whenever he was in proximity. If she was going to be spending the next stretch of days up close and personal with Drew Williams, then Ally needed to strap on Kevlar, because he infected her like a computer virus, scrambling her mind and heart every time. The idea that she had gotten tangled up over her ex-boyfriend was cute — their mess traveled down to the roots.

They might've kept it a secret from their packs and families, but Drew Williams was her mate.

Ally tugged her freshly highlighted hair back into a ponytail and clapped a hand on her scarred thigh as a reminder. Drew had changed, and so had she. They weren't the same people they'd been two years ago before she'd dumped him. Before Drew had joined up with the enemy and split their pack apart.

The knock sounded on her door again.

Ally splashed icy water on her face and headed out of the bathroom. Her pulse pounded in double time when she approached. *Nerves over the mission, obviously.* She was two steps from the door when it creaked open on its own.

"We don't have the thousand years necessary for you to finish getting ready." Drew's droll voice echoed through the house as he strode inside. The familiar tone made her bare her teeth on instinct while her mountain lion lunged in her chest.

"Try an ounce of patience, Williams," she responded through gritted teeth. "Not even asking for an average amount. An ounce."

Drew shut the door behind him and turned to face her. A breath hitched in her throat at the full sight of him. Even though he was a bad decision in human form, Drew's looks placed him in Hollywood territory. He had a jawline sharp enough to slice, an arrogant nose that fit him all too well, and tan skin that glowed like he'd spent days basking in the summer sun even though early spring had just arrived. His hair, long enough to tug, gleamed like molten gold and the wicked arc of his eyebrows complemented his mocking smile.

"Well, we both know I'm not average in anything — even my lack of patience," Drew drawled, hooking his thumbs through his belt loops. He leaned against the wall.

"Excuse me while I eyeroll myself into a seizure," Ally shot back. She dipped down to snag her blue tote from beside the couch. Even after living here a couple of months, she thought of this place as Lana's, not hers. Probably because her bestie's name was still on the deed—Ally just acted as caretaker for the cheap rent. Besides, any day now, Lana and her fearsome Tribe mate would be returning for a temporary stay to make this house comfortably crowded.

Ally sucked in a breath and made her way to the door. She'd had to argue with Dax for days to take this recon assignment even though the prospect terrified her. But her alpha's mate, Sierra, was due in less than a month with the first cub or pup between the united Red Rock and Silver Springs packs. Dax needed to be there for the birth of his kid. Ally wouldn't budge on that one.

"Let's get this misery tour on the road," Ally said, flicking off the lights. She followed Drew out to the landing and locked up behind her.

By the time she'd spun around, Drew had slipped his aviators on and sauntered toward his Cadillac. "I'm driving," he called.

Cocky asshole.

Ally tugged the tote at her shoulder and followed him to the car, to hop into the passenger seat before he'd even stepped in. She hated the way the familiar scent of vanilla and smoke stroked at her nerves, evening her breaths. How she sank into these worn cushions like an old memory.

Drew turned the key, bringing the engine to life. Music blared through the speakers, the same acoustic rock he'd always listened to. He didn't say a word as he pushed on the gas to speed out of the development before she could even cast another glance to Lana's house. She could understand why he wouldn't want to linger.

Her fingertips traced the scar on her thigh on instinct. The silver had burned her flesh beyond repair when the pipe bombs had gone off through this neighborhood. The bombs Drew and his defection had been behind.

And she'd been good on hating him too. She'd gotten real good at that. Until the bastard had returned to town and told them of how Mackey Kendricks had used compulsion, forcing Drew to commit horror after horror. Ally might've pretended she didn't understand how fucked up his whole situation was, mostly because hating him was better than the alternative. But then she'd experienced Mackey's compulsion for a flicker-flash of a second, *and holy hell*.

Ally rolled the window down. This car was getting way too stuffy.

"So, what's the plan, Williams?" Ally asked. She placed her hands behind her head and leaned back in the seat. "I'm assuming your lengthy history with the Landsliders gives you some indications here."

Drew didn't need to tilt his aviators up for her to feel the intensity of the gaze flashing her way. "Williams is what folks called the old man." He tipped his glasses down on his nose, passing her a scorching look. "I prefer babe, darling, light of my life. Sir, if you're feeling kinky."

"You'll be called dipshit next if you keep at it," Ally shot back. Drew Williams had been the one person on the planet to keep up with her acerbic humor, to let her unleash when she sank into a mean mood, because they'd always worked the same way. He might've deceived most of the pack into believing he chewed up their hatred and spat it back out in droll one-liners, but she'd always known better.

"We're heading to World's End State Park to narrow down where the hell Mackey planted his secret lair. So, while we sleuth out the specific location, we'll be staying at a cabin in the interim—it'll be our home base."

"World's End? How fucking poetic," Ally responded, tapping her fingers along the ledge. Focusing on the breeze and sunlight proved better than thinking of spending nights in the same room as Drew Williams. Close proximity and a flat surface to fuck had always been her kryptonite when it came to him. "Does Mackey Kendricks choose all of his spots for maximum dramatic impact?"

Drew snorted. "You have no idea. The bastard's a full-blown prima donna."

The sun winked at her as they sped across the highway leading away from their territory. Soon they'd be heading into different pack territories, hence their stay in the public cabins used by human hikers. Even with the warmth radiating through the car and the gentle scent of lilac traveling with the breeze, a chill swept through Ally.

"Ava's spell on Mackey's device—that's all that's keeping him from using it to blow our packs into ash, right?" Their clever shamanic friend had placed a spell over the anti-shifter device they'd fought Joe Ganzorig for. They'd lost. However, Drew and Lucas had calculated that one, a minor loss for the greater victory of tracking her spell's signature to the general vicinity of Mackey's lair, a secret that had eluded them for far too long.

"That's the rumor," Drew responded.

She and Drew had been waiting for the call to hunt down this lair at last. If their packs stood any hope of stopping Mackey Kendricks or his Landsliders, they needed to catch him in his home base.

"Are you ready to confront him?" Ally asked, her sharp edges softening. "Ava fixed the bond between you and Kendricks through the Landsliders' mark, right?"

Drew's cocky grin faltered. She didn't need the mating bond to sense the terror gripping him tight. "Our friendly neighborhood shaman did me one better. She managed to reverse the bond—I can resist his compulsion. At the end of the day, either one of the East Coast Tribe takes him down, or me. Luc and Navi have too much to lose, so you can bet I'm going to be the one to end his life, even if I go with him."

His words stung, though she didn't have any right to the hurt. Drew wasn't wrong. They weren't dating, and most of his former pack and family barely tolerated him. Only Lana had welcomed him back in, but Ally's cinnamon roll bestie couldn't hold a grudge. Hell, Lana would forgive a bumblebee for stinging her, so why not Drew?

Ally tugged out the flask of Jack Daniel's she'd packed and took a swig.

"We're five minutes into the drive and you're drinking?" Drew arched an eyebrow.

Ally saluted with the flask. "The astounding new lengths you bring me to. Also, you're the one who wanted to drive so badly."

What she could never admit aloud was how much his self-sacrificing pissed her off. His actions made her flip the mirror back around and look a little too hard at all the desperate maneuvers she'd pulled as beta. How she'd thrown herself into fighting fang and claw against Landsliders, even mutated ones, without a blink.

Her mountain lion prowled inside, restless, needing to fight or run. Her mother had always told her she was a firework—all flash before the burnout, and she hated, hated to prove Rylie Coleman right.

"Oh, we're making a detour along the way," Drew mentioned offhandedly.

Ally gritted her teeth—she'd wear them to nubs by the end of this recon mission. "Didn't think of mentioning at all? You know I'm not the type of soldier to fumble along blind."

Drew placed a hand over his chest. "No, really?" The sarcasm reached eleven. Even though he drove, Ally considered the option of reaching across to strangle him. "Luc asked me to check on a pack out here," he continued. "He wanted to gauge if Mackey had them under his thumb or not."

"Like Mackey hasn't pulled together enough shifters to form a fucked-up little family? What's his damage?" Ally leaned along the window, her hair rippling out with the breeze.

"Mommy and Daddy issues puts it lightly," Drew drawled before flicking a quick glance her way. "And you thought we were bad."

"How dare he," Ally responded. "Didn't you tell him I don't share the spotlight?"

Her comment earned a genuine grin from Drew, one that made his eyes crinkle at the edges. One that made her heart thump hard. Once upon a time, she'd have set a forest on fire for one of those smiles. If she were even an ounce honest with herself, she still might. Ally's gaze drifted to the trees ahead of her. Her brow furrowed. She hadn't been serious.

Smoke trailed from the trees, the dark plumes billowing with increasing urgency.

"Hey, Drew?" she asked, sitting up in the seat.

A frown creased between his eyebrows. "Looks like there's a fire in the forest."

"That wouldn't happen to be in the direction we're heading…" Ally let her words taper, unable to dispel the tug in her gut. Mackey might be behind this too.

"One way to find out," Drew said, slamming hard on the pedal. His Caddy soared across the highway even as a cool competency settled over him. Like this, he seemed so different from the cocky upstart she'd fallen for. He exuded a maturity she wasn't used to seeing in him.

Her claws pricked out in anticipation for a fight. She needed somewhere to channel all this nervous energy beyond bickering with Drew.

In the distance, the fringes of buildings signaled an approaching town, and Ally half-expected to see the properties alight with crimson and gold flames. So many times, her mind transported to the night of the pipe bombs, and her thigh ached. Drew slowed when he neared the town, the slate smoke coming from the left past the main stretch of Mildred. The small bone-white church and red-bricked post office ahead lay untouched, even as folks pulled to the side of the street to gawk at the big plumes of what was building into a rager of a fire.

"We're getting close," Drew murmured, his tone darkening with the same seriousness that had settled over her. "The pack lives just beyond the town, nearer to the creek."

Ally's nose pricked with the charred scent of smoke beginning to pervade the car. Drew veered down a side street, farther away from the town.

"And you said a pack of shifters lives here?" she asked, even though she knew the answer. Mackey and his Landsliders had wreaked enough havoc on her own pack to dispel any delusions that he might show restraint. That he might not tear families apart in his quest to destabilize the region.

"He doesn't care." Drew's voice had distanced, the same as his eyes, as if he'd gotten trapped in memories of a different life from that of the man she'd known. "Mackey hates the packs. He hates his kind, maybe more than the Coalition does."

Her stomach flipped. This monster's hatred radiated like Hiroshima, the effects stamped all across their region, their homes and their packs.

Drew turned down another side street. Ranchers and two-story colonials sprawled out around here, short driveways and lengthy yards bursting to life with the careful blossoms and sprigs of spring's first breath. The acrid stench of smoke grew even stronger when they neared the column of black pouring into the sky.

Drew reached the end of a cul-de-sac facing thick brush and towering oaks. Flames glimmered in the distance, and the cries echoed through the air, faint from here. Ally's blood thrummed, her body prepared to move, to fight, to lash out at the first bit of trouble to step in her way. He parked at the edge.

"The pack must be deeper in," he said before stepping out of his car. Ally vaulted out of her seat, her nails shifting to claws. Drew met her eyes on the other side of his Cadillac. "Let's shift and check the area."

This was the sort of job for the East Coast Tribe—most packs stuck to their own kind and stayed out of each other's business. But the escalating threat Mackey Kendricks had brought to this region affected them all. This might not be her pack, but she couldn't let innocents suffer. They both started stripping their clothes off to prepare for the shift.

"Follow my lead." Drew gave the command. He'd been spending too much time around the Tribe. As much as Ally wanted to argue on reflex, the *thump-thump-thump* of her heart drowned out any response. She nodded and began to shift.

Her bones transitioned and fur pricked out along her arms. Her mountain lion took over, the form coming as naturally as breathing. The second she crouched on all four paws, the scent of the smoke grew overbearing and the screams reverberated through the forest, clearer than ever. Beneath the stench, she caught the other trails of the wolf pack who resided around here.

Before Drew gave the cue, Ally launched into the woods. Drew raced alongside her within seconds, keeping pace like he always did. Her mountain lion never needed the confirmation that he was her mate — he'd always been able to keep up with her in every aspect of their lives when no one else could.

Even though the fringes of trees had begun to spark, the fire focused on a different target, one that became clear the deeper in they ran. A pack cabin similar to their own lay in the middle of these woods, one accessible by a thin dirt road lined with cars. The pack must've been in the middle of a meet, all of them gathered together when the Landsliders had struck.

And now, those innocents burned.

Home of Erotic Romance

Sign up for our newsletter and find out about all our romance book releases, eBook sales and promotions, sneak peeks and FREE romance books!

About the Author

Strong women. Strong words.

Katherine McIntyre is a feisty chick with a big attitude despite her short stature. She writes stories featuring snarky women, ragtag crews, and men with bad attitudes—high chance for a passionate speech thrown into the mix. As an eternal geek and tomboy who's always stepped to her own beat, she's made it her mission to write stories that represent the broad spectrum of people out there, from different cultures and races to all varieties of men and women. Easily distracted by cats and sugar.

Katherine loves to hear from readers. You can find her contact information, website details and author profile page at https://www.totallybound.com

www.ingramcontent.com/pod-product-compliance
Lightning Source LLC
Chambersburg PA
CBHW031451260626
47154CB00016B/836